52 Broad Street

A novel

by

Diane Dorce

Copyright © 2007 by Diane Dorce'

All rights reserved. No part of this book shall be reproduced or transmitted in any form or by any means, electronic, mechanical, magnetic, photographic including photocopying, recording or by any information storage and retrieval system, without prior written permission of the publisher. No patent liability is assumed with respect to the use of the information contained herein. Although every precaution has been taken in the preparation of this book, the publisher and author assume no responsibility for errors or omissions. Neither is any liability assumed for damages resulting from the use of the information contained herein.

This is a work of fiction. Names, characters, places, and incidents either are the product of the author's imagination or are used fictitiously. Any resemblance to actual events or locales or persons, living or dead, is entirely coincidental.

ISBN 978-0-9774126-3-1

Library of Congress Control Number: 2007902500

Published by FireFly Publishing & Entertainment

Printed in the United States by Morris Publishing
3212 East Highway 30
Kearney, NE 68847
1-800-650-7888

Acknowledgements

I would like to thank all my well-wishers and supporters while writing this book. I would like to thank my family for always believing in me and listening to me while I generate yet another idea, and allowing me to bounce those ideas off of you time and time again. Thanks to all the wonderful writers who came before me, the ones I admire and often return to just to make sure I got this writing thing right. You are my teachers, my mentors. Thanks to my lovely new blog family, Saadia, Dee, DC, Rich, Cortney, Shai, Sheletha, Lance, Justme, IYMS and the LoZone. You have been an inspiration to me...you keep me on my toes and writing daily. Thanks to my party crew, Debra, Candy, Ann, Nikko, Cynthia ...you all allow me to let my hair down and I have needed a lot of that this year. Thanks to spiritual supporters, and friends, Janet, Deanna, Gwen, Furnetta, and Mike C.

I dedicate this book to the loves of my life,

Jenna and Frantz!

PROLOGUE

It was the first of the month, and just like every first of the month, Grady Memorial hospital got its share of crazies. Couple that with a weekend and a full moon, and it was likely that Dracula himself would step through the door, but it wasn't like that. Instead, crazy had been turned inside out and what looked like normal wasn't really normal at all, at least that is what Gerard thought when he saw Miss Thang. She was about 5' 2", petite, cute haircut, wearing jeans and an Old Navy brazened t-shirt, nothing fancy but cute enough to catch his eye. He was gearing up to use his famous line on her "What's up cutie?" but came to a dead stop, when she yelled.

"Where's my baby? I need to find my baby!"

Gerard retreated five steps, turned on his heels and proceeded to go in the opposite direction, but he wasn't fast enough. Her arms flailed like tentacles, desperately reaching, grasping at anything, anyone who could help—finally latching onto him. Even up close she was still cute, older than he had first thought, but doable.

"My baby," she pleaded. "I need to find her." He wanted to help her, but he didn't know nothing about her baby. The last woman that had asked him about a baby, come to find out the baby wasn't even her's.

"Look Lady, I'm sorry," he said, peeling her fingers from his arm, "I don't know who you are looking for." He tried to move, but the woman was relentless.

"Listen," the lady said pressing her hands against his chest. "She's about five-five, brown skin, long hair," speaking so fast each word seemed to erase the other, leaving him with only bits and pieces of her conversation. Although she was talking directly to him, her eyes dodged around the room like searchlights, to the door, down the hall, and back at the elevator.

Gerard had heard enough. He didn't know about no girl coming in here. All day long he had to deal with this kind of shit. Hell they weren't paying him to be no receptionist either! It made him mad just thinking about it. "Like I said, I don't know nuthin bout no girl!"

"Please," she said, wiping huge tears from her eyes. "She was with my grandson, Rashawn. He's four years old, brown skin, with curly hair and he got these big, puppy dog eyes. He..." She paused and struggled to speak. The way she was choking up, he didn't know whether to answer her or call for a doctor. "They told me, they were brought here," she said in a breathless whisper. "I need to find them."

It had been a hectic evening, so many patients. Almost impossible to discern one from the other, but the night so far had delivered only one small child fitting that description. He looked back at the lady and couldn't help but sympathize with her.

"Through those doors," he pointed, "they might be there."

The woman blew past him, leaving behind a scent of peaches and cigarettes, a smell that stayed with him long into the night... He watched with a heavy heart as she entered the Trauma Center. It seemed rubbernecking didn't just happen on highways, everyone including him stopped to watch. Others behind him whispered questions, and comments about this lady and her daughter. Gerard had a good mind to tell them to shut-up, but wasn't he just as bad. She stood in the middle of the emergency room. But Gerard would later remember that that was more of an understatement, she seemed to do more leaning than standing, as if the world had tilted and she was the only one who felt it. She clasped one hand over her mouth, and wrapped the other around her head, covering it like a wrap. Her eyes fixated on a door, a table, whatever he couldn't quite see— but from her expression, he didn't really need to. As the door eased to a close, he and others crept forward, afraid they would miss something, but no one was bold enough to grab the doors or prevent them from closing. The woman dropped to her knees, her mouth was open, but nothing came out. Nothing. It was like the room had been sucked of all sounds. Eerily quiet. The door finally shut and he not knowing what else to do, turned to walk away when a piercing scream reverberated through Grady Memorial Hospital making his six foot frame shudder from head to toe. "Shantique!"

CHAPTER 1

For Shantique, luck was something that happened to rich, white folks or people like Baby Boy, who had been shot five times and still lived to talk about it. Luck was the one thing she never had, no matter how bad she wished for it, no pot of gold, no Ed McMann and not one lottery ticket worth a damn. Luck was an elusive son of a bitch, but that didn't stop her from believing that one day luck would be on her side. She had never been a stupid child, that's the one thing old folks always said; *she had her wits about her*. Shantique never quite knew what that meant, but it must have been good because they kept saying it even after she got pregnant. Pregnant at sixteen, not a dropout and still smart enough to graduate in the top half of her class, that wasn't luck that was wit. And if having wit, meant she would have to work at some things, make some luck, build some dreams on top of this hell hole, then she would. Miracles happened on television, but in the SWATs, the ATL, the Dirty South, miracles were made, even on 52 Broad st.

* * *

Shantique sparkled like a brand new penny in her shiny, silver lamet halter; white leather mini-skirt and four-inch diamond studded stiletto heels. It was both classy and hot, a lot like her. She especially liked the way it barely covered her breast and exposed all of her stomach. Sexy, sexy, sexy!

"Go Shantique! Go Shantique! Go!" The crowd chanted. You would have thought she was barefoot the way she moved in those heels. Shantique loomed over the other dancers and took the spotlight in the middle of the stage. She could hear rapper/singer Crazy X singing "Bump it! Uh huh, uh huh, grind it! Uh huh, uh huh!" And there she was standing right next to him, moving and swerving her hips to the music. She was smiling and he was smiling! She couldn't believe it, even her mama screamed from the audience.

"Shantique, Shantique! Pick up the phone!"

Shantique moaned, turned over and placed her pillow atop her head. Who would call her so early on a Saturday morning, the morning she reserved for sleeping in. She moved the pillow from her head and reached for the phone, that's when she caught sight of the time. Eleven O' clock. She had forgot all about the mall.

"Hello" she said, yawning.

"Shantique, you sleep?" Nikko asked.

"Yeah girl, what's up?"

"I thought we were going to the mall today. You gonna be ready by twelve?"

"Yeah! You talked to Martinette?" Shantique said rubbing her eyes.

"Yeah, she's gonna meet us there. What you wearing?"

"Damn, I ain't even thought about that yet, some jeans and a halter, I guess. What about you?"

"Girl, I got this slamming sun dress, its lime green with tiny flowers."

"A dress! Damn Nikko, ain't nobody gonna be at the mall. Why you getting dressed up?"

"It ain't dressy! It's cute. You know this is NBA weekend, or did you forget? There may be some ballers hanging out and I for one ain't taking any chances. You know how it is during NBA Weekend"…she rattled on. "Girl them hoochies be everywhere and I am not about to let them show me up. You know what I'm saying."

She reached for her nail file and began to file down a chipped nail on her left hand. "Yeah! So what's Martinette wearing?"

"She wouldn't tell. I don't know what she's so secretive about, it ain't like we going to be dressed like twins or nothing. We don't even have the same taste in clothing. Anyway, Miss Diva said she would meet us in the food court."

Shantique paused when hearing Rashawn's laughter. "Cool, look I'll call you back when I'm ready."

"Alright then, hey your mama gonna keep Rashawn?"

"Girl, I haven't even asked her yet. To tell you the truth I ain't looking for no drama. I'm thinking about taking him over his other grandma's. She been complaining to Taye that she don't see him that much."

"Taye? Now that's a name I ain't heard in a while. You talked to him lately?"

"Girl, me and Taye ain't got nothing to talk about. That's ancient history; all he need to do is take care of Rashawn. Anyway I got my eyes on a bigger prize."

"All do tell girlfriend. You met somebody?"

"Not yet, but I will."

"Shantique," her mother clicked in, "excuse me ladies but I need to make a call."

"Mama!"

"Five minutes Shantique," her mother said and hung up.

"Girl, good luck on getting her to baby sit, call me when you ready."

"Alright Boo."

As soon as Shantique hung up the phone, Rashawn her four-year-old son busts through her bedroom door and jumps on the bed.

"Hey mommy! You sleep?" He asked. He was still wearing his Pokemon pajamas, with lots of blue spots and covered with grape jelly.

"Hey baby." She gave him a big hug. "Oooh, you sticky. He giggled. Somebody's been fixing jelly sandwiches. I wonder who?"

"Not me!"

Shantique ran her hand through his curly hair. "Uh huh. I just bet. Did you brush your teeth?" He nodded. "Now you know I can tell. Open up." Rashawn opened his mouth wide. "Uh huh, I see monsters on top, in the back, oh my there all over!" Rashawn screamed and ran to her mirror.

"I don't see no monsters mommy."

"I do, so you better go brush those teeth, or all of them teeth are gonna fall out." He ran out of her room as fast as he could heading for the bathroom. Her mother knocked at her door.

"Shantique," her mother said. "I got to run to the store and then I'm stopping by mamas for awhile. What you got planned for you and Rashawn?"

Shantique was always amazed at how young her mother looked. It had to be something in the genes because her grandmother looked young too—just something that ran in the family. Shantique wasn't mad at her, standing there in the doorway, looking every bit of twenty, with her hip hugging bellbottom jeans, and DKNY fitted T-shirt. Her mama could pull from the same crop as her if she wanted. But her mama hadn't been on a date in over 5 years, at least that's what Shantique thought. Her mama only seemed to care about a few things, one being Rashawn, Shantique and three, playing her numbers, everybody and everything else fell somewhere in between and some even landed on the "I don't give a shit list'. Her mama always fussed about not needing no man, and she tried to drive the same thing into Shantique's head, almost every day. But Shantique wasn't hearing none of it. If her mama didn't want no man, that was fine for her, but Shantique was going to have the man of her dreams, and the life.

"I'm going to the mall with Martinette and Nikko. Can you take Rashawn with you?"

Her mother rolled her eyes, reached into her purse for a cigarette and lit it before responding. It was only after her second puff did she speak.   "Look Shantique, we not going to start that shit again. I told you, when you had Rashawn that I had raised all the children I'm gonna raise and you were not going to be dumping your babies off on me. Seems to me you forgot whose Rashawn's mama is?"

"All mama, it ain't like that. Rashawn hates going to the mall with me, but if you got something to do I understand. I'll call over to Miss Berry's to see if she can take him." Shantique could feel her mother's eyes burning at her back. It was a low blow to mention Mrs. Berry, especially after the last incident between the two. Miss. Berry and her mom only managed to be respectful to each other and that usually happened only at holiday gatherings. Even when Shantique and Taye, Rashawn's father were dating, her mother adored Taye but loathed his mother. They could hate each other all they wanted as long as it didn't interfere with her and Taye's relationship. So, for the past 3 years all that mattered in her life was Taye and Rashawn, but now even that had changed. Now her life centered on raising Rashawn and spending time with her friends, sometimes not exactly in that order.

"Oh hell no!" her mother shouted. "You're not taking my baby over no damn where!"

Shantique tried to look serious, but couldn't especially after her mom started screaming.

"Rashawn! Rashawn," her mother screamed. "Come on in here boy so we can go visit Grandma Ann. You think you funny!" She said pointing at Shantique.

"Mama, I'm not, what's up?"

"Girl don't play with me. Rashawn, what are you doing? You better not be playing in that bathroom!"

"I'm not Nana."

"Okay sweetie, just hurry yourself along so we can be on our way." She turned back to Shantique, looking her up and down. "Since you so smart you can stop by Victoria Secrets and pick me up some of that peach lotion I like."

Shantique stretched out her hand.

Her mother looked at it and said, "With your money! I already done told you, ain't nothing free!"

"Mama!"

"Mama nothing."

"Dang, gonna charge me for taking care of your own grandson. Some kind of grandma you are," Shantique teased.

Her mother gave her a stern look, the kind you just didn't question or play with.

"I'm just kidding," Shantique said wrapping her long arms around her mothers' shoulders. "You know I love you."

"Yeah, alright, I love you too! Just don't have your ass out all night. You hear me?"

Shantique slightly turned her head, breathing a sigh of relief.

"Rashawn!" she called. "Come give your mama a hug before you go."

Rashawn was always a bundle of energy, and bounced through the doors, running at full speed, collapsing onto the bed. It was hard to believe that he would be starting school this fall. Her little boy was growing up so fast and right before her eyes. Shantique lifted, squeezed, tickled and hugged Rashawn until both of them were out of breath. She couldn't help but notice how much he looked like Taye, the left dimple, his eyes, even his coloring was closer to Taye's. There was no real reason to be sad, especially with how things had been going in her life, but thinking of him, and looking at Rashawn tugged at her heart. *When will it ever be over?* She gave Rashawn a big kiss. "You be good at grandmas and don't eat too many sweets, remember about those monsters."

Rashawn nodded and hurried off behind his grandma.

The house was finally quiet, a guilty pleasure she'd come to miss. Every since having Rashawn her world was not only turned upside down, but filled with diapers, pull-ups, Barney, kissing boo boo's, and the pitter pattering of little feet all day long. She never regretted having Rashawn. She loved him more than anything, but she also realized that having a child is no joke, and certainly no small task. It was a lifetime of responsibility, and even though Rashawn was only three, the last three years seemed like a lifetime. With Taye off in college and her mama being hardheaded about her taking care of her responsibility, it left her little time to kick it like she used to, but then again her mama wasn't as hard as she likes everyone to think she is. Rashawn is her heart. Everybody knows that. So on occasion she gets a pass and gets to live her life like a regular twenty-one year old.

After a hot shower, Shantique went through her closet and found a two piece bright orange halter and short skirt with side slits. She tried it on and it was cute as ever. Shantique turned up her boom box, and there was that song again by Rapper Crazy X. "Bump it! Uh huh, grind it! Uh huh". She remembered her dream from last night, her onstage with the rapper, and the center of attention. This was a premonition! Shantique didn't know when Crazy X was coming to town, but whenever, wherever... she was going to see him, and maybe if she was real lucky, she would even get to meet him.

* * *

Nikko and Shantique arrived fifteen minutes late and Lenox Mall was packed with people. Shantique had a good mind to cuss Nikko out for taking so long, but she wouldn't at least not until she got back home. Nikko was not only one of her bestfriends, but always the chauffeur. Shantique didn't drive, didn't have a driver's license and had no intention of getting one anytime soon. Nikko was a good driver and so was her mom as long as they could get her to and from the train station or bus stop she was doing alright.

Nikko was able to secure a parking space in front of Macy's. A stretch away from the food court, but it was cool. On Saturdays the mall was like a club, filled with pre-teens, teens, some hip-hop, and quite a few older people as well. Shantique's mom refused to drive all the way out to Lenox. She said they were too pricey and had too many kids hanging around. But that is what Shantique and her friends loved about Lenox, and the fact that every now and then you could spot some real true ballers.

The two of them stepped out of the car to a symphony of cat calls and whistles, coupled with a few "Hey shorties" and the like. There seemed to be very little separation when it came to appreciating the fine. Young men, old men, Black, White, Asian, it didn't matter, all of them necks whipped around when Nikko and Shantique passed by. This is exactly what they wanted! They loved the attention! Shantique pulled on her short skirt and checked herself again in Nikko's driver mirror while Nikko pretended to check herself as well. Nikko was a perfect size 1, but she didn't look skinny, because she was what you called petite, a little over five foot and just short of five-five in her favorite heels, which she wore better than anyone. Shantique would swear that Nikko was born in heels. She could outrun, out walk and out dance anybody in five inch heels, which to her seemed like an incredible feat, amongst other things....like dancing. Nikko was and had always been the premier dancer, in school and out. On the dance floor she was a different person, fierce is the word that comes to mind. A small woman with the courage of a lion. Shantique met Nikko during her sophomore year in high school when Nikko tried out for cheerleading. All of the other girls were so jealous of her, and pretty much dissed everything she did, kind of like what they did when Shantique tried out, but Shantique knew that Nikko was special. She had the body, the moves and the face, three parts dynamite, and so she would stop at nothing to get her on the squad.

   Born of a Vietnamese mother and black father, Nikko seemed to inherit the best of both worlds, honey colored with jet-black hair and rounded out Asian eyes, she was the picture of cuteness. Her body was much the same, tiny waist and arms, but with a well-pronounced derriere or like the brothers called it a "sista booty". Nikko was most proud of that!

   The two of them headed for the food court amidst the hoops and hollers from their male admirers. By the time they got to the Food Court they saw Martinette was surrounded by a cadre of men, handling her business, as usual. She was so busy flirting; she didn't see the two of them coming. As far as Shantique could remember and for as long as she's known Martinette, Martinette has always been the center of attention. Shy by no means, mouthy and cute, often got her into a lot trouble, both at school and at home. Her and Shantique first met in the 9th grade and even their meeting was filled with drama, when two girls threatened to jump her in the bathroom, Marti was the one person who came to her defense and ended up beating up both of the girls. The two had been best friends every since.

Nikko and Shantique watched from aside while Martinette shook down a group of guys. Martinette would chat with any man who paid her attention. She liked to flirt, but anything else would cost you and she was the best at making men pay. Martinette saw her two friends and waved them over. "What's up girls?" She shouted from across the food court.

"Nikko and Shantique replied. "You girlfriend!" When all three got together they hugged and giggled at the attention they were getting. The men were lusting and the women look disgusted.

"Come on you ready to go shopping?" Shantique asked.

"Yep! Wait a minute, one of you got a pen?" Martinette asked.

Shantique and Nikko both gave her a look of surprise, because the man she was about to give her number to looked old enough to be her father. Nikko handed Martinette a pen. Martinette wrote down her number and handed it to the man. After careful speculation, the other two agreed, he sort of dressed nice; Rolex watch, then he smiled, and bling bling. Okay, they agreed, he may have money, but he's no baller, too old!

Martinette handed the old guy her number and planted a kiss on his cheek. Shantique and Nikko were shocked.

Shantique asked. "Who was that?"

"Oh, so now you want to know." Martinette smirked. "I shouldn't tell y'all, I seen the way y'all was looking at me when I gave him my number. I ain't stupid! "

Martinette rolled her eyes, popped her gum and made them wait before answering." He just happens to be the road manager for the group 'Too Hot'."

"You lying!" Shantique said. "Girl, they in town? Where they staying? We need to hookup tonight!"

"I love 'Too Hot'! You know that song, 'In the bedroom', girl the lead singer is so fine!' said Nikko.

"I know! Look, he's supposed to call me on the cell once he gets back to the hotel. They're doing a concert in Macon tonight and he thinks he can get us backstage passes, limo, all that shit." The three of them screamed.

"Girl, I got to get me a new outfit for that and I wasn't even planning on spending any money here today." Shantique said. "Nikko you got your credit card?"

"Yeah, why?" Nikko rolled her eyes, "You still owe me for that Fourth of July outfit. And anyway it's about maxed out, so I'm using cash today."

"Look don't you two start in about money and ruin my day. You know we got enough stuff at home between the three of us to come up with a banging outfit. Alright!" Martinette put her arms around her two friends and whispered "We gonna blow them muthafucka's away!" The three laughed and slapped hands. "Come on, let's go to the music store and look at their CD so we can see who we want."

"I know who I want!" Nikko said, "The smooth, chocolate lead singer, Laron! With his fine ass! Ooh!" She bounced.

Shantique said. "Well, I like him too! But since you about to piss on yourself, I'll take his twin Taron." Both her and Nikko slapped hands.

"You all are so crazy, but the finest member of the group is the bass player, Ty! Shit, have you seen that man's muscles, especially in the CD cover when he is wearing that white wife beater and those black leather pants. Girl, I swear, I almost wet myself. Ooh! I love me a black man, and he is as black as they come!" Martinette turned to give high fives to her friends. "Am I right?" They all nodded in agreement.

From there the threesome went to Macy's because they were having a sale, and Nikko had a Macy's card.

Martinette wanted to look for some shoes so that's where everybody headed. She found a pair of Gucci Lizard skin slip on's and was about to try them on when she spotted Taye by the perfume counter and he wasn't alone either. She nudged Nikko and Nikko looked around for Shantique, because both knew how Shantique felt about Taye. Shantique was in the designer section, looking at some Nine West slip on's . She had already sat down to try them on and seemed oblivious to anything else taking place in the store. Martinette recognized the girl Taye was with and from her expression, you would have thought Taye was her baby's daddy.

"Nikko! That's the same Trick who was messing with Malik! Nikko turned to check the girl out.

"Damn, if it is she sure does get around! First Malik, now Taye."

Look at her. She thinks she all's that swinging that fake ass ponytail, like it's hers. I can see the tracks from here! The cheap bitch can't even pay for a good weave! What's wrong with Taye? When did he become so low class?"

Nikko waved her hand. "Girl, I don't know! He was always on top of his game in High School! I just hope Shantique don't see him."

"Go over there and distract her, maybe I can get him to leave"

Nikko left for Shantique, hoping to head her off before she saw Taye. Martinette waited until Nikko got with Shantique, then caught up with Taye at the Clinique counter.

"What's up Taye? I didn't know you were back in town." Taye seemed too surprised to see Martinette but that didn't stop him from holding the hand of the pretty Puerto Rican girl standing at his side. Martinette gave her a once over look. She was cute, but her girl Shantique was far prettier, and this girl had no taste in clothes. Looked like some K-mart stuff to her. Martinette rolled her eyes in distaste.

"Hey Martinette! Yeah, well I'm just here for the weekend. So where's Shantique? I know she can't be too far behind?"

"She right over there." She pointed. "But, I don't really think you want her to see you and Maria here. You know how Shantique is! You my boy and all, but when it comes down to Shantique or you, you know who's back I got."

Taye nodded in agreement. "True that. Look, you know me and Shantique ain't together no more, so why she got to be tripping? I am not thinking about that girl. This here is my new girl, and that's that, the rest is history."

"Alright, whatever! But don't say I didn't warn you! Y'all need to be stepping before Shantique sees you, especially since you didn't even call her or nothing, or go by and see Rashawn."

"Damn Martinette! Why you all up in my business? I was going to see Rashawn today if you want to know! Look, gone over there with your friends and tell

Shantique don't be coming over here tripping, cause I am not for her mess today. Alright!"

"Whatever! You just better get your girl out of here before she gets a major beat down."

Taye's new girlfriend stepped up in Martinette's face.

"Look bitch, I'll take on all three of you's. Fuck this shit, Pappy. Who this fat bitch think she is?"

Taye pulled his girl out of the way, just before Martinette swung and missed. That got his girl started and the two of them, wrapped around Taye like a human burrito, each of them pulling, screaming, pushing and shoving, until he had had enough and pushed Martinette to the side.

"Fuck you Taye and your taco eating bitch. I hope Shantique kicks both your asses, and I plan to help her."

Her hollering and pushing caused the other shoppers to gather and look. One of the store clerks called Security.

Nikko had Shantique pretty much covered until Security ran past them.

"Oh shit!"

"What?" Shantique asked, turning her attention to the commotion taking place on the other side of the store. "No that ain't Taye over there! What is Martinette doing and who is that other girl Nikko?" She dropped the pair of shoes she held and sprinted across two aisles to get to them. By the time she got there Security had broken up the trio and asked all of them to leave the store. Martinette was still running her mouth when Shantique and Nikko arrived on the scene.

"I'm gonna get you bitch! There better not be no scratches on my face! One mark and you are mine. You here me! Your boy will not be able to protect you, J-NO bitch!"

"Miss, please calm down. You have to leave the store now." The Security guard said, pushing Martinette along.

Shantique didn't know what to say. There was Taye with some other girl who looked like she just got whipped, and from what she could gather, Martinette did the whooping. Martinette was about to be thrown out of the store and she couldn't be more pissed. She hadn't seen Taye in over three months. She hadn't even spoken with him once. The last she remembered, her mother said he called about two weeks ago to speak with Rashawn. Now here he was standing in front of her and looking every bit of good, if not better! Her emotions were like potluck on Sunday, a hodgepodge of hate, filled with disgust, and a dash of attraction. When she last saw him he had some short twists, but now his hair had grown out and he sported it wild and natural, making him look more like Maxwell than she wanted to admit. Taye stood six-foot-two, all muscle, but still a little too lean for the pros, at least that's what all the sports commentators said. Yeah, even though they wasn't together she still kept up with his games and silently rooted for him every chance she got. He was one fine chocolate brother, still, and she was at a loss for words the moment their eyes met. She was angry, but how could she ignore those sexy eyes that were once, only for her, or those thick lips she tried to swallow whole? How could the love of her life and her baby's daddy come to town without a call or anything and then have the nerve, the audacity to be out shopping with some other bitch? Shantique slapped Taye hard across the face. Taye didn't flinch, took the shot like a man, while his girlfriend attempted to retaliate.

"You bitch!" she said flinging her arms at Shantique.

Taye stepped in between the two and took the blow meant for Shantique.

Shantique said nothing but her mind rambled on like she was having conversations with three people. *How the hell could he show up herewith some other girl on his arms? And how come, she couldn't stop the tears from falling from her eyes.*

"Fuck you Taye! What kind of shit is this? You take your new girl friend shopping before even visiting your son. You ain't shit for a father and I'll be sure to let your son know that!"

* * *

CHAPTER 2

    Nikko felt sorry for Shantique! All the way to her house she cursed and cried about Taye. She really loved that boy! Shantique started talking about not going out, but Nikko convinced her it would do her some good to go out and have fun with a bunch of ballers and Martinette wasn't even hearing it. Not after what she went through. Nikko dropped Shantique off at her house then headed to her home in Tucker to get dressed for the night.
    Thirty minutes later, Nikko pulled into her tree-lined subdivision, Emerald Pointe and instantly felt at peace. It always amazed her how quiet it was here, compared to Shantique and Martinette's neighborhood. There were no boom-boom car radios blaring or music coming from the windows of houses, no kids running and playing in the streets, just quiet. Too quiet some times! But today, she appreciated it, especially after all that drama at the Mall. Nikko knew better. She should have never let Martinette run interference with Taye. No matter what Martinette said, Nikko had a sneaky suspicion that she started the whole mess. Martinette never really liked Taye, or let's just say, she seemed envious of Taye and Shantique's relationship or maybe it was the fact that Taye was predicted to go pro in the next year or two. She probably didn't like the idea of Shantique nabbing a baller before her. But no

more! Shantique and Taye were through! All that remained was little Rashawn, and now that relationship was in jeopardy. Damn! She should have warned Taye at the mall, not Martinette, now everything got all fucked up over some silly bullshit. Well, it wasn't really her problem; all she had to worry about was what to wear tonight and sneaking out of the house before her dad found out. Now that was Nikko's most pressing problem. Nikko's cell phone lit up and rang as soon as she drove up to the house.

"Hello!" she answered.

"Nikko! It's Martinette. Girl, "Too Hot's" road manager just called and said for us to meet them in the Marriott Marquis main lobby. We will ride the limousine down with him and his staff to the concert, so I thought that we could meet at my house and leave from here around six o'clock. The concert starts at eight and it's about an hour drive to Macon."

"Alright girl! I'll be over to your house at five-thirty. Okay!"

"Cool! I'll call Shantique and let her know. You talked with her yet?"

"Just in the car, she's cool though! At first she was talking like she didn't want to go no more, but she's okay now."

"Good! Okay, I'll call her and let her know the time. See ya!"

Before Nikko could hang up her phone good, she noticed her mom peeking out the front window at her. Nikko's mom was very protective, but nothing like her father. He just happened to be both overprotective and strict. Although Nikko would be officially turning twenty-one in December, he still treated her like a child, issuing curfews and wanting to know where she's going or where she's been. Nikko loved her parents, but she hated their ultra conservative ways. Nikko's mom didn't approve of the way she dressed or who she hung out with. She didn't understand, in America everyone dressed like this, unless they were old. Her mom spoke to her in Vietnamese. Nikko hated when she did that, because she still understood very little of the language.

"Mom" she said, "English please." She placed her bags on the small wooden table at the entry of the house and removed her shoes. It was customary. Her mom spoke to her again, this time in English.

"Nikko, it's late! You've been shopping again! Why do you spend so much money on these little clothes? They are so tight! So unbecoming of a lady!"

Nikko huffed. *Here we go again.* "Mom, I just bought a few things for tonight."

"Tonight! What tonight Nikko?"

Nikko could tell from her mom's tone where the conversation would end up. "I'm going to a concert with my friends. It's really no big deal mom so please don't tell daddy. I really don't want to fuss or have a scene tonight."

"Nikko, what do you mean don't tell your dad? What am I supposed to say? I will not lie for you Nikko. You know your dad will be totally against you going to some concert. Come now, go wash up, its time for dinner." This was her mom's way of giving in. She hated to argue with her and yet she was more liberal than her father ever would be. Nikko leaned over and kissed her mom. She knew her mom would keep her secret, mainly to keep the peace in the family. Dad could be a hell storm when he wanted to be and her mom hated to anger him.

Her mom grabbed her hands and said. "Your father is downstairs, you should go speak to him."

Nikko's dad was once a Captain in the Air Force, stationed in Korea during the Vietnam War. He met her mother at a local bar, where she worked as a cigarette girl. He told Nikko, the moment he laid eyes on her, he knew that she was the one. The woman he would spend the rest of his life with, although that would come some years later, and well after the war. Through no fault of their own, the two were separated soon after they met. It took her father nearly ten years later and several trips overseas before he located his beloved Sing Lee. He found her working in a clothing factory where conditions were terrible and wages were low. In the spring of nineteen seventy-eight, they were married in Korea, and he immediately brought her back to the states to live. Two years later, Nikko was born their first and only child. Her mom conceived again after that, but her pregnancy ended in a miscarriage and she learned that she could not bear anymore children. Nikko's birth was also difficult and as a child, she had been plagued with many childhood illnesses. This only caused her parents to be more so protective of her.

Nikko descended the stairs to her fathers' hobby room, where she found him working as usual on building another model fighter airplane. This was his favorite past time since retiring from Lockheed, where he worked as Floor supervisor after returning from the war. Every since leaving Korea, her mom never worked. Her job was to take care of Nikko and her dad. Nikko's dad leaned over his stool, his face and eyes covered with goggles while he inserted another piece and quickly secured it with his glue gun. He was unaware that he was being watched and Nikko would never dare sneak up from behind. That would scare the bejesus out of him. She had known that since childhood. Daddy never turned his back on anything or anyone. He was so paranoid of someone sneaking up behind him, that he normally set facing every door. Nikko believes his fear and that terrible war would haunt him forever. Nikko watched from the stairs. He had always been such a strong man to her, with big strong arms that would swing and cuddle and large hands that not only tickled and smoothed, but were also handy when it came to wiping tears. His hair was nearly white now and seemed to glow against his dark bronze skin. He was ever so handsome! She could see why her mom fell in love with him and he with her.

"Can I help?" She sheepishly asked.

Her dad turned around, gave her a big smile and removed his goggles.

"Hey sweetie! Sure you can."

Nikko leaned over and hugged her dad around the shoulders.

"Where you been all day?"

She scooted another stool up next to her dad and began to recount her day, minus the fight at the mall.

"Mom says dinners ready. She wants you to put down your toys and come eat." She smiled knowing she had lied just a bit.

"Oh my toys, huh. Well, my toys paid for that car you driving out there and your mothers' new curtains. That's pretty good for toys, don't you think." He ran his hands over her hair. "When you gonna let your hair grow back?"

"Dad! I like my hair like this. No maintenance required."

"You look like a boy!" He laughed.

"I do not! Quit! Come on, mom's waiting." She grabbed her father by the arm and the two of them went up for dinner.

Her mom had the table laid out with the fine china, rice bowl, sesame chicken, vegetables and hot tea. After washing their hands, everyone sat down for dinner, but not before a blessing from her dad. Dad rarely attended church, but he always blessed their food before they ate and prayed with her as a child before bed. These were their traditions. Over the years their two distinct cultures had merged and found a comfortable place. Nikko looked across the table at her parents, both seemed a lot older now, and yet they seemed as much in love as if they had just met. This was the type of love she was looking for, everlasting, to die for love. How will she ever find a brother like that? She knew he probably wasn't in the clubs, or the malls where she headed every Saturday with her friends, and yet she still kept looking. It's not like she was trying to get hitched already, that was not the situation. She just admired her parent's relationship, and was sure she wouldn't settle for less than that. Her goal right now is to make that big break and she wasn't letting anything or anyone stop her from achieving that.

Nikko studied dance all her life, ballet, modern, tap etc. She was an excellent dancer, had even received a scholarship to Juilliard, one she hadn't accepted yet. She liked ballet and all, but she was more passionate about Hip-Hop! If only she could get just one lucky break dancing in a video, she could take off from there. What she really wanted to do was to choreograph. She was that good! Just one lucky break and her star would shine. Perhaps tonight was the night! Tonight, her star would shine so brightly she wont' be missed. Like Martinette said, "We gonna blow them away!"

She had the slamming outfit, attitude, now all she had to do was get out the house without daddy finding out. That was going to take some careful planning and a little help from her mom.

After dinner, Nikko helped her mom clear the table and wash the dishes. Her dad retired to the den for a nap, and she knew this would be the only time she would have to escape. Nikko packed her clothes into a small bag and placed them in the trunk of her car. She called her Cousin Kim and told him to be expecting her at his house in about an hour. She told her mom the truth; she would be visiting Kim, and may even spend the night.

"Nikko, you don't want to upset your father. Please!" She said before giving her baby girl a kiss on the cheek. "He only worries about you, because he loves you so much, and so do I. We know you have to find your own way, but hanging in the streets is not it dear. I only pray that you will learn that soon enough and without much pain."

Nikko almost felt sad about sneaking out after that lecture. Her mom always had a way of making her feel so guilty about nothing. After all, she hadn't done a thing, at least not yet!

Nikko kissed her sleeping father lightly on the cheek, then headed out the door for Kim's and a night of what she hoped to be fun and excitement.

* * *

Martinette's patience grew thin waiting on Juanita to fix her hair. She couldn't believe how busy they were this afternoon, and it wasn't even Friday. She looked around the room and counted not one or two, but at least three other customers waiting for Juanita, two of them with wet hair, waiting to be set, and herself needing a touch-up, but settling on a wash and weave. She didn't know how it could be done in less than four hours. She thought about leaving and going elsewhere, but she knew it would be a wait wherever she went. That's just how it was at black hair salons. Juanita leaned from around the glass partition looking slimmer than she looked in months, but also dead tired.

"Hey Martinette girl! Look don't be mad! I know I'm running a little behind, but I promise to have you out of here by six."

"Alright Nita, you know if you wasn't my girl, I would have been gone." They both laughed.

"What you having today?"

"Wash and weave."

"You already pick up your hair?"

Martinette nodded.

"Bring it here, let me see."

Juanita raised the hair up to Martinette's head and checked the color and the texture. "You did good girl! Okay, go ahead and take out your ponytail and I'll get Muffin to wash you." She hollered "Muffin! Wash Martinette when you done with Crystal, alright!"

Martinette walked back to her seat up front and removed the weaved ponytail from the back of her hair. She was glad it came out easier than braids, taking them out could take all day. Next time she looked up, all the chairs were nearly full up front, and each beautician's seat and the dryers were occupied. Damn it was busy today and it was getting louder and louder by the minute. Black beauty salons were a trip! A melting pot between the Holy and the Hell bent for sure. In one chair you'd have someone praising the lord, trying to save everyone in the salon, then sitting in the chair next to her, somebody be talking about who fucking who! Martinette checked her watch once more, it was nearly four o' clock already and her head hadn't been touched. Muffin called from the back.

"Martinette." She drawled. "Come on back!"

It's about time, Martinette thought. *Damn if this girl wasn't slow!* Martinette made her way through the "valley of the damned", that small stretch of space between each of the beautician chairs, pass the dryers and to the wash area. She could feel at least 48 evil eyes on her, and with only 6 chairs, 6 beauticians and 6 clients, meant quite of few of them were doubling up on their haterade. Oh, but she loved it, and purposely switched every bit of her big ass as she went by. She couldn't stand them bitches! They hated on her for no reason. She tried to be friendly at first. She would speak to them, "Hey Nee-Nee! Hey Marcia! Hey Timone!" Not one of them spoke. They just looked her up and down, scrutinizing her from head to toe. But they couldn't say anything, because she always had it together.

Shit! Fuck'em. I'll give them something to hate!

On her approach, heads turned, eyes rolled, and Nee Nee, the shop owner whispered to Timone, but loud enough for Martinette to hear," I can't stand that bitch!"

Marcia turned not just her head, but her whole body and her client around to avoid looking at Martinette. Martinette grinned as she walked by loving every minute of it. Muffin waved her over.

"Why you be tripping like that? You know you be pissing them off, don't you?"

Martinette sat down and leaned her head back into the sink.

"Like I care! Anyway, how you been? I ain't seen you here in awhile." Muffin ran the warm water across Martinette's hair, which was now nearly shoulder length, then mixed in some shampoo and started to scrub.

"I been working at JC Penny's in the evenings most time but I still shampoo for Nita when I can. You itching anywhere?" She continued to scrub.

"Naw girl, you got it! I thought you was gonna get your Hair license. What happened?"

"I am. I just couldn't finish school, but I'm going back in the fall." She wrapped a towel around Martinette's hair. "Okay, you can get combed out. I'll talk with you later girl. Mookie! Come on back!" She hollered.

Martinette took a seat in Nita's chair.

"Hey Marti girl," Nita said. "Girl, your hair is really growing. Soon you won't need a weave."

"Girl, I'm always gonna need weave, cause I don't like to do no hair."

They laughed. Nita finished combing and smoothing and then sent Martinette to the hairdryer. "See, now wasn't that quick. Give me forty-five minutes under the dryer and I promise to have you out of here by five o'clock."

Martinette found herself a hairdryer, then picked up a "Hairstyles" magazine. She passed the time under the hairdryer by flipping through the pages of the magazine in search of a new look. After approximately fifteen minutes, she had located that perfect hairstyle for tonight's activity. She would most definitely be able to pull off that hairstyle, especially with what she was wearing. A smile crossed her lips. She didn't mean to gloat, but she had done well, despite the shouting match between her and Taye. She didn't even want to think about Maria or whatever. She thought. *That bitch would get hers, eventually. It was all her fault anyway, shooting off at the mouth, like she was running something. I wasn't even talking to her. She swings at me, trying to beat a sister down, and I'm just supposed to stand there? Oh hell no! Don't nobody play me like that! I'll kill that bitch over some dumb shit! She was messing with me, messing with my girl's Shantique baby's daddy. She deserved a beat down, and I was ready to giver her one. If it weren't for Taye, man I would have hurt that girl, seriously. She just messed up everybody's mood. Had Shantique talking about not going tonight! Can you believe it, after I scored one of the biggest deals of the year, she want to get ill over that want-to-be player, ex-boyfriend of hers, cause he got him a new piece, and she ain't even all that! I told Shantique to chill with that shit! We all going out, we gonna look good and we gonna have a damn good time. No doubt.*" Martinette's dryer stopped and she checked her watch. It was already four-thirty-five that gave Nita less than an hour to whip up her new do.

Nita not only did an excellent job on her hair, but also finished in record time. Martinette sped off in her ninety-six, red convertible mustang. She had about fifteen minutes before Nikko and Shantique would arrive at her house, and she hadn't even showered yet. Thank God, her apartment was only five minutes away.

"All hell no!" she cursed as she pulled up in front of her apartment and found her older brother sitting on her steps, smoking a cigarette and looking like he just escaped prison detail. She watched while he smashed the butt between his fingers, then smiled and waved at her as if she had been expecting him. Things couldn't get any worse. Here she was already running way behind, and who should shows up but Calvin, the dark, dark sheep of the family. He stood as she exited her car door.

"Hey baby sis, what's up? With his arms outstretched, he reached for her. She returned his hug and was greeted with the stench of days old funk, liquor, blunt and cigarettes. What would it be today?

"What's up Calvin? What you doing way over here?"

"I just came to see my little sister that's all. Ooh!" he danced around her. "Look at you, girl! You look just like... what's that girl, Beyonce! I like your hair! Girl you know you looking good!"

Martinette couldn't help but smile. Damn! He always had a way of getting to her.

"What you need?"

He smiled back, exposing more gum than teeth. He was actually looking worse than she ever had seen him.

"I just need a little change to get back to my place. You know like five or ten dollars. I start a job next week!"

Martinette handed her brother twenty-five dollars. She knew it was more than he asked for, and probably far more than what he needed.

Calvin thanked her for the money and promised again to pay it back, although she knew better. Martinette hugged her brother outside her apartment and watched him as he strolled down the street to the bus stop, until he was no longer in view. He was one of the main reasons she had to get her hands on some real money. Her brother was the only family she had, and yet he spent most of his life on the streets. He wouldn't live with her, because he couldn't see himself relying on her for his daily needs, so he chose the streets, always, no jobs, between jobs, and in and out of addiction. Calvin life hadn't been right since he returned from Vietnam, she wondered if it would ever be.

If she could just hook up a big money deal, she would take care of all of them, no doubt! Tonight may just be the night she had been dreaming of. She checked the time, and got shocked back to reality, she only had ten minutes before Nikko and Shantique arrived, and less than an hour before getting to the hotel. Martinette snatched off her clothes and placed a plastic cap over her head while starting the shower. After a five-minute shower, she rubbed her entire body down with baby oil then walked naked through her apartment to air dry. She had read in a magazine that air drying her body was best for the skin. Martinette surprised herself by being ready at five-thirty on the dot, hair, make-up and clothes. She took one long glance in the mirror, and she happened to be very pleased with what she saw. Her dress fit perfectly and accentuated all of her natural curves. It was a colorful mixture of royal blue, passion purple and fuchsia, organza and silk, one-armed sleeveless with a diagonal hemline. It was a designer rip off, but it looked just like the one seen on the cover of the August issue of *Cosmo*. She topped off the outfit with silver stiletto heels, with purple gems and a matching bag of the same. This was a special occasion so Martinette brought out the ice, two-carat diamond and platinum teardrop earrings, and her diamond and platinum, Bulova watch courtesy of her last boyfriend, Malik... Martinette turned around and checked out her backside view, an all she could say was "Whoa!"

> *   *   *

Shantique was pissed! Mad as hell about seeing Taye at the mall with some Puerto Rican girl. Then to top it all off, him, Martinette and his supposedly girlfriend gets all of them thrown out of Macys. She didn't even get the shoes she wanted. Everything was messed up, and Taye acting brand new and shit, like none of this was his fault. Damn him! Shantique slammed doors and drawers, still angry about the situation as she prepared to go out with Nikko and Martinette. Earlier today, this had been a dream come true. They were finally gonna get to hang with some ballers, meet the right kind of people, people who could definitely enhance their careers. Then Taye had to come along and fuck every thing up. He had made her so mad that she almost decided to stay home.

Martinette was right. She still wasn't over Taye. She grabbed her bottle of baby oil and began to smooth it onto her legs, thighs and upper torso. Shantique knew she had to get over Taye and she wasn't afraid to admit that this obsession with him was going to ruin her entire life. One thing for sure, she had never loved any man, the way she loved Taye. He was her very first love; hell he was her first everything! More importantly, he's Rashawn's father. There would always be a connection between them, always! She knew what she had to do! Starting tonight Shantique was going to find her a man! Not just any man mind you, a baller! And when she got through with him, he was gonna love him some Shantique, then Taye could go to hell, him and his Hoochie bitch!

* * *

The girls made good time getting to the Marriott Marquis. All of them were in high spirits and ready to get their party on. Nikko brought along a camera to record their night out with "Too Hot's" crew and the three of them didn't waste any time taking pictures the moment they stepped out of the car. While Nikko played photographer, Shantique and Martinette struck poses in front of the very glitzy, lighted water fountain that graced the Marquise motor lobby. Before they knew it, they had a crowd around them, some of them thinking that they were celebrities themselves. One older white male asked Shantique "Are you with that group 'Destiny's Child'? Shantique laughed and said no, but that didn't stop the older gentleman from giving her a compliment she would not forget. "Well, I didn't think so, because you are so much more beautiful!" That brought a much-needed smile to her face. Shantique had a lot on her mind, Taye, Rashawn, now her mother was even barking at her about working again. She needed tonight, just to kick it and have fun! She took her time in choosing the perfect outfit; a sheer lime embroidered tulle pleasant blouse by Richard Tyler and a pair of black leather shorts. Nikko on the other hand chose an extremely beautiful and sexy Dolce and Gabana black silk, halter style dress that stopped at her thighs, and whose halter dipped low in the front and in the back it ended just above her butt line. She also wore her ice to compliment her dress. A diamond and platinum bracelet, earrings and ankle bracelet! It was going to be a night to remember.

* * *

Martinette enjoyed playing the game. If they thought she was a celebrity, why not go with it.

"Sure sweetie, what's your name?" Martinette signed her name on the back of some man's checkbook.

"Marti what are you doing?" Shantique hollered.

Marti was about to answer when she noticed Mr. Bling Bling himself walking toward them in a Black and white pinstriped suit, black silk shirt, matching tie and carrying a walking cane. Shantique started laughing.

"He thinks he is so fine. Look at him, old player, I bet he was something back in the eighties with his Big Daddy Kane suit on."

Martinette elbowed her.

"Shut up girl, that's our ride, you messing with. And he ain't really all that bad, just a little dated."

Martinette stepped forward and held out her hand.

"What's up baby? You looking mighty fine there, you think we gonna be able to ride with you?"

Mr. Bling smiled at the compliment, bent down and gently kissed Martinette's hand. He held onto her hand and turned her around three hundred and sixty degrees, getting an eye full.

"Damn girl, I didn't think you could get much finer, but you damn show did." He pulled her into his arms and squeezed. "I think I'm gonna have to keep you to my self."

He laughed and Martinette caught a whiff of what smelled like garlic and shit. She nearly gasped, but played it off by laughing along with him while pulling away. She stepped out of his reach, caught her breath which she had been holding for nearly a minute and called to her friends.

"Shantique, Nikko our ride is here. You know my friends don't you?" She introduced everybody and tried to get as far away from Mr. Bling Bling as possible. That was going to be a difficult task, especially while in the limo, but as soon as they got to the concert and after party, she was going lose Big Daddy. That was for damn sure! In the mean time, she would have to deal with it.

* * *

Nikko was awestruck, not by the limo, but the man standing near it. He was hard to miss, tall, dark and very handsome. He smiled and introduced himself to the threesome.

"Good evening ladies, my name is Butter, I'll be your driver tonight." He said with the confidence of a man who knows what he wants and how to get it.

Nikko was immediately drawn to the charcoal colored brother with the engaging eyes. His black pants and white shirt hung loosely on his taut body, and she could only imagine what his skin would look like next to hers. Butter held out his hand and like a very experienced gentleman guided her into the back of the stretch limousine. Nikko couldn't help but notice his smooth skin and well-manicured hands. She liked a man that took good care of himself.

"Where did you get the name 'Butter'?" She asked.

He smiled and leaned forward, close enough to her that she got a good whiff of his cologne, and boy did he smell good! There ain't nothing like the smell of a man with some good cologne.

"Let's see, it's what my friends call me."

"I don't get it. You don't look like a Butter". There's got to be more to it."

"Yeah there is, but that's a story for another day. I hope." He winked and smiled almost simultaneously.

"Oh, okay." Nikko responds, although silently she's thinking, "I hope so too!"

* * *

Shantique was glad she came. She marveled at the fine and luxurious interior of the limousine, running her hands across its white, baby soft leather seats. *This is something I could definitely get used to.*

. Martinette spent most of her time fending off Mister Bling while Nikko carried on a conversation with Butter. With nothing left to do, Shantique closed her eyes and settled in for the long drive, dreaming of better days to come.

The nearly hour drive went by so fast that none of them seem to notice that they had arrived in front of the auditorium, amidst a crowd of fans and concert goers. Everyone was so excited. It was the very first time they arrived at a concert or anything in a limousine, well not since their High School Prom. Martinette reached into her bag and refreshed her makeup and lipstick, while Nikko nervously pulled at her dress and Shantique applied dabs of perfume.

"This could be it." Shantique thought. "The day they had all been waiting for, the day she dreamed of. It was at least very close to it, only one thing was missing, Crazy X."

"Alright Ladies and Gentleman, We have arrived." Butter announced from up front. "I'll be pulling up to the door in less than a minute." He lowered the window and addressed them directly. "You Ladies look wonderful. Oh and you too, Sonny! Have a good night tonight. I will be waiting for you when the concert is finished."

"You real smooth man. Smooth like butter. Give me some!" Mr. Bling reached his hand through the divider glass to receive his dap from Butter.

"Alright man, you take care of them ladies, especially this one." He points at Nikko and she smiles back.

"You got it man. They with me and nothing but royalty rolls with Big Daddy."

"What I tell you, he thinks he's Big Daddy Kane." Shantique whispered to Nikko.

Nikko not paying much attention to the exchange, whispered back, "Butter is real nice."

"Yeah, he's alright for a chauffeur, but we got bigger fish to fry. Come on girl, it's time to get our roll on. It's our night, you know." Shantique said.

"Yeah, you right, I was just thinking…"

"Well quit thinking and come on, we got to go."

Butter opened their door and helped them out of the limo, one by one. He held onto Nikko's hand and said.

"You have an especially good time." Nikko smiled back and couldn't help but be swept up by his kind eyes and smile.

"I'll see you later." She said.

"Can't wait." He replied.

"Me neither." She said back, halfway not believing it. This was new for her. In all her young years, she had never been attractive to the average man, let alone a working man. Since the time she had become interested in dating, she had always aimed high, dealing with nobody but the best and the best had to have money and lots of it. Butter was different. Not only was he kind, funny and fine, he had class. "If he only had some money." She thought. "He would be the perfect catch."

The crowd outside the theater wrapped around the building, lingering into the adjoining streets on both sides of the theatre. Groups of women by the dozen stood scantily dressed along side a few couples and even fewer groups of single men. Vendors of all types yelled from the sidewalks, selling everything from posters and t-shirts to CD's, hats and other paraphernalia. Martinette especially enjoyed the attention they were receiving once they exited the limousine. People were looking at them like they were celebrities and she didn't have any problem with giving the people what they wanted. She was all attitude as she strolled up to the door of the theater, arm in arm with Mister Bling. Martinette smiled and waved to the crowd of playa haters and barking men. Shantique graciously followed behind with Nikko by her side, in awe of the attention and a little bit nervous. She felt her legs tremble as she walked. Her voice shook when she whispered to Nikko.

"Girl, I ain't never seen nothing like this."

"Me neither, I guess we better enjoy it. Times like this don't come every day."

"Yeah, but I got a feeling, this only the beginning for us."

Mister Bling handled them backstage passes, which they draped around their necks while two very big body guards ushered them in the door and led them past a row of screaming woman to four front row seats. Bling set in the middle of the ladies, between Martinette and Shantique, with Nikko at the end. The two seats next to Martinette were empty and she contemplated moving one over to put some distance from her and Bling. She was really getting tired of him holding onto her, placing his arm around her like she was his. She thought if no one sat in those seats by the start of the concert, she was moving, but first things first. She reached deep into her purse and pulled out some mints, offering one to Bling. Shantique caught Martinette's eye and mouthed "Thank You". The two of them broke out in laughter, which broke up when it seems every woman in the house screamed at the top of their lungs. That's when Shantique looked up onstage and couldn't believe what she saw. The host, a local deejay introduced the reason for the mania, and surprise walk on guest.

"Yo! What's up! Can you believe it? Crazy X is in the house!" They slapped hands and hugged brother style.

"What's up, What's up Macon!" X said.

"Man, what you doing here?"

"I'm chilling, checking out my boys "Too Hot", you know just holding it down." He looks out into the crowd and then directly at Shantique. "Man, Macon got some fine woman up in here!" The women screamed. Nikko pushed at Shantique.

"Girl, he was looking right at you."

"So you gonna stay awhile?" The deejay asked.

"Yeah, sure. I'll be here."

"Alright then, Macon, GA let's give it up for Crazy X!" The crowd screamed while Shantique sat in awe. Before he left the stage, he caught her eye once more, this time winking and pointing. Everyone, including Martinette caught that exchange. She leaned over Bling to speak to Shantique.

"Girl, you are in there!"

Shantique held onto her chest as if it would drop to the floor if she let go. She smiled back at Martinette and then leaned over to give her a high five! Everything was happening so fast, everything she wanted. She could hardly catch her breath. Nikko whispered to her that the playa haters were pissed, but she could care less, tonight was her night, and her night alone.

The concert began with a local rap group, who happened to be very good, but not good enough to hold the attention of this rowdy crowd. After seeing Crazy X, they were more than eager to get to the main act. Martinette eyed the two seats again, she thought about moving over now, right before "Too Hot" came on but then her plans were ruined when she saw a large man and woman being ushered her way. The woman could have been her twin, dressed sharp, upper-class Hoochie style, big boned, high yellow with lot's of weave, and she walked in like her shit didn't stank. It wasn't until they were just a few feet away and she saw Martinette that she grabbed her man's arm.

"Damn well better." Martinette thought, even before she knew who he was. She leaned over to Bling and asked. "Who's that?" Bling stared at her like she was crazy or something.

"Shit girl, that's Big Ro, Rotando Watson. He plays for the Lakers! Cash money baby! Multi-million dollar contract. He's the baddest center in the league!" Bling said in awe.

"Oh!" She replied calmly, then crossed her legs, exposing the lengthy split that rose up to her hips. Martinette turned slightly to her left, giving Ro and whoever else an eyeful while acting uninterested and unaffected by his fame or fortune. She could tell by who he was with what he liked. As he sat down the row of seats rocked. "Damn he was big!" She thought and he really wasn't bad looking either. Dark skinned baldheaded, no facial hair, and nice teeth, certainly doable. He spoke to her and the others.

"Good evening!"

"What's up Ro?" Bling said. He almost jumped all over Martinette to shake this man's hand.

Ro returned the handshake but concentrated his attention on Martinette.

"Hi." Martinette said extending her hand to Ro. "I'm Martinette and this is Blin... I mean Sonny, and next to him are my two girls, Shantique and Nikko."

Shantique and Nikko waved from down the way.

"Pleased to meet you ,Martinette."

The first thing she noticed about this handsome and extremely rich baller was that he couldn't take his eyes off of her. That was a good sign and secondly he never bothered to introduce his date to them. Now what was that all about? Surely, Miss Thing had to be pissed. Martinette looked her way, trying to catch her eye, but she stared straight ahead, seemingly engrossed in the show. Martinette knew better, it was all an act, girlfriend was about to explode. At least she would be had he dissed her like that. To tell you the truth, that shit would never happen to her, no matter who the man, rich or not. She rolled her eyes his way as if he had just dissed her.

Ro caught Martinette's eye action and said.

"Excuse me?"

"What?"

"Did you just roll your eyes at me?"

"No! What makes you think that? I mean why would I roll my eyes at you. I don't even know you." *Damn he's been checking me out the whole time!*

"Not yet you don't."

His lady friend tapped his shoulder.

It was about time that girl stepped up. Martinette tried to keep from looking over at them but curiosity got the best of her. It seemed Miss Thing had finally gotten some balls because the two of them were involved in a heated exchange. Martinette turned away when she unexpectedly caught Ro's eye. Miss Thing seeing all of this, yanked hard at his collar and it was on then, there once quiet exchange turned loud. The only thing that saved them and Ro's reputation was the loud booming voice of the radio deejay announcing the main act, "Too Hot". The crowd went wild, women were screaming, men barking, band playing, all drumming out the argument taking placing between Ro and his woman friend. By the time "Too Hot" took the stage Miss Thing was leaving and Ro turned his attention to Martinette.

"It's all your fault." He leaned over and said to Martinette.

"I don't think so."

"It's all your fault I no longer have a date. So tell me, how you going make it up to me?"

"You the one with shifty eyes. You just wrong and you got what you deserve!"

"Damn you mean! Can't you cut a brother some slack? Look at me, I'm lonely, I just lost my date and..."

Martinette turned his way for the first time since his girl left.

"Stop it! You are so pathetic. You can have anybody you want, so why you playing with me?"

"Because, I don't want just anybody. I want you."

"Yeah right! That's smooth. I guess all the girls just drop their drawls with that line." He laughs.

"Damn you rough too! I like a roughneck!"

"Roughneck!" Martinette snapped back and rolled her big eyes. "You tripping! If you wanna know I'm all woman and I like to be treated like a lady."

"Will you be my lady?"

"No! Now be quiet so I can watch the show."

"Pushy too! Oooh I just might be in love."

Martinette laughed. She really enjoyed their exchange. Not only was Ro fine and rich, he was also funny. She liked that. But she also knew that he didn't exactly treat his women like royalty, at least that's the impression she got thus far. Now that's a negative and something she absolutely could not deal with it. Maybe she would give him her number tonight, if he plays his cards right. *I'll just have to wait and see.*

* * *

Nikko sat mesmerized while lead singer Laron serenaded the crowd. It was a love ballad and nicely sung by the handsome twin. She couldn't believe how much he sounded just like the CD and how fine he was in person. The other twin was just as cute, but she thought that Laron was much finer. There was something about him that was so cool, yet adorable. He wasn't as rough acting as Crazy X, but he had a hardness to him that was so sexy. She sat there dreaming as if he was singing that song only for her. Nikko sat on the edge of her seat, bracing herself for when he made it to the end of the stage. She thought, maybe she could touch him, shake his hand or something. Laron was singing on the opposite end of the stage where he kneeled down and sung to a crowd of screaming women. Nikko screamed with delight along with the other two thousand women in the theatre. Her hands began to sweat as he made his away along the stage, now heading in her direction. Like her, all the women seated in the front row on both sides of her made their way to the stage, with arms reaching out, all of them trying to touch Laron. Nikko barely made it up front at first, but she squeezed her small frame through the group and thought she was as close as she would ever gonna be to the man of her dreams. He touched hands all around her, but not hers.

Nikko was a little disappointed, but still she held out, hoping that there was still a chance. She couldn't move away if she wanted, the crowd behind her had moved up closer and was now mashing her body up against the stage. The song was almost over and he still hadn't kneeled down like he did at the other end. Nikko was beginning to lose all hope of that private serenade when the music slowed to a drumbeat and he spoke to the crowd.

"What's up Macon?" Laron shouted. The crowd screamed. "I said what's up Macon! Y'all in here?" The crowd screamed again. "Now I hear you." He laughed. "I just wanted to thank you for having us here. We've been traveling all over and it's good to come to a town where you are appreciated. What's up ladies? Fella's I hope you don't mind if I talk to the ladies for a moment.

Y'all my dogs and all but there's something I want to say to the ladies. Ladies!" The women scream. "You know it gets real lonely on the road. Traveling from town to town, hotel to hotel, and not having anybody to call your own, nobody to hold, and nobody to hold me. Sometimes a brother just got to break down. You know what I mean. A brother like me needs love! I was just wondering if I could get some special lady to come onstage and dance with me. Can a brother get some love?" The crowd screams and women from the balcony, to the eastside and the west begin making their way to the stage. Nikko's body was slammed even tighter into the stage. She tried with all her might to raise her hand, but she was hurting and as much as she wanted to be on that stage, she also wanted to get out of this crowd. She tried turning around, but she couldn't, she could do nothing but stand and take the punishment.

Nikko almost cried out in pain when a really big sister swung her arm over and knocked Nikko in the head.

"Dammit!" Nikko screamed. "At least you could do is apologize." She said to the woman.

"Ain't nobody trying to hit you, they pushed me." The woman said back, never apologizing.

That was it. Nikko thought. She was getting out of here, if she had to fight, kick and bite her way out, but then someone grabbed her hand and when she looked up it was Laron pulling her onstage. The other women around her screamed and pulled at her clothes and torso as if to hitch a ride. But surprisingly none of it bothered Nikko her eyes stayed glued on Laron lifting her out of the crowd like a baby then placing her gently down on the stage. She pulled at her dress and tossed her fingers through her hair while he held tightly onto her hand.

"Would you dance with me pretty lady?" Laron asked.

Nikko nodded too excited to utter a word, too shocked and bruised to do anything. Laron started singing again cradling Nikko in his arms. She felt like she was dancing on air. Although the crowd was screaming and Laron was singing, Nikko could hear none of it. She was obviously too busy living her dream to even notice that he had finished the song. He whispered into her ear before ushering her back off the stage.

"Meet me backstage after the show."

She floated off the stage into the waiting arms of Bling who assisted in getting her through the crowd and back to her seat. Shantique was pulling at her clothes, screaming loudly in her ear while Martinette was shouting her name, but the only thing Nikko heard was Laron's voice, asking her to meet him backstage.

CHAPTER 3

By the close of the concert everyone was feeling pretty good about how the night was going, everyone that is except Bling, who was pretty pissed that Martinette and Ro was hitting it off so well. He kept giving her dirty looks throughout the night, so much so that she insisted on moving to the empty seat on the other side of Ro. Bling cursed and turned his attention to Shantique, but she wasn't having none of it and told him so. He tried to go off on Shantique when Ro stepped to him, taking him outside for a little talk. When the two returned everything seemed to be fine. Martinette didn't know what transpired between the two, but she suspected that big as Ro was he didn't have to say much to shut Bling up. She wondered if they would still be going to "Too Hot's" after party, since they were after all Bling's guest. She leaned closer to Ro and asked.

"So you going to the after party set for "Too Hot"?

"Yeah, as a matter of fact I am. Your boy Bling invited me outside; in fact, I've decided to hitch a ride with y'all. You don't mind do you? I mean, I won't be cramping your style, invading your space?"

"No, not at all. I just thought you had your on limousine. Bigshot like yourself."

"As a matter of fact I do, I just don't have the same delightful company." Martinette smiled and thought, *Boy he is slick!*

The concert ended and Bling ushered the group backstage and away from the crowd. He seemed to be in better spirits, but still not quite as friendly and big on himself as before the concert. Shantique and Nikko were all smiles and nerves as they followed closely behind Bling to the back of the stage.

"Girl, that was the dopest concert I have ever seen!" Nikko said. "I swear I was dreaming. I don't know how we gonna top this."

"I know what you mean. I don't think I ever want it to end, this night I mean."

"You think we'll see Crazy X backstage?"

"I sure hope so. You been checking out Martinette with that baller? They sure are getting pretty close."

"Yeah, I know. Bling looked pretty messed up about it. I saw him trying to get next to you. What was that all about?"

"Girl, he was tripping, but his ass just got tripped up. He's stupid. He knew Martinette wasn't interested in him then he gonna get pissed because she hooking up with Ro."

Bling turned around like he heard his name or something and both Nikko and Shantique smiled. Martinette joined them at the curtain with Ro not too far behind her greeting lots of fans, mostly women trying to get next to him.

"What's up girls?" Martinette said. "Is this the shit or what?" They all silently screamed, getting Bling's attention again. He turned around saw Martinette and damn if he didn't roll his eyes. Martinette winked and said. "I love you too Baby."

"Fuck you!" Bling said under his breath.

"Ooh, don't you wish."

"Martinette!" Shantique said. "Girl, are you forgetting that's our ride back to Atlanta, and our ticket to the after party. You gonna fuck things up for everybody."

"Girl, He ain't nothing but a gopher and don't worry about the ride back to Atlanta or to the party, Ro has us covered."

"Ro! You just met him. He could be playing you. Look, just be nice okay, for all our sakes."

* * *

Nikko didn't say much her eyes were glued to that backstage curtain as she caught glimpses of Laron and his brother. She knew that Shantique was right but she couldn't be bothered with that now, this might be her only chance to get with Laron. There were about thirty or so women waiting in the wings along with their small group of five, all of them were trying to get with "Too Hot" and "Crazy X". That made it like six to one, the odds were against her. All of them just as pretty, decked out from head to toe, all invited backstage. With everything being the same, the only thing that stood out, was that they were actually with "Too Hot's" manager. That was the good thing. The bad thing was, he wasn't exactly in the best mood and Martinette wasn't making it any better.

"Alright, alright!" Martinette said. "I'll be cool! I promise!"

She grabbed Bling by the arm and pulled him close, whispering.

"Look, I'm sorry about that! I, we really appreciate you bringing us to the concert."

"It's cool baby, I know what's up. You see I've been in this game a long time. A girl's got to do what a girl's got to do! Word!"

Ro placed his large arms around Martinette waist, just barely missing the exchange between her and Bling. But she didn't leave Bling hanging, when Ro wasn't looking she caught Bling's eye and gave him a wink.

All of a sudden, Bling's mood lightened up and he was back to his old self again, shucking and jiving like before. He turned to Shantique and Nikko.

"Come on ladies, y'all ready to meet the guys?"

The two of screamed. They didn't know what Martinette had said or done, but whatever it was it sure made a difference. Bling flashed his credentials to the two heavy guards at the dressing room and indicated to them that the girls were his guests. They had no problem letting Ro get by, but not before getting an autograph first. Bling knocked on the dressing room door, three times then twice. It seemed more like a signal to the girls. Shantique turned to Nikko and said.

"What was that all about?"

"I don't know and don't really care. I just want to get in."

The first knock went unanswered so Bling repeated his patterned knock then yelled.

"Yo, it's Sonny man! I got guests." The door cracked open and a cloud of smoke drifted their way. "What's up man, it's about time." Bling said to the man in the door. "Look, I got some people with me. Y'all straight?" The door opened wide and the tall smoking man peered around Bling, checking out Shantique and Nikko. Shantique recognized him and turned back to Nikko.

"Girl, that's Ty, the bass player, Martinette is going to freak!"

She tried to catch Martinette's eye but she was too busy charming Ro to notice who was standing in front of her wearing his signature white T-shirt and leather pants. Ty seemed to be pleased with what he saw, speaking first to Bling.

"Damn man, what you do hit the lottery or something nigga?"

They slapped hands and Bling was all smiles.

"Naw man! I brought them up from Atlanta in the limo. You know me nigga, I cop like that!"

Shantique couldn't stand listening to Bling brag about picking them up, like they were his hoes or something.

"Move out the way nigga so we can come in!"

Ty stepped aside then held out his hand to meet Shantique and Nikko.

"What's up ladies? Damn you sho is fine! What yo name is shorty?"

"I'm Shantique." She smiled and turned to Nikko. "This is my girl Nikko." She pointed behind her and said, "This is my girl…"

"Ro! Rotando Watson!" He shouted stepping past Shantique, Nikko and nearly stepping on Martinette to get to Ro. They slapped hands. "Damn man it's good to see you!"

Shantique could tell from the look on Martinette's face, she wasn't happy about being ignored. She moved around the two, and made her way up front.

"What's up girls?"

"Girl, did you check out Ty? He is so fine!" Shantique said.

"He looks just like his CD cover don't he?" Added Nikko.

"He's alright! Rude though!" Martinette smacked. "Motherfucker nearly took my foot off trying to get to Ro." They laughed.

"Yeah, I caught that. So what's up with you and Ro? Y'all hanging pretty tight there." Shantique asked. Bling turned to the three women and asked.

"Y'all coming in or not?"

"I'll tell you all about it later." Martinette said.

The three of them followed Bling into the dressing room, filled wall-to-wall with women of all types. Bling nearly jumped out of his pants at the sight. Shantique and Nikko were not surprised, but they were damn sure disappointed. Shantique searched the room for Crazy X, while Nikko looked for Laron and Martinette strolled around like the Queen bee looking down at every woman in the room. Bling said something then quickly disappeared behind another door, leaving the three of them standing in the middle of the room. Martinette was the first to speak.

"Now this shit is whacked. I did not come all the way from Atlanta to be sitting up here in a room full of women, waiting to be picked up. This is a fucking meat market!"

"I didn't see Crazy X in here, so to tell you the truth I'm ready to go." Shantique added.

"I knew it was too good to be true! This makes no sense, what they gonna do with all these women?" Nikko asked.

"Fuck them!" Martinette said. "They probably try to do every last one of them! Look at them! Some of them look like they came right off the street. Girl, fuck this shit, I might as well hang with Ro!"

"Well you better get him before he comes in here!" Shantique said crossing her arms like the rest of the girls.

Martinette went back outside with Ro and Ty. She returned about ten minutes later.

"Come on, Ro is going to take us to the after party. Y'all ready?"

"Yeah." Shantique said dryly. "Any place is better than here."

"Girl, I been ready." Nikko added.

All eyes followed the threesome as they headed out.

Bling came out of the locked room just in time to catch the three leaving. He staggered over to them all red-eyed and smelling of weed.

"Hey! What's up ladies? Where y'all going? I thought y'all wanted to hook up with "Too Hot"?

Martinette leaned around Shantique and Nikko and motioned to Bling to come closer. He leaned over to her and she said.

"Look, we ain't got time to be waiting around with no group of chickenheads. You see what I'm saying. We riding with Ro to the after party, so maybe we'll see you there. You taking us back to Atlanta right? Don't get too fucked up and forget you got passengers Bling!"

Bling stood there for a moment in a daze before laughing and shouting out loud. "Chicken heads! Damn girl you right!" He looked around the room and pointed at the ladies leaning against the wall. "Ain't nothing in here but a bunch of Chicken heads! Let's roll! Where Ro at? I'm riding with y'all." He grabbed onto Shantique arm. "Damn girl! What you say your name is, you sure is fine! Fine as wine!"

Shantique gave Martinette an evil look. Martinette laughed.

"Let's go then, Ro is waiting."

Nikko turned to Bling and asked. "So who was in the room with you?"

"Everybody, you know. It was fucking party in there! Stuffy as hell though."

"Everybody like who? Laron, Taron?"

"Yeah…Taron. I ain't seen Laron. He the sneaky one, ain't no telling where his ass is? Laron the lover! You like him don't you?"

"No! I was just asking. I don't even know him."

"You lying girl. You wide open! I saw you up there dancing with Laron! Laron's the quiet one, you know. You gotta watch out for the quiet ones. Laron the lover!"

"Why you keep saying that? Laron the lover!"

"Cuz that's what he is. He loves all the ladies and all the ladies love Laron. Like you!"

"Excuse me! But I don't love Laron!" Nikko rolled her eyes.

"Not yet!" Bling said under his breath

* * *

Butter saw the ladies first with some guy and then Bling. He blew his horn and flashed his lights. Nikko was the first to see him.

"There's Butter over there! She pointed.

"We riding in Ro's limo to the party Nikko, Bling says Butter will be driving "Too Hot". Shantique said.

"Oh." Nikko said a little disappointed. She waved at Butter from across the way. He waved back and hollered.

"You have a good time?"

"So, so!" She said walking toward the limo. The concert was real good! I guess I'm just getting a little tired."

"You going to the after party?"

"Yeah, Martinette got us a ride with Rotando Blackmon."

"Ro! So that's who she's with. I was wondering who that was. Well, I hope you're not too tired to save a dance for me."

"You gonna come in?"

"Yeah! That's the best part about driving for the group. I get to party too!" He laughs.

Bling walks up.

"What's up BUTTER? Man look, I'm gonna catch a ride with Ro, so I'll see you at the spot."

"Alright man! You take it easy alright!" They slap hands.

"You got it baby!" Bling said and pimps away. Butter turns his attention back to Nikko.

"So, I'll see ya later?"

"Definitely!"

Martinette hollers from up ahead.

"Nikko come on!"

"I gotta go."

* * *

"This party is off the hook!" Martinette shouted across the table. She seemed to be the only one having a good time and why wouldn't she? Shantique thought. Everything was going her way. Not only was she the life of the party, she had caught a mighty fine fish, not to mention rich! All eyes were on her and Ro! Shantique had to admit they did make a cute couple. She just wished she was having as much fun as they were. Martinette downed another shooter of Tequila, chasing it with a glass of Crystal. Shantique thought, Ro had better watch himself! She knew first hand what Tequila does to Martinette. For some reason the image from that commercial where hundreds of people are running down an alley, falling and tripping over themselves, running from a big, wild, bull, that was Martinette on Tequila. This was not the time or place for her to show her ass. She checked around the room for her girl Nikko, and spotted her holding up a wall near the bar, looking just as bored.

"What's up girl?"

"Shantique, in about five more minutes I'm gonna start drinking shooters with Martinette and Ro! You know what I mean! Shit, I didn't come all the way to Macon to be bored. At least if I catch a buzz I can have a little fun, except I ain't seen nobody in here I want to have fun with." *Where is Butter when I need him?*

"I know what you mean." Shantique said, bobbing her head to Crazy X's song. "Damn! Where is he? Come on let's order a shooter!"

"Alright girl, it's on!" Nikko got a hold of the bartender and ordered the drinks. Martinette hollered from across the way.

"That's what I'm talking about. It's about time you two decided to join the party!"

Nikko and Shantique downed their shooters and sipped at their champagne. It was just what they needed. The two of them began to loosen up a little and enjoy the scene around them. This was the first

time they had ever been in a VIP section and it was kind of nice looking out over the dance floor, being served and observed. After about two more shooters the three of them were up dancing with Ro and he couldn't be happier. Although from time to time some girls from the dance floor made it up to the VIP section by bribing a security guard, he didn't seem to pay much attention to any of them. He only had eyes for Martinette and she gave him plenty to look at. They all danced another song then flopped onto the circular couch, out of breath and thirsty. Martinette told a joke and they all laughed so hard that the manager and some of the waiters came over to see what the commotion was all about.
Martinette told the joke again and sent them away as well in tears. Everyone was so busy laughing that no one even noticed the small crew approaching.

"Damn Ro! What's up? It looks like the party is over here!" Crazy X spoke then turned to Shantique and said. "Don't I know you?" Shantique nearly fell over, face first into the table and her drinks but she would later remember that it was purely the liquor that made her speak up.

"No, but you will!"

Nikko screamed. Martinette and Ro fell back into the couch in another laughing fit.

He reached out his hand and grabbed hers.

"I'm X and you are?"

"Shantique. Pleased to meet you and it's about time you got here."

"You been waiting on me?"

"All my life."

That did it. She had him hooked. He waved his boy's goodbye and grabbed a seat next to Shantique and Nikko.

"You were at the concert right, sitting in the first row?"

"Yep! That was me. I'm surprised you noticed."

"I've always had an eye for beauty, especially a chocolate sister like you. So where you from? Macon?"

"No. I'm from Atlanta."

"Hotlanta! I love Atlanta. I got some family there too! So what y'all been drinking? Whatever it is I want some, cause y'all pretty wired over here." Shantique and Nikko laughed.

"You sure you can hang?"

"As long as you got my back."

* * *

Nikko tried not to listen to the conversation between Shantique and X, but she couldn't help it. She didn't really have anyone else to talk to since Martinette and Ro was kind of into some things over in the corner and she wasn't about to interrupt that so she pretended to be listening to the music. She thought that this would be a good time to make a bathroom run, hell why not, it ain't like anybody is paying attention to her, and she was right, no one was. She excused herself from the table and made her way to the restroom, which thank God was not far. She couldn't believe how many drinks she had tonight, much more than she probably has ever drunk in her entire life. She knew she wasn't much of a drinker, but tonight she was handling things and it did take the edge off and allowed her to have some fun. Now, she thought everyone is in couples and things, and she was pretty much alone. After tinkling for what seemed like ten minutes, she spent another ten to fifteen minutes in the mirror fixing her makeup and messing with her hair. Although nothing was wrong with either, she just wanted to waste some time before going back to the table. She reached in her purse, locating her eye drops because her eyes were getting red and irritated from the smoke. Her eyes cleared up in a matter of seconds. Well she thought, can't do much more to look good, I guess I better just go out there and make the best of it. Whatever that means!

Nikko turned the corner from the restroom and couldn't believe her eyes, standing at her table talking with X and Shantique were none other than Laron, Taron, Ty and Butter. She caught Shantique's eye and who winked at her from across the way. She didn't know whether to walk or run to the table, but she did know for sure that she stood there at the restroom door another five minutes deciding on what to do next. Martinette must have seen her standing over there and shouted from the table.

"Nikko, girl come here!" That's when everyone turned around and looked her way like she needed that shit! More pressure! She waved back and made her way to the now crowded table of superstars.

"Hey!" She said to no one in particular, scooting down in the seat next to Shantique. Ty and Taron spoke then left for the bar, while Butter waited on the outside of the table looking debonair and cool. Laron on the other hand took the seat next to Nikko surprising her both with his undivided attention and questions.

"Where were you? I thought you would be back stage?"

"I was, but it was a little crowded." Nikko was having a hard time looking him in the eye. She looked down at her now sweating hands, then at bar and back to her hands. "Me and my friends weren't feeling the vibe, so we left. Came here instead."

"Yeah, I'm sorry y'all weren't feeling the vibe." He says half mocking her. "I guess I'll just have to find some way to make it up to you."

"Yeah?"

"Yeah! So you came here with Sonny?"

"Sonny?" She looked confused for a moment, then noticed him pointing at none other than Bling. " Oh Bling! Yeah, I mean we rode to Macon with him, but we came to the party with Ro."

"Bling? Who's Bling?" He laughs.

She notices that he has pretty teeth like Butter and she likes his laugh.

"Nobody, just a nickname we gave Sonny."

"Oh, I see because of his teeth and all that jewelry."

"Yeah, exactly."

"Nikko. That's a tight name!"

"Thanks!" She wonders about Butter again, but when she looks up, he's no longer there. She was glad. She was kind of enjoying talking with Laron. He's cool for a superstar player. She stares at him closely, taking in all of his assets. Damn his eyes are deep; a woman can lose her soul in those eyes. He catches her staring and she looks away quickly.

"You looking for somebody?"

"No."

"Good! Cause I was hoping you and I could kick it awhile. I mean if you don't mind."

*   *   *

Shantique couldn't see, but she could hear Martinette gearing up to go off on somebody. She hadn't cursed yet, but Shantique knew when Martinette was upset. Her voice rose about five octaves, somewhere around extremely high soprano, or to put it simply think Minnie Ripperton or Mariah Carey just before they hit that note that left the majority of us gasping for breath. Marti could speak that note and when she did, somebody was about to take an ass whooping. Shantique kept her cool but she was becoming concerned about her girl, especially after she heard her holler "Fuck you Bitch", from across the way. X stood up to look along with everyone else then turned to her and said.

"Hey, you better go check your girl! That girl she messing with is a banger. She don't be fucking around."

Shantique immediately got up from the couch, but it was too late, within seconds all hell broke loose!

CHAPTER 4

The bitch had it coming. Her and Ro was having a good time, just chilling, drinking Crystal getting to know one another when this hood rat come shaking her ass all up in Ro's and her face. She tried to ignore her at first, but the more she drank the more pissed off she was getting. The bitch wasn't even pretty or nothing and she couldn't talk worth a damn, slurring her words, pronouncing everything wrong, sounding and looking just like she was, a hood rat! She was sporting one of those ghetto funk styles, with mounds of somebody's hair piled on top of her head, then shooting straight up to the sky, kind of like a tower. The rest of her head was covered in strands of hot pink crinkles, and cropped bangs. First of all, she was way too black to be wearing pink anything, and by the way, how did she get up here in the first place and what the fuck is she doing shaking her ass all up in my face. That was it, the last straw.

Martinette scooted to the edge of her seat and shouted to the dancing diva. "Bitch can you move your ass out of my face please?"

"Who you calling bitch?" Her voice was deep, scratchy and heavy.

"Oh, excuse me. I mean MAN BITCH!"

Ro busted up laughing and so did Martinette when the girl pulled a knife. Martinette see's it, but doesn't half believe what is going down. When she realizes the girl is seriously thinking about cutting her, she loses her high in a matter of seconds. *Ain't no bitch ever cut me and I wasn't about to be cut this time either.* Ro wasn't laughing anymore.

"Move Martinette. She got a knife."

Martinette heard him pleading with her to sit down, but it was too late for that. That bull had pushed her buttons, crossed the line, stepped on the wrong fucking toe and worst of all she wouldn't stop talking shit.

The last time she waved that piece of knife in her face, Martinette picked up the closest thing to her, which happened to be an opened and very expensive bottle of Crystal. And without thinking she cracked that bottle over the girl's head, sending blood and glass as far as the dance floor.

* * *

Shantique saw the melee of security guards, other patrons, then Ro and Martinette all scrambling here and there, and the scream, somebody was screaming but she couldn't see who.

"Martinette! Martinette! What happened? You okay?" She hollered.

Martinette waved back and hollered that she was, but then she was being escorted out of the club along with Ro. Shantique tried to follow, but the security guards stopped her, until she told them that she was riding with them, and Marti was her sister. She went back to get Nikko, when X grabbed her.

"Hey! You leaving?"

"Yeah. Marti got mixed up into some trouble and her and Ro were put out, so I got to go."

"Alright, well I'm going to. Ain't gonna be no fun in here without you. So where yall heading."

"I don't know yet. I guess home." Then she remembered that they rode here with Bling and his crew, not Ro, which made her think of Nikko again who she spotted standing next to Laron. "Nikko!"

* * *

Nikko couldn't believe what went down, but she should have. Wasn't it Martinette that got them thrown out of Macys just today, and now her ass was being thrown out of the club for popping somebody with a champagne bottle. It wasn't just Marti's crazy ass temper that got her into trouble, most times it was her temper coupled with liquor that brought out the worse in her. Nikko was getting real tired of Marti's mess. She looked over at Shantique with X and thought, tonight could have been the perfect night, now she had to go and ruin for all of them. She was surprised to see that Laron didn't' have much to say about what happened. In fact, she would remember how he laughed when Marti hit that girl. He laughed very loud. A little too loud for her taste.

"Look, Nikko I'm gonna go outside and see what's up with Martinette, you want to come?"

"Yeah, I guess we better. I hope they ain't locked her ass up." Two of X's guards guided them through the crowded club and outside the doors to the waiting limousine, and Butter.

"What's up man? You see where they took Ro and his girl?" Laron asked.

"They ain't come out here, they must still be inside." Butter slapped hands with Laron like two old friends, then his eyes couldn't help but roam over to the beautiful women in their company. His eyes found Nikko again. "Y'all want to wait inside the car? I'll let you know as soon they come out."

"Yeah man, that would be cool. Nikko, Shantique, X, let's get in and wait." The three of them followed Laron into the car, Nikko being the last. She stopped for a moment to speak with Butter.

"Hey! I thought you owed me a dance."

"I still do."

He winked and helped her into the car. She was glad he wasn't mad at her for hanging with Laron, and quiet as it's kept, she still kind of hoped her and Butter could hook up, but she would never mention that to her girls, they would think she was crazy or something.

For awhile-there things were tense in the limo, no one was saying much at all, everybody was just sitting back looking out the window and waiting on Ro and Martinette. No sooner than everyone had got into the limo that the police arrived, that's when everything got tense and it didn't tend to loosen up until Bling arrived. Bling provided comic relief for the entire crew, and no sooner everyone was laughing and drinking again. Shantique wiped tears from her eyes after laughing so hard.

"Damn, I needed that." She said to no one in particular.

"Yeah, that was tight man! You need to be on stage you got mad skills man, I swear!" Said X.

Bling shook his head and waved his hand.

"Naw man, I'd get onstage and freeze, this just for fun, that's all man."

"Alright," X said, "but you funny as hell! Damn you could be like Chris Rock or somebody, blow up big time. You know, quit tromping off behind your boys and be your on man nigga."

Bling shifted in his seat and didn't say much else.

Laron interceded. "What you trying to say X? He the manager and a damn good one at that! Ain't that right man?" Laron slapped hands with Bling.

"Show yo right! I'm the manager of the hottest R&B group this side of the Atlantic!"

The door opened and everyone was startled and surprised to see two uniform officers staring them in the face. The one white officer with the extreme case of bad acne spoke first.

"Good evening ladies and gentleman." He said with a twang. "I apologize for interrupting you festivities but we gonna have to ask you a few questions about tonight's altercation and for your convenience we can do it here, or we can have y'all follow us downtown." He smiled slyly.

No one said anything at first and no one expected X to be the one to speak up.

"What is it you want to know, officer?"

"Well, I like to know what you all saw in there? It's obvious we got a badly hurt young lady; I hear requiring some stitches to her head, claiming she was jumped. On the other hand, we got a superstar basketball player and his pretty little girlfriend who just about everyone we talked to say she was the one doing the hitting. One thing for sure, we know y'all was together and were closest to the action, so somebody had to see something! I need to know what you all saw! Nobody is leaving until we get the real story." He pulled out his pad, tapping the pen against the paper. "One by one, name first and then description."

* * *

The night ended pretty much the way it had started, back in the limousine, back to Atlanta, but without the hype. In fact, everyone was just dead tired.

Shantique turned her very heavy head to the side, trying to ignore the constant ringing taking place inside and the pain. But, no matter what she did the ringing didn't stop, another reminder of last night's drinking binge, although she didn't really want to be reminded of just about anything from last night. X being the exception.

"Shantique!" Her mother called from downstairs. "Pick up the phone!" Shantique rolled over; obviously upset that anyone would call so early in the morning, probably was Martinette. She thought.

"Huh?" She said to no one in particular and reached for her phone. "Yeah?"

"Yeah? Damn! You sure are cranky in the morning!" Shantique was only halfway listening to the conversation. She had a monster headache, a queasy stomach and no tolerance for bullshit. "Who is this?"

"Oh! It's like that huh? Look, I guess I caught you at a bad time...I thought we might hook up for some breakfast or lunch..." The voice went on.

"X? I'm sorry! I just, I was sleep. What's up?" Shantique tried her best to perk up, once realizing that X was on the phone. She sat up way too fast and felt the rush and spins send her back to her pillow.

"Damn!"

"You alright?"

"Yeah! Just got a monster hangover. How about you? Where you at anyway?"

"I'm fine. I wasn't drinking like you. Anyway, I'm laid up at my cousin's crib in East Point. I think I'm gonna get me a room though. I swear these niggas running a damn boarding house over here! Nigga can't get no peace over here. I ain't slept yet!

"Damn! That's ill! So where you gonna go?"

"I don't know, probably downtown. Maybe the Ritz?"

"That's cool! What time we eating?"

"What time you'll be ready?"

"I don't know. Say about twelve or one?"

"It's already eleven, you sure you can get dressed that quick?"

"Yeah! I can do anything, if I put my mind to it."

"Alright then. Where you want to meet?"

"I'll meet you downtown at the Ritz. You go ahead and get s settled and I'll meet you in the lobby."

"I ain't sure yet! Look, I'll call you back after I make some reservations. Cool?"

"Cool"

"Alright Baby girl, I'm out."

Shantique held the phone up against her chest, considering the many possibilities. She couldn't believe this was happening to her and she couldn't believe he called her "Baby Girl." She was feeling better. That was until her mother came into the room and the chatter began.

"Shantique! What was that all about? I know you not thinking about going out again today. You practically stayed out all night and slept in all morning."

Shantique turned over in her bed, not wanting to hear any of it. Not while her head was banging against her temples.

"Your trifling behind haven't even got up once to check on Rashawn. No Miss Thing, you and I are about to have a serious conversation."

"All ma!" Shantique placed a pillow over her head.

"All ma nothing! I'm serious Shantique. I thought I raised you better than this. You running around at all times of the night, now you gonna go meet some boy at a hotel! Hell no! I know I raised you better!"

"Mama, it's not what you think. This is X mama! You know the multimillion-dollar rapper I always talk about. X, and we are only gonna have lunch."

"I really don't care who it is. It's not right Shantique, you leaving Rashawn all the time chasing some celebrity around hoping to get next to him, hoping to be the one. Don't be no fool Shantique! Do you know how many girls they meet traveling? How many like you running behind them?"

"Mama, please! I am grown and I'm not chasing behind anybody. He likes me. He invited me out and I'm going."

"Well, I guess you gonna be taking Rashawn with you, Miss All Grown UP with a Baby. You told him about Rashawn?"

"No! It hasn't come up and no I'm not taking Rashawn. If you don't want to watch him, I'll find somebody who will."

"Fine Shantique! Do what you want, but remember I warned you. Just one more thing, since you so grown and all and can handle yourself I think it's about time you got your grown ass a job, and maybe you need to be looking for another place to stay as well. I'm giving you three months to get it together, you hear me three months." She slammed the door behind her.

Shantique knew she had upset her mother but she didn't expect that coming. Her getting a job has been an issue for quite sometime, ever since she dropped out of Junior College. She had every intention of returning, but she hadn't repaid the student loan yet, and there was no way they would accept her back until it was paid. Finding a job wouldn't be a problem, she just wasn't working at no Fast food joint, that would be disastrous and beneath her, plus they didn't pay nearly enough to accommodate her livelihood. Now finding a place to stay is going to be a challenge, one she wasn't looking forward to, even if it meant she would finally have some privacy and could get out from under her mother. The phone rang, and she picked it up after one ring, hoping it was X again.

"Hello!" She said.

"Shantique, its Taye." Shantique held the phone, but said nothing. She expected that Taye would call but she just wasn't ready for it. Hearing his voice on the other end made her angry and quiver at the same time. "Shantique". He said again. Her mother's voice broke in.

"Taye, is that you? How you doing baby? You calling to talk to Rashawn?" Her mother asked.

"Oh, how you doing Miss Jackson. I thought that was Shantique who picked up. I'm doing fine. Is Rashawn there?" Shantique said nothing. She just listened to the two of them carry on as if nothing ever happened. Of course her mother didn't know about their blow up at the mall, but surely she knew that she wasn't in to him like that, and yet she carried on like they were the best of friends. Shantique thought just to get back at her.

"Yes baby he's here. Rashawn, it's your daddy. Your daddy's on the phone." She handed the phone to Rashawn.

"Daddy! Hi! You coming to pick me up?" Shantique covered her hand tightly over the mouthpiece. Rashawn's reaction to his father calling stirred up all kind of emotions in her, another thing that took her by surprise.

"Hey Rashawn! Boy, I sure do miss you man. If it's okay with your mom, I wanted to take you to Chucky Cheeses today. You want to hang out with your pop?"

"Chucky Cheeses!" Rashawn screamed and turned to his grandma to ask. "Grandma, can I go to Chucky Cheeses with daddy? She nodded yes and he screamed again. "Grandma says I can go."

"Good. I'll come by around twelve and get you okay. Let me speak to your grandma." Rashawn handed the phone to his grandmother, while Shantique almost exploded at everyone, because no one consulted nor asked her permission and yet she still said nothing.

"Hey Taye, yes it would be fine for Rashawn to go with you. No, it's no problem, Shantique has something to do today anyway and I plan to be out an about myself. So you say you will pick him up at twelve. Okay, I'll have him ready. Thanks baby. See ya later. Yeah I'll tell her."

Shantique slammed the phone into its cradle as hard as she could. She was angry! Angry with her mother for interfering and angry with Taye, for dammit, just being Taye. As angry as she was she knew better to engage her mother in another heated discussion. She would just have to deal with it and let Rashawn visit with his father. It was after all, the right thing to do, no matter how pissed she was at Taye. Rashawn needs his dad and she needed to get the hell out of Dodge before he arrived. The last thing she wanted right now is to see Taye. She had better things to do. Like spending time with one of the most eligible, fattest, attractive rappers on the planet, X. Soon, Taye would regret the day he ever let her go. Soon, everybody would envy her.

* * *

    Shantique hated riding the trains. It was however the quickest and most inexpensive forms of transportation outside of a car in Atlanta. She rode in silence. Even amongst the revelry, she held her focus outside of the window, dreaming, wishing and hoping for a better life and the promise of things to come. The stank of unwashed bodies mixed with the many perfumes and colognes that traveled in and out caused her stomach distress and she began to feel sick. The conductor announced almost too loudly, "Five Points Station." Shantique exited the train and the station, in need of fresh air. She could have ridden another stop to Peachtree Center, but the walk would do her good, even if it was a good two to three long country blocks.
    Downtown Atlanta bustled with the sounds of cars, buses and street vendors selling their goods on every corner. The day was windy, but warm and she enjoyed the breeze even more so after being in the confines of the train. It was nearly lunchtime so the streets were filled with people walking. She wished she could work downtown. It was where everything seemed to be happening. Men and women dressed in their business

attire, with suits and ties, carrying their laptops and briefcases, chatting on cell phones. It was a whole different world from Decatur. Though she never thought about holding down a corporate job, as she looked around the city and the people she thought she might like it, if it paid well. It would certainly be better than working at a fast food joint. She had arrived at the corner of Peachtree and International Boulevard and the Ritz Carlton stood just across the street from her. Shantique checked herself out in the windows of Macys before heading across the street. Her attire was casual hood chic, but fly as well. She chose a pair of black shiny Fubu jeans, T-shirt and jean jacket with a chain link belt that dipped ever so slightly down the center of her crotch. Her hair was still damp from washing this morning, its curls cascaded down her back and around her face. The wind had done her some good in that department. Shantique applied a dab of orange flavored lip-gloss to her lips. The one thing she couldn't stand was chapped lips so she always carried her gloss. Other than that, she wore little or no makeup at all, just some liner on her eye's and on special occasion's a bit of eye shadow. After giving herself a thorough look over, she turned to cross the street when someone grabbed her from behind. Shantique screamed loudly, causing people to turn and stare.

"Hey girl, it's just me."

"X, you scared me to death! What are you doing out here? I thought we were going to meet at the Ritz?"

"We are. I just came out of Macys. I had to pick up some things there." He stepped back and looked at her from head to toe. "Damn girl, you look good! I didn't think you could look much better, but I was wrong."

He ran his fingers through her hair, pulling at the curls surrounding her face. "You got good hair too! I like it curly. You look a lot like Chili from TLC."

"Yeah, I hear that all the time." She smiled and thought he was looking real good too! He wore his baggie Roca wear jeans and jacket in a deep blue and a white do rag on his head. Shantique couldn't miss the nearly three carat diamond studs he wore in both his ears, nor his diamond studded watch. But most impressive of all, was that million-dollar smile he wore, that simply melted her heart.

"What's up? You ready to go?" He asked.

"Yeah."

"Come on then girl, I'm hungry like a muthafucka!"

* * *

Shantique spent the next few hours and almost the entire day having the time of her life. Her and X, ate, went shopping, to the movies, to the zoo, ate again and then settled back into his room at the Ritz Carlton. His room was the size of her entire apartment. From his window, she could see the glare of lights at Turner Field and everything in between. The room was elaborately decorated with plush furnishings, cherry wood furniture and fresh flowers on the tables. She had only been there an hour, but she knew that she never wanted to leave. This would be a day she would never forget. No matter what else happened or didn't, she would always remember this being one of the best days of her life.

"You alright?" X asked.

"Yeah, why you ask?" She turned from window to find him standing shirtless behind her. She was caught off guard and her mouth dropped as she stared at his fine, chiseled physique. He smiled that million-dollar smile and moved closer wrapping his arms around her waist.

"Cuz, I want to know how my baby girl is doing. Alright?" Shantique nodded. She was nervous, more nervous than she had ever been before. He held her tightly, and she felt warm all over. Damn. She thought. This was too fast. Everything was happening too fast. She had to get a grip, but damn if he didn't feel good. It was against her better judgment to sleep with anyone on the first date. But X, wasn't just anyone. He was X; the rapper and he could have anyone he wanted. Her mind did battle while his hands began to explore and their bodies swayed in harmony. She thought she should walk away right then, before anything else happened, but she didn't want blow it, didn't want to piss him off, but things were going way too fast. She opened her eyes to find that his was closed. He was really feeling her too! This was too much! Damn, damn, damn!

"You know, you are really sweet and I had a great time with you today...."

Oh here it comes. She thought.

"Girl, there is nothing I want more than to get with you right now. You know that don't you? But, it wouldn't be right. It would be disrespectful and I want you to know that I'm the type of man who respects women. That's the way I was brought up and you the type of lady that deserves the utmost respect. So, what I'm trying to say is for right now, I just want to enjoy holding you." He tightened his arms around her. "Like this, if that's okay."

* * *

Martinette turned over, but she found she had nowhere to go. Ro was lying so close to her, wrapping his extremely large legs around her, like a baby with his teddy. She didn't mind though. It's been quite sometime that she's allowed a man into her bed, an even longer time that they saw daylight together. She checked out the time, it was way past noon. He moaned.

"What's up?"

"What's up with you Boo?" She asked, purposely turning her head away from him, trying to spare him that morning breath.

"Nothing, just chilling with my baby." He pulled her tighter.

"You know what time it is?"

"Don't care."

"Oh, like you have nowhere to go, nothing to do. Mister big time basketball player has some free time?"

"Yep! I'm exactly where I want to be. Exactly where I'm supposed to be. You got a problem with that?"

"I ain't saying all that. I was just asking that's all, just trying to keep things straight. I ain't the kind of woman that likes to sweat a nigga."

"Yeah, I know that. Nigga's be sweating you, right?"

"Naw, it ain't' like that."

"Sure it is. Girl, as fine as you are, you ain't even got to play me like that. I know niggas be checking you, everywhere you go. But it's cool, I wouldn't settle for anything less."

"Who say's you settling?"

"Who say's I'm not? Just one thing though."

"What's that?"

"I think you need to invest in a bigger bed."

"Only if it's long term."

"No doubt, like I said. There's no place I'd rather be."

Martinette turned around, forgetting all about her morning breath and planted a kiss on Ro's lips. She knew he was turned on, because she could feel him poking at her backside during the entire conversation. She liked that. She kissed his neck and his chest and then proceeded under the covers. The sweetest sound she ever heard was Ro moaning her name. This time she had hit the jackpot.

CHAPTER 5

Nikko turned over again, this time placing the pillow on top her head in an attempt to muffle the noise taking place in the next room. Her cousin Kim and his girlfriend Tammy were arguing again. Damn! She thought. She wasn't feeling like breaking up no fight this morning, especially after last night's drama. She pressed the pillow down harder, but to no avail, she still heard the screaming and then a bang. Nikko jumped up from her bed, nearly tripping on the covers and ran into the hallway to see what was happening. This time Kim had Tammy by the neck, while she kicked and swung at everything and anything in her way, knocking down lamps and ashtrays mostly. Nikko hollered.

"What the hell you doing Kim stop!" At the site of Nikko, Kim let go of Tammy who turned around, punched him right in the eye, and laughed.

"Bitch, I'll kill you." Kim hollered and went after Tammy again, until Nikko stepped in between them.

"Tammy, I think you need to go! Now!" Nikko hollered.

"Fuck him. He ain't nothing but a punk anyway. Fuck you Kim! You want some more? Huh?" Tammy taunted, while slowly backing up towards the door. It took all of Nikko's strength to keep Kim from going after her.

"Kim. Kim! Let her go, please!" Nikko pleaded while still holding him back. She didn't let go until she heard Tammy's car drive off. "Damn! Why all the drama? If you all got to fight every time you get together what's the point and dealing with her Kim? I don't understand and I really didn't need this shit so early in the morning. Damn!" She fell onto the couch, exhausted from holding back Kim.

Kim paced the floor before sitting down beside her.

He reached over and grabbed her hand.

"Sorry about that cuz. You know how she gets sometimes."

"Yeah, but ain't you tired of that shit or are you just like her and like to get your boxing on?"

"Naw. I just love her that's all. I know she can be messed up in the head sometimes, but most times she's sweet, and she loves me too!"

Nikko looked at him like he had lost his mind.

"What?"

"I guess that's what you call Crazy Love."

Kim laughed.

"That be it cuz."

"Crazy can get you killed."

"She ain't trying to kill me, just hurt me."

He stood up, stretching his arms out, examining the new scratches on his shoulders and arms.

"You want to grab some breakfast?"

"After all of that, you want to eat?"

"Yep. Fighting builds up an appetite. Come on. Go get dressed and we can head out to Waffle House and you can tell me all about your night out, hanging with the ballers."

* * *

Nikko remembered the first time she had met Tammy. It was a year ago at a gathering for Kim's birthday. Kim was turning twenty-one and his friends threw a party at Dugan's pub on Ponce De Leon. Tammy showed up with two of her stripper friends. From the looks of her, you really couldn't tell that she was as evil as she is, but you know looks can be deceiving as hell. Tammy stood about five feet nine, high yellow with long black hair and thin. She could easily be mistaken for a model. She was syrupy sweet and Kim was crazy about her. Now a year later, both had records with the police department, due to the numerous complaints made by both when fighting. It really was a shame. Nikko thought. Kim was such a good man, responsible, smart and a budding and talented tattoo artist. He was the man, when it came to tattoos. In fact, his shop was rated number one in Atlanta, two years in a row. Kim came by it naturally too! No real training or anything although he apprenticed for some time at a local shop, after about three months he struck out on his own and opened a shop down in Little Five Points. In less than a month it took off. That's where he met Tammy. She had come in for a tattoo. She wanted paw prints on her breast, just like Eve. Of course, he obliged and the rest is history. Her cell phone rang.

"Hello."
"Hey girl." A male voice spoke.
"Hey." Nikko said.
"Nikki?"

"No, I'm sorry you have the wrong number." Nikko was about to hang up when the man interrupted.

"Wait. I mean Nikko. It's Laron."

Oh shit! Nikko thought. She was just about to hang up on Laron. Laron of "Too Hot".

"Laron! Hey yourself. What's up? I didn't recognize your voice."

"I see. Damn girl. It's been a long time since a girl hung up on me. So what you doing?"

"Nothing." She sat down on the bed. "So where you at? You in Atlanta?"

"Yeah." He stopped and hollered at someone in the background. "Ah I was going by the studio for a minute and wanted to see if you were free later. Maybe we can grab a bite to eat or something?"

"Sure. I really don't have any plans for the day. So what time is good for you?"

"Say about four. I should be done with my tracks by then."

"Cool!" Nikko paused. She heard women laughing in the background. "Who was that? Sounds like you having a party over there."

"Naw, just some friends, some of my crew and a few chickenheads."

Chickenheads, no he didn't

.He covered the phone and hollered something. "So, you where you live? I can have Butter pick you up."

Nikko thought quickly. *All hell would break loose if Butter came up to her house.*

"No that's okay. I have my own car. I can meet you somewhere."

"Cool. You know Fellini's Pizza on Ponce?"

"Yeah, I love that pizza."

"Alright, meet me there around four. I'll call you on your cell if I'm running late or something."

"Okay Laron. Four it is." Nikko was all smiles. This was a dream come true, first meeting Laron, now actually having a date with him. She couldn't wait to tell Shantique and Martinette. She quickly dialed their numbers but was interrupted when Kim called.

"Nikko! You ready yet? I'm hungry!"

"Okay." She hung up. She would have time to check with them later. "I'm coming."

"Hurry up girl and call your daddy. He called this morning to check up on you. I forgot all about it because of Tammy and all. Call him before you go. I don't want him getting all mad at me about not giving you the message."

"Alright, give me five minutes." Damn, if daddy called, he must know I went out. Now how am I going to get out the house again to meet Laron?

* * *

It was a Saturday afternoon and Ponce was popping. Not only was there a lot of street traffic, but foot traffic as well. The area near Fellini's had a sudden upgrade, instead of broken down, drug infested houses and abandoned buildings located on every corner we have instead a multitude of newly built and decorative dwellings. Nikko looked from right to left and couldn't believe how much the area had changed from slum to high income. Lining the streets of Ponce were condominiums and townhouses ranging from the low one hundred thousands to the high two hundreds. Not too far down the street and across from one of her favorite Mexican restaurant, stood an elaborate structure housing lofts ranging from the low 200's to the high 300's. Midtown had it going on! Nikko made a left turn into Fellini's and parked. It was exactly noon and Laron was no where to be found or seen. She waited in her car another five minutes; primping and he still hadn't arrived. Nikko stepped outside, deciding to see if he was perhaps already there waiting in the restaurant, but he was not and she was getting pissed. She hadn't brought many clothes with her over to Kim's so her favorite, no name hip hugger jeans and one shoulder strapped fatigue printed top would have to do. There was no doubt that she looked every bit of good because all of the men were ogling her from the moment she stepped out the car. Even the waiters tried to step to her, but she wasn't even in the mood, even if he was kind of cute in that raw Hispanic way, then maybe she thought, if Laron didn't show up soon, she might give it a thought. She heard a lot of noise coming from behind the building, then saw a brother wearing one of those wife-beaters shirts, talking loud and walking like something was left up his ass. She tried not to stare, so she turned her head quickly when he caught her eye.

"Damn man, check out Shorty over there?" He said, eyeing Nikko then moving her way.

Oh shit, Nikko thought now it was really time to go, until she saw Butter followed by Laron emerge from the back of the building. Butter was looking real good, dressed casually so in some sagging jeans and a walnut colored sleeveless sweater vest that made his dark skin glow and exposed the very well defined muscles in his arms. He smiled when he saw her, but she also saw something in his eyes that looked like disappointment. Laron on the other hand was designer chic from head to toe, Sean John jeans, jean jacket, T-shirt, and hat that he wore backwards. He smiled as well and Nikko nearly fell on her face, because he was fine too! He didn't have the same fine physique that Butter possessed; he was slim and too cute for his on good, especially his smile and those dimples.

"Hey baby". Laron said walking towards her and wrapping his arms around her like they had found a home. "How long you been here? You know Butter and this nigga here is Bino, my homey from way back. Damn!" He turned her around you are too cute!"

Okay, you couldn't wipe the smile off Nikko's face. Not only did he look good, he felt good, he smelled good and she was feeling everything he was saying.

"Hey yourself. I've been here about fifteen minutes, waiting in the car. Hi Butter. You look different."

Butter gave a short reply then turned his attention back to Laron. The two of them slapped hands. "Hey man, I'm out. Bino you riding man?"

"Man, I don't wanna be hanging on no hard leg. I want to be like because here; find me some soft honey to hook up with. So Shorty, you got somebody you can call, Bino asked.

Yeah, Cops. Didn't none of her girls want to hook up with no wife-beater wannabe that's for damn sure. She wasn't giving him an inch, less than any inclination that she would call someone for him, all she wanted was for him to leave, so she could spend some quality time with Laron.

"Oh, I'm sorry Bino, all my friends are busy today, maybe next time."

"Hey man, come on I know where you can find some honeys, ride with me, let D handle his bizness. Alright?"

"Yeah man, Stop hating." Laron jived. "Look, I'll catch up with you two later. We still shooting pool right?"

"Alright cuz. An you sweet thing, don't do nothing I wouldn't do."

"Come on Bino man. Alright D, I catch you later. Nikko you be good, alright!"

Nikko watched Butter get into a very shiny, very new looking silver BMW 700 and it blew her mind.

"That's your car?" She asked Laron.

"Naw, that's Butter's car. Oh shit!" He started laughing. "I bet you thought Butter was just a limo driver."

"Yeah, isn't he?"

"Hell naw, Butter owns the limo service. He's got a limo business in 3 cities, but his most profitable is in New York, that's where he's from."

Nikko could not hide her surprise, Butter a business owner, possibly rich, a baller.

"You should see your face. It looks like you just seen a ghost. You alright?"

"Yeah, I just thought, I mean why did he drive you all if he's the owner?"

"He just does it to hang out with us. We're all old friends, attended high school together, so anytime I have a concert down south or even in NYC and he has time, he does the driving himself. Butter's a stand-up nigga, now that's my real homey. Come on, let's get something to eat, that weed got me hungry like a muthafucka."

* * *

Fellini's lunchtime crowd was primarily made up of White middle-class yuppies, a few buppies and the rest generation x'ers. Nikko enjoyed pizza and the conversation wasn't too bad either, although she had to listen to Laron talk about himself for the majority of the conversation, but it was all good. Laron had the big head about his success. All he wanted to talk about was how the girls were sweating him. Nikko was getting bored and tired of listening to his bragging about himself and his conquests. They were interrupted only a few times with autograph seekers, while she sat quietly by watching him at work, flirting, like she wasn't even there. She would be mad, but had no reason to; it wasn't like they were hooked up or nothing. This was the first date, nothing more and yet still she wondered if she would be able to handle the constant interruptions and female attention he received. She couldn't help but think about the scene in his dressing room after the show, all those women hanging around, all waiting to kick it with him. She knew she was thinking way too far in the future and the idea itself could be considered farfetched since she wasn't even sure she liked him very much. He was fine, there was no question about that, but she needed to see who he really was, in the inside, something he hadn't shown her as of yet. The conversation finally switched back to her.

"So, Nikko tell me about yourself. You in school, work or something?"

"Not yet in school. I'm enrolled for the winter quarter. I'll be attending the School of Art, majoring in Fashion Design. I guess I'm just kicking it right now."

"Fashion Design huh, I can see that, the way you dress is pretty tight."

"Thanks."

"So you'll be going to New York?"

"No, the campus I'm attending is in Savannah."

"That's cool, so you'll be close by."

"What difference does it make if I'm close by?"

"I don't know, I just thought you'll be close to Atlanta, so I can come check you out some times."

"Really, like you have time to come check me out. Be serious Laron, I mean I'm no dummy. You got women clamoring for your attention everywhere you go. I saw it for myself after the show so you don't have to fake it with me. I know your reputation, in fact that's all you've talked about since we been here."

"Hold up Girl! I wasn't bragging or nothing about those situations, it's just such a trip to me how women throw themselves at me. I mean, I ain't gonna lie to you, the shit is flattering and I do get more sex than I could ever dream of, but still that's not the kind of life I want to live. And to tell you the truth, I don't want my lady throwing herself at no man, just because he's in a singing group, playing ball or whatever."

"Oh, so you telling me you ready to settle down?"

"Naw, I ain't saying that either. I'm just saying it would be nice to have a real relationship with someone. Someone nice, smart… a good girl like you. You know somebody you can call after a show and just kick it with, converse with. I ain't had that in awhile, and I miss it. You seem like someone I would like to get to know better. Come on Nikko, I picked you out of a crowd of thousands, don't that tell you something?"

Okay this shit was really blowing her mind now. Here she was sitting across one of the most popular, pecan fine, smooth talking, dimple wearing brothers of the century, who could sing his ass off as well, and he was pushing up on her? This cannot be real, she thought. She couldn't help but stare at him while he talked, the brother was really too fine, and she didn't normally date really fine men, mainly because they were always too conceited. Nikko didn't really know what to make of this revelation, this change in direction, this masterful courting taking place. But she did no one thing, all of sudden her most comfortable jeans, had her squirming and it had nothing to do with the heat. While she twisted and readjusted herself in her seat, she replied.

"Not really, that's part of the show. Everywhere you go you pick a girl out of the crowd to dance with."

"Okay you got me on that one, but let me tell you, this time was different. I swear! Girl when I saw you, I got all nervous and shit, something I hadn't felt since high school. You were perfect, like a china doll standing there next to me. I felt something and I know you did too!"

"I don't know Laron, you've got me really confused right now, but I'll tell you what we can take it one day at a time and see where it goes."

"That's all I ask girl. Look, I'm gonna show you I'm not this superstar-player you perceive me to be. And I'm gonna start with today. So what you got planned for the rest of the day?"

"Nothing really. So what's up?"

"Alright good. I'm gonna take you to all my favorite places to hang out in Atlanta. You game?"

"Yeah, sure. But what about your boy and Butter, I thought you were gonna hook up with them later."

"All forget about them niggas. I hang with them all the time, today I rather be hanging with you, if that's alright?"

"Like I said. Sure, I'm free."
"Cool, but first I gotta take a leak."
He stood up and excused himself to the restroom. Nikko couldn't really believe what was happening here. How Laron wanted to prove something to her, boy what a turn this has been, she thought. Here she was at first going goo-goo, ga-ga over him and just when she was about to exit, he did a three-sixty on her. She wasn't sure whether to trust his; "I'm not really a player" soliloquy. A lot was left to be seen, but she was impressed with his openness. That's a lie, she was more than impressed, she actually felt warm all over, despite her protective shield up and armed, he was able to find a weak spot and he was working his way via a narrow path to her heart.

CHAPTER 6

    Shantique was in another world. The weekend she spent with X was more than she had expected. Instead of being the crazy, high-strung rapper he was known for, he had showed her a totally different side, a kinder gentler side. She hadn't felt this close to anyone since Taye and that was saying a lot. She practically had stopped dating after Taye. Their breakup was devastating and left her hating men altogether then after the hate, she felt there was no one out there worthy of her time. She had her girls and Rashawn and they kept her busy. Her mother told her a long time ago that a man would come and go, but her girlfriends would be there forever. Shantique reached over to her nightstand and pulled a single yellow rose from the dozen X had given her on Saturday. They were just as beautiful as the day he had given them to her. She inhaled the sweet fragrance and languished in the memory of last weekend. She wished she could lay there all day just dreaming about X, but that was out of the question. Today she had to find a job or else.
    After the tenth application and some four hours later, Shantique started to question her choice in shoes. Her feet were on fire and to think these were her most comfortable pair. They never hurt her when she wore

them out, but she found out it was a different thing sitting around in four inch heels and walking in them. She took a seat outside of Underground on a concrete ledge and removed the heels. No sooner had she removed them that her feet began to come alive. The numbness was gone and she could actually wiggle her toes. She must have looked strange to passerbies with her feet dangling from the ledge, but if anyone got a look at her shoes, they would understand. Although her job search hadn't yet netted her an offer, she was happy with what she had accomplished. In fact, she thought about just calling it a day and calling up Nikko and Martinette to see what they were up to. She talked briefly with Nikko on Sunday, but she hadn't heard from Martinette since the concert. Nikko said she was shacked up somewhere with that basketball player and knowing Martinette, Nikko was probably right. Martinette had always been successful with hooking up with ballers. Before Ro, she was dating one of the Atlanta Braves, a guy by the name of Dwayne Mulberry. As far as Shantique knew they were still dating, but Dwayne was on the road, at least that's what Martinette told them. Dwayne was crazy about Martinette. He put her up in a nice apartment in Midtown, paid the rent and even furnished it with everything she wanted and still Martinette was out there looking. She said she liked Dwayne, but he was square and a just a baller wannabe. Hell from the looks of it, at six million dollars a year he was every bit a baller, so there had to be something else wrong with him. Martinette didn't want to tell her at first. Shantique had to prod and prod, and when that didn't work, liquor did. On one of their girls night out, and after Dwayne had refused to buy her a diamond tennis bracelet Martinette was more than ready to spill her guts.

"I can't stand him. Who the hell he think he is? Hell, I make him look good. He couldn't keep another woman, even if he tried. He can take that rubber dick of his and stick it up somebody who cares and buy some Viagra while he's at it." Martinette downed the last of her shot and pounded the bar for another.

Nikko let out what sounded like the cross between a yelp and a cry, before shouting, "He's soft? Maybe it was just a bad night, girl."

"That motherfucker has a bad night, every night. I feel like I'm fucking a Nerf ball. Never did a damn thing for me and I'm fucking tired of faking it. Ahh, Ahh Dwayne!" she mocks, "You so good baby! Fuck that!"

"Damn Martinette. He is so fine. Well, he does take care of you, right? You got to give him that." It was hard to believe that this fine, well-chiseled athlete could not perform in bed. At least that's what Martinette had them believing. Even with Dwayne's lukewarm performance in bed, Martinette kept stringing him alone, "a bird in the hand was worth two in the bush", she said. Now, with Ro in hand, she wondered what Martinette was thinking.

"Excuse me," a woman interrupted, "Girl I just had to tell you, those are some slamming shoes."

"Thanks, but they are no good for walking or job searching."

"Oh, you looking for a job?"

"Yeah, I've been putting in applications all morning."

"Well we're hiring. I work about a block from here, across from the park. The shop is called Et Cetera. Stop by, I might be able to hook you up."

"For real? Wow, thanks."
"No problem. By the way my names Nia."
"Shantique." The two shook hands.
"You think you gonna be able to walk again? If so, you can follow me down there now. I was just on my lunch break."
"Girl, don't you worry about me. As bad as I need a job, I'll go barefoot if I have to."

* * *

After nearly eight hours of looking for work, with help of Nia, Shantique accepted a job offer with Et Cetera Fashion boutique. The pay was just above minimum wage, but with commission, she could make a lot more. She felt good about getting a job in just one day of looking, and felt even better after seeing the merchandise, which was off the chain. The boutique's owner designed most of the clothing herself, but also carries some name brand designers like Prada, DKNY, Versace, Roca wear, FUBU and Sean John, just to name a few. To top it all off, she would get a twenty-percent discount on everything and fifty percent on clearance items. Shantique had already picked out a couple outfits she wanted. She settled in to her seat on the Marta train and dreamed about having her own apartment, or house, and maybe owning her own boutique someday. Shantique loved fashion. She even thought about attending Atlanta's School of Fashion, but that was before Rashawn. Having Rashawn changed everything for her, but she wouldn't give him up for anything in the world. She would just have to make things happen for herself, one step at a time.

She had everything going for her right now, her health, Rashawn, a new job and a new love interest. Although it was too early to think of X as her boyfriend, she couldn't help daydreaming about them as a couple. Even when she wasn't trying, his face would pop into her mind, and something he said would make her smile. Shantique didn't like riding the train, but it was her only mode of transportation and she was lucky to have found a job near a train stop, without her having to catch a bus as well. For the most part, her train ride downtown and back was uneventful, and to her surprise quite relaxing. She closed her eyes and rested while the hum of the train rocked her to sleep. Sleep led Shantique exactly where she wanted to be, in the arms of X. Her dream was almost identical to the one she had some nights ago. She was dancing on stage next to X. He was singing the same song, but then something happened. She couldn't see what, but people were running, screaming and she was alone but she could still hear his voice in a distance. Shantique woke up, shaken and disturbed by her dream. She tried to shake the feeling she had, of dread, of loss when she heard X's voice again in distant. She turned to the voice and found herself staring into the face of a pimple-faced teen, nodding and rapping along to his CD player.

"What up Shorty?" he asked, showing off several gold teeth, his head bopping up and down to the beat.

Shantique didn't answer him, just stared at his tarantula styled hair, avoiding his beady eyes and brass smirk. She had the funny feeling she knew him, but knew they had never met. Being in that space with him gave her the strangest notion of deja vu.

"Decatur station," the train conductor announced Shantique gathered her things and exited the train without a word but with one thought *where was X and was he okay?*

*   *   *

Martinette's phone had been ringing all night and she knew exactly who it was. That's why she took the phone off the hook because Dwayne wasn't going to stop calling and she wasn't ready to deal with him, yet. She turned over on her side, rubbed her satin sheets and relished the memories of last night's date with Ro. That man had it going on in the sex department. He was as big as he was tall and instead of carrying it around like a peg leg, brother had a power drill. A tiny smile crept up and she exhaled. She could really get used to this, but first things first, she was gonna have to get rid of Dwayne for good. From past experience she had learned that was no easy task.

Dwayne unlike Ro, was a punk, easily led and misled and Shantique had led him around for years. It wasn't her intent to dog him out. She actually liked him when they first started dating, before the sex. He would take her out to Justin's and Bones two of her favorite restaurants in Atlanta, sparing no expense on anything she wanted and she could eat and drink with the best of them. Dwayne lavished her with expensive gifts and trips, had even bought and furnished her townhouse, but still she didn't love him and didn't think she ever could. Over the two years, she had served her purpose, his eye candy, and he had served as her Sugar Daddy. Now with Ro in her life, she didn't need him anymore. Ro made more money than Dwayne and could take care of her just fine, just the way she was used to being treated and on top of that, Ro knew how to do her in bed! She knew Dwayne wouldn't take the news easy. He might even do something drastic like try to put her out of townhouse. But that shit wasn't happening because Martinette had the ownership papers drawn up in both their names, so no matter what went down, the townhouse and everything in it was hers to keep. It was a nice place, in a nice neighborhood, right in the center of Midtown and close to Five Points. She was smart enough to choose a location that had since grown, and tripled in price. In the last two years, her townhouse among many others had nearly tripled in price not to mention the number of new condominiums, townhouses and lofts popping up nearby selling close to a quarter of a million dollars.

    Martinette was sitting on some prime real estate, so even if things didn't work out with her and Ro, she could sell this place and make a fortune. Instead of chasing ballers, she would be her own damn baller. Now that was a thought. Everything she had done in life had prepared her for this moment, but she wasn't there yet, not quite. A million dollars was good money, but not enough, not now, not when she was dating Mister Sixty million, himself. Yep, that's right; Ro's last contract was worth sixty million dollars. He was one of the highest paid basketball players in the country, and he was about to be hers. All she had to do was play her cards right and not fall in love, at least not until the marriage certificate was signed and dated, then there will be plenty of time for love. Martinette never gave much thought to love, not ever. She had seen love ruin too many folks, her family and friends included. Love put her mother on the street, after she fell in love with some wannabe pimp, who for loves sake, had her fucking every Joe and John up and down Stewart Avenue. Then left her to die after she contracted AIDS. Love had her brother Calvin strung out on heroin, crack and alcohol, after his wife of fifteen years left him for a twenty five year old man. Now he's living in the streets, going from shelter to shelter, to street corners and back. Love even had her girl Shantique messed up and strung out over her boyfriend Taye two years after they had broken up. Naw, Martinette thought, fuck love, what she needed was finance. Finance before love, equaled success and happiness. With money, shit she could buy love, because she loved her some things, jewelry, clothes, and food, not exactly in that order.

Money was love, and Ro had all the money she could hope for. Ro was her future, now all she had to do was make him fall in love with her. Martinette knew exactly what to do; tonight she would lure her big catch with a homemade southern meal. That was one thing she had to thank her mother for, teaching her how to cook, because there was no quicker way to a man's heart, than through his stomach, and tonight she wasn't pulling out any stops. Ro would get the works, a fine meal, and a fascinating dessert.

* * *

Nikko worked on her application for nearly two hours without any breaks. Her temples throbbed and her fingers began to cramp from all of the writing. This was big for her, not quite as big as meeting Laron, but close. Getting into school and fulfilling her desire to study dance was something she dreamed about since a young child. She never thought she would become so consumed with being a professional dancer when she took her first dance lesson at the age of five. She remembered crying the day her mom dropped her off at Little Stages Dance School, but that all changed in just ten minutes of being there. Nikko loved to dance and soon became Little Stages star pupil and featured dancer. For the next ten years, she would be their premier dancer, lead ballerina and part time teacher. Landing the part in Atlanta's Ballet's staging of "The Nutcracker" really clinched it for her, she would dance professional, be it ballet, jazz, or hip-hop, this was what she wanted to do. Convincing her parents was a different thing; neither of them approved of her desire to dance professionally. Her father wanted her to study medicine, and her mother always went along with what her father said. It was frustrating and heartbreaking not to have anyone on her side. She understood the difficulties. Nothing was predictable or promised when it came to show business, but it was her dream and her life and she would be the one to make the decision. For the first time in her life, her parents and her were at odds about something, but she wouldn't give, whether they paid for it or not, she was going to be a dancer. Nikko received a partial scholarship from the Atlanta Ballet, which would cover up to two years of her schooling or contribute fifty percent for four years if she majored in dance. To cover the rest, her only alternative would be to apply for a student loan. *Would you be applying for Federal Funding, i.e. Grant Student Loan?* She stared at the question for some time, knew the answer but she also knew with all honesty she could not obtain a student loan without a co-signer and that's the one thing she didn't have.

"Nikko what are you doing?" her mother asked in Korean from behind her. When Nikko didn't answer, she asked again, this time in English, "Nikko what you doing?"

"Nothing ma."

"You do something. You been in your room all morning," she said walking around Nikko's room picking up things.

"Ma, you don't have to do that," Nikko said getting up. "I'll clean up. You do enough around here for us. You don't have to pick up after me."

"I like picking up after you and your father. It is what I do. It is what I like to do, so you go back to doing nothing and I'll pick up."

Nikko's mom made her way over to her desk and stared blankly at the application. "School?" she asked.

"Yes Ma, for school." Nikko didn't really want to have an argument this morning about school, so she took a folder and placed it over the application.

"You study medicine, right?"

"No Ma, not medicine. I want to study dance. We already went over this. That's okay," Nikko said, throwing up her hands. "You know what, it doesn't matter, because if I can't get some more money, I study nothing."

"Your father has money, for medicine, but you want dance. Dance a beautiful thing. Art and movement grace and style. You have passion for dance, I know, but dance not profitable. Medicine is."

"Mom, I know. I've heard it all before from both you and dad, but it's what I want to do, and I will, whether you help me or not."

Her mom stared at the application, not saying a word, then reached over to Nikko touching her face, "you have a strong will Nikko. You are like your father. I believe you will be dancer. You will find your way."

Nikko could not believe what she was hearing. Was her mom encouraging her to dance? "Ma," she started to say, when her cellular phone rang. She reached in her purse on the floor and answered, "Hello."

"Hey Nikko, what's up? This Laron."

When Nikko looked up, her mom had already left the room, "Hey."

"You sound strange. You alright?" he asked.

Nikko couldn't explain, and she didn't know if he would understand, but all of sudden she felt a load being lifted off her. "Yes, I'm fine. What's up?"

"I'm shooting my video today and thought you might like to come down and check it out. That's if you are free."

"Sure, what time?"

"The video shoot is at six, but I have to be on the set around four. I thought we could grab a bite to eat before the shoot, if you are game. We can meet up at Justin's."

"Justin's, alright, I'll see you at four."

CHAPTER 7

"So when you gonna start?" Shantique's mother asked from the kitchen. "Shantique!" she hollered again. "You hear me? When you supposed to start?"

Shantique ran from her room to the hall, half dressed in a short leather skirt, leather boots and her bra. She only had twenty minutes to get ready before meeting X for dinner. "I'm going in tomorrow." She hollered back.

"Tomorrow? Shouldn't you be resting up then, getting ready for your big day, instead of going out?" She said stirring the pot of chili, then sipping from the spoon. "Umm, Umm, Umm, grandma done went and put her foot up in this." Rashawn moved in closer. "You want a taste, little man?"

He nodded. Lifted his chin to the spoon and slurped the rich brown liquid.

"Good ain't it? What I tell ya. Your mother gonna miss all this good chili, cuz you and me gonna make chili, chili dogs, chili corn carnee."

"What's Chili corn carne?" Rashawn asked, wrinkling up his nose.

"Baby that's some good stuff. That's when you take some of grandma's cornbread and crumble it up in the chili. Ooohwee, I'm talking bout some good eating there."

"Ooh you made chili?" Shantique asked walking into the kitchen.

"Yep, and you ain't getting any?"

"Whatever mother, put me some in the fridge. I'm out and I promise I will be home early, okay. Come here boo," she called to Rashawn. "Give mommy a kiss, and hug. Okay, now you be good to grandma, and don't let her eat all the chili?" The phone rang. Shantique checked the caller ID. It was Taye. She passed the phone over to her mother and mouthed, "I'm not here."

Her mother grabbed the phone, confused about Shantique's behavior until she too saw the caller ID. "Hello," she answered. "Oh, Hi Taye. How you doing baby?" She gave Shantique the evil eye; "no she ain't here. She out somewhere with her friends. Okay baby, I will. Yes, he's here. You want to speak with him?" Shantique was shaking her head no. She knew if Rashawn spoke with his father, he would tell him she was standing right there. That boy didn't have a dishonest bone in his body. Her mother recouped, "Look Taye, he's a mess right now. I'll have him call you after his bath. Okay baby, you too!" She hung up. "Now you got me lying to your ex, and by the way that's the last time, okay?"

"Okay Ma. It's just that my business is my business. Taye," she began then changed, "he don't need to know my business. It's over, he's moved on and so have I."

"Have you really? Then why all the lies?" she said shaking her head. "Girl you don't fool me a bit. You still want him and you just don't want to admit it. You ain't over that boy."

"Mama! Look, I'm not gonna get into this now, especially not in front of Rashawn, plus I have to go," she said walking to the door.

"Damn that nigga must really be something to have you out catching trains in the dark."

"I'm not catching the train. He's picking me up."

Her mother stopped stirring and faced Shantique. "Then where he at. I didn't hear no doorbell. How you know he here? You got ESP or something?"

"Grandma what's ESP?" Rashawn asked.

"Evidently it's something your mama has."

Shantique walked over to the window and looked down below. X was where he was supposed to be waiting outside. A wide grin stretched across her face. "Come here ma?" She pointed below to the black SUV limousine waiting outside their apartment building.

"Damn! The nigga picking you up in a limo and you just met him. Shantique what's going on?" She whispered, "You not going to bed with him are you? Baby men with money like that to throw around got women chasing them everyday. You hear me, don't be no fool!

"Grandma, I'm hungry," Rashawn said pulling at his grandma's T-shirt.

Shantique kissed her mother on the cheek, "Don't worry, I haven't done what you asked. And I know you didn't raise no fool. Your girl ain't no fool. You hear me."

"Yeah, I hear ya baby girl. But remember women are a dime a dozen to those types. Don't sell yourself cheap."

*   *   *

For the second time in less than a week, Shantique found herself riding in a limo. She would have enjoyed the ride even more if X had paid her some attention, but from the time she had got in the limo, X had been on the phone. She didn't know who he was talking to, but suspected it was his manager or some company exec since it was all about business and contracts. She tried to busy herself with the view and even took the time to pour herself a drink from the well stocked bar. That was all fine and good but what she really wanted to do was spend some quality time with the fine man by her side. Even in his most casual wear, X looked impeccable. His smooth black skin glistened in the dimly lit car; occasionally he would smile at her, although he didn't seem happy at all. X raised his voice more than once, and cussed just about every other word. She pulled out her cell phone and dialed Nikko's number, who answered after a few rings, but promised to call her back because she was at a video shoot with Laron. So she dialed her girl Martinette.

"What's up girl?" Martinette answered.

"You hoochie! What you up to?"

"Girl, you will never believe it. This is a first, okay. Something I have never done for any man." Martinette sounded really hype about something and Shantique was sure it had something to do with Ro.

"Damn girl, what you doing?"

"Cooking girl. I'm cooking a four course southern meal for Ro, who I might mention is on his way over right now. I've got the Corona's chilling in the freezer. Hold up, I need to make sure they didn't freeze."

Shantique could hear the refrigerator door open and close and Martinette cussing.

"Alright, those bad boys were almost frozen."

"Martinette, you, cooking?" Shantique said laughing, which got X's attention and he smiled back at her. "I can't believe it, wait till I talk to Nikko, she is going to trip."

"Yeah I know. I'll save y'all some if there is any left." Her doorbell rang. "Look, Shantique I gotta go, my man Ro is here."

"Alright girl, I'll check with you tomorrow." Shantique hung up the phone and X reached for her hand.

"I'm sorry about the phone call. Damn girl, you look especially sweet tonight. You trying to break a nigga down!"

Shantique was all smiles. "Thank you, you don't look too bad yourself." She wasn't going to ask him about his business. As far as she was concerned, his business was his business. "So where we going?"

"I thought you might show me around. Where do you usually go on a Wednesday night?"

"I don't," she hesitated, wondering how much to share with him. She hadn't told him about Rashawn, but it wasn't like she was keeping it from him, she just didn't initially feel it was necessary to share. But for some reason she was feeling different about things. "I spend most of my nights with my son."

"Your son. You have a son?"

Shantique couldn't tell if he was upset about it or what, but if he was, she didn't have a problem jumping ship. "Yeah, I do. He's four years old. His names Rashawn."

"Oh, you sure don't look like you had a baby. You must have been working your pretty little ass off to get back in shape."

"No, not really. I was pretty physical during my pregnancy and after, so it was easy."

X got silent. "So, how about your baby's daddy? Y'all cool?"

"Yeah, we alright. We broke up not long after Rashawn was born, but we cool."

"Word. A son needs his father," he said looking out the window. My mom had me, when she was in her teens. Yeah, but I never met that motherfucker."

"Never?"

"Well, not when it counted. Not while I was growing up, getting beat downs, watching my mother fuck other niggas just to make ends meet. Naw, that motherfucker never was around, not when I needed him." He turned back to her and she could swear he had tears in his eyes. "But it's all good, all good now. Mamas living like a queen. I give her everything she want, when she want, no doubt."

"That's good. She deserves it."

"Hell yeah, if for nothing but putting up with my bullshit all those years. Shit my mama would have to run my ass down!" he said laughing, "I ain't lying. She would literally chase me down the street with a broom. All the kids on my block used to jones me about it! That shit was funny as hell! Damn!" he smiled, "I ain't thought about that shit in a long time. Long time."

Shantique hadn't thought X would open up to her like that, but she was glad he did. She instantly felt closer to him. Something she hadn't felt with another man, since Taye. He held her hand tighter, pulling it to his chest and placing it on his heart.

"So," he asked, "when I'm gonna meet your boy, Rashawn?"

* * *

    Nikko swiveled around in her chair trying not to look bored or annoyed. She was glad that Laron had invited her to the recording session but she wasn't prepared, nor did she expect to be sharing him with a cadre of groupies and homeboys. The scene was no different than from backstage after the concert. Different place, same scene, lots of scantily dressed women vying for attention, wannabe singers and rappers acting like they were somebody and then there was her, sitting in a corner wishing like hell she was somewhere else. Laron was in the booth finishing up a ballad for his new album, away from the chaos and it seemed miles away from her. Nikko didn't know how much longer she could take it, the waiting and the absurdity of it all. Hell, she thought, she wasn't like them. She wasn't no groupie! Yeah, she liked Laron, and didn't mind hanging out with him, but she wasn't about to strip down to her underwear or give a crewmember a blowjob just to get next to him. She didn't have to.

    "What's up Shorty?"

    Nikko came face to face with wannabe rapper Skeezer, another Lil Jon wannabe. He even dressed like him, wore an obviously fake grill and tried his best to wild out his hair but he didn't come close. "Hey," she responded flatly.

    "You in the game or what?" he asked leaning in closer. "Who you with?"

    Nikko turned sharply away from him and his hot breath that stank of beer and shit or some other nasty combination. "What?"

    "I said who you with?"

"She's with me," Laron said. "Damn man, ain't there enough women in here? You got to go messing with my girl."

Nikko was beaming with pride and happy to be relieved of Skeezer's company. Skeezer backed off, apologizing to Laron and nodding at Nikko. Laron grabbed Nikko's hand, pulling her up from the chair. "Let's get out of here," he said.

*   *   *

Laron's hand had slid up under Nikko's bra and before she knew it he was rubbing her nipples. She should have stopped him, but she was just as hot as he was and despite the surroundings she considered letting him go further.

"Hey, what you doing?"

"What? You don't like it?"

"I'm not saying that. I'm just saying...where do you think this is leading?"

"Wherever you want it to lead? You game?"

Nikko straightened out her blouse, and gave it to him straight.

"All I know is, I'm not about to give it up at no drive-in theatre. I'm not like that Laron."

Laron adjusted his clothing, pulled at his crotch and stared straight at the movie screen. Several minutes passed before either of them spoke and Nikko was getting pissed. What was with the silent treatment? "Laron," she asked. "What's up with you?"

"Nothing," he said not looking her way.

"Nothing? Then why you get all quiet, and stuff?"

"I'm watching the movie. If you don't want to watch it then get the fuck out!" he hollered.

Nikko didn't know what to think. She stared at him not halfway believing what he said, when he quickly reminded her he meant business by shoving her body against the passenger side door and screaming again.

"What you death? Get the fuck out of my car!"

"Laron, what is wrong with you?"

"Nothing, like I told you, I ain't got time to be fucking around with silly, young bitches. I can have any woman I want," he shouted slamming his fist into the leather seat, "right here, right now!"

Nikko acted on instinct, and her first instinct was to get the hell out of that car, so she opened her door and climbed out into the cold. Her mind was everywhere. What would happen to her now? Who would she call? What had she done wrong? Tears fell from her eyes as she looked at the vast wasteland of cars with people she didn't know and then looked back into the car to see Laron on his cellphone, probably calling up some other heifer to take her place. She started walking towards the concession stand when he called out her name.

"Nikko. Hey wait a minute." He ran up behind her and put is arms around her shoulder, which she shrugged off.

"What Laron?"

"Hey baby, look I'm sorry," he said. "Really sorry. I was tripping back there, just got a lot things on my mind and I'm sorry I took it all out on you."

"Laron, I don't appreciate being called no bitch, okay. And I'm nobody's fucking punching bag. I've seen too much of that shit with my cousin. I'm not the one, okay."

"I hear ya baby. I'm sorry, really sorry. Please," he grabbed her hands and kissed them, "forgive me. I can take you home if you want or maybe we can go back and enjoy that movie?"

"I don't know Laron. You were really tripping."

"I know, I know, but trust me, I won't do that again."

He pleaded with her and despite all he had done she found herself falling for him all over again.

"Please come back," he started to sing, "Baby please". That's when someone in the other cars recognized him.

"Hey, that's Laron from the group "Too Hot"; one girl shouted heading their way. Her boyfriend wasn't amused and muttered something that sounded like "so fucking what." But that didn't stop her from coming over and asking for an autograph. All of that took just about enough time for Nikko to get over her anger and start to appreciate what a fine catch she had.

Back in the car, they cuddled like before when Laron pulled her closer, "Look at you," he said. "You are one the most beautiful women I have ever laid eyes on and you are especially cute when you all pissed off. He pulled her chin and lips up to his and kissed her soft, slipping his tongue into her mouth. Nikko was happily surprised by his gesture. His kiss stirred something in her and she didn't know if she had the power to fight him off this time. "Ummm, you taste so good, so sweet." His hands moved under her blouse again and this time she didn't stop him. His fingers gently caressed her nipples one by one and then he raised her shirt even higher and wrapped his warm lips around each one. Nikko enjoyed every bit of it, his touch, his mouth on her breast, when he unzipped her pants and cradled her mound in his hand. "You are so wet," he said. And she was, it was like she had urinated on herself, but she hadn't. Laron caressed her and inserted his fingers in her warm spot. Nikko moaned when he moved them inside and out, and back again. Laron kissed her again, his tongue swimming with hers. He used his free hand to guide her, but she didn't need much help. Nikko found her way into his pants and wasted no time touching and caressing him. He was big for his size, although she really didn't have much experience with guys; the two guys she had touch seemed smaller than Laron. Laron moaned in her ear and she returned the moan. Everything was happening so fast. She didn't have time to think about what she was doing, or how far she would go. His hands felt good all over her and she didn't want him to stop.

Laron whispered in her ear. "Come for me. I want you to come for me Nikko." He said that over and over again, almost rhythmically, in time with his movements, in and out, he whispered, "Come for me Nikko." Nikko could feel herself working against his fingers, harder, more forceful, she felt herself rise up as she tried to escape the thrill. Laron moved his fingers and concentrated on removing her underwear. She slid out of them with ease, while the world around her melted into a cloudy haze. She hadn't planned to go this far with him. *No she hadn't planned on any of this*. Yet still, she didn't stop him. There was pain at first, and she gasped to catch her breath as Laron drove himself deeper until she cried out.

"Sorry baby, you okay?" He paused to ask. Nikko nodded her head and moved along with him.

She liked it when he slowed it down and met him stride by stride. Laron moaned with pleasure and whispered her name repeatedly in her ear. Nikko could feel the heat rising from her loins. She heard herself screaming and wanted to stop, wanted to laugh, because she sounded like her cat the day her dad ran over his paw, but worse. Laron joined her, issuing his own moan of sorts, and he was funnier than she was. When the two became quiet and all you could hear was their breathing, Nikko became aware of her surroundings. She was fucking in the middle of a drive-in Theatre with someone she had only known for less than a week. But then again, this wasn't just anyone, this was Laron of, "Too Hot", and to her that made the world of difference.

CHAPTER 8

Shantique ran the steamer over the designer dresses she had just unboxed and ticketed. After her second week on the job, the owner, Marisela put her in charge of stock. Although she spent most of her time unboxing, steaming and tagging clothing, she found herself liking the time alone. She was around clothes all day, and she loved it. Shantique enjoyed everything about working at Et Cetera, especially dressing the mannequins. Marisela told her she had good fashion sense and an eye for detail, a requirement in the fashion business. She was all smiles after that and tried to do everything she could to impress Marisela with her displays.

"Titi you did it again," Marisela said approaching from hallway. Marisela was a Cuban born, American bred, bleached blond, just shy of five feet, even with 4-inch stilettos. Shantique had never met anyone quite like Marisela. Marisela was like her mom's chili, hot, spicy, and sometimes gave you heartburn. A fashion madam by choice, what her money couldn't buy, she bartered. She loved sharing her stories of success and Shantique loved hearing them. "Titi", she called out again. She started calling Shantique by that name since the day she hired her. It was a first for

Shantique, having a pet name. Even her mama called her by her full name. "Hey Titi!" She said reaching up to Shantique and giving her a hug and kiss. She was dressed in a white leather mini, with matching white pointed toe boots and a pink angora sweater that hung off her shoulders. The Easter Bunny came to mind and Shantique smiled at the thought.

"So, how's the new shipment coming?"

"Great! You like the display?"

"Like it, girl I love it! The colors, mixing the burlap bag with the crushed velvet skirt. It's so hot! Where do you get these ideas?"

Shantique welled up with pride, "I don't know, I just see them in my mind and go for it."

"Oh my Titi," she said cupping her hands over her mouth, "It is a gift. You have a gift." Marisela ran her hands through the just steamed clothing, "and you are also the best steamer I ever hired. Everything is beautiful!"

"Thanks, how was New York?"

"Terrible, the traffic, the people, everybody running here and there. Who am I kidding, I miss it already. You've been to New York, right?"

"No."

"No? Oh my goodness girl. You need to see New York! And there is so much to see and do. Not like here, not slow and everybody speaking like this and that. It is fast, fun, and exciting. Next time, next trip I will take you with me."

"Really!"

"Of course darling, me you and Nia, will all go. Close the shop down and spend a weekend in New York. I will show you guys all around town, we can get a manicure, and pedicure at Sophia's, and even take in a Broadway show. You know Yuri can hook us up some tickets for a play, or even a Nick's game. Whateva girl, we can have a ball."

"I'm game." Shantique said, forgetting where she was or who she was with. "I mean yeah, that would be great Marisela."

"All girl, cut the proper crap. I'm down; you know what I mean. Look, I gotta run, you and Nia close up shop and I'll see y'all tomorrow. I am dead tired and Yuri is in town so I got's to get my beauty rest. Alright Titi," she said planting another kiss on Shantique, "I'll talk with you tomorrow."

"Okay Marisela, have a good night."

When Marisela left, Shantique spent most of her time daydreaming about New York, and hanging out at all those fine places Marisela had talked about. She sat there daydreaming like that until Nia interrupted her.

"Shantique," she called.

She heard Nia's footsteps rounding the corner, and it sounded like she was running.

Shantique jumped up from her chair, afraid that something was wrong and ran straight into Nia in the hallway.

"What's up? Something wrong," she asked.

Nia seemed to be out of breath, but laughing and smiling at the same time, "girl do you know who is out there asking for you?"

"Nia, who?"

"Girl, damn, okay, I got to get myself together. I can't believe this shit! Okay, X. X the rapper is in our store and he asked for you."

Shantique was just as excited but for different reasons. She hadn't seen X in weeks, not since their limo ride around the city. The day after he had to leave for a 2 week tour of Japan. It had been the longest they had been apart since they started dating, and although he would call at least twice a week, it wasn't the same. She was thrilled he was here and nervous too. She tried to act cool, and not let her nervousness or anxiousness show.

"X is here."

"Yes, did you just here what I said."

"Okay," Shantique said and made her way towards the front room.

Nia blocked her way. "Oh hell no, you are going to tell me how you know X! Girl, I am tripping up in here."

"Nia, I promise to tell you everything as soon as he leaves. Now let me get out there before we have a store full of groupies all over my man."

* * *

Shantique didn't make it in time to stop the groupies. There was already a group of young women surrounding X and his entourage at the cash register and more were coming through the door. X was looking good, and despite the madhouse handled himself pretty well with his fans. He signed autographs and took pictures but when Shantique entered the room, he stopped cold.

"Hey baby," he said moving away from the crowd. Shantique felt all warm inside and quite special at that moment, especially when every eye in the room was on her. "So this is where you work. I like it! It fits you, classy, upscale and sexy, just like my Boo."

"X, X they hollered from every corner," his fans weren't having none of that mushy stuff, and they didn't give a damn about Shantique. They pushed their way to him, blocking her, until his bodyguards took hold of the situation and moved them all back and out of the store. By the time Shantique had a chance to get next to him; X's demeanor had changed from quietude to utter frustration.

"What are you doing here?" she asked. "I thought you were out of town."

X grabbed a hold of her, squeezed her tight and kissed her on the cheek. "I needed to see you Ma. Needed to feel ya."

Her whole body tingled. He had a way of doing that to her. Damn! She couldn't believe this. Couldn't believe him and what was happening to her, to him. In just a couple of weeks they had become so close, and she knew exactly how he felt, because damn near every waking moment she thought of him. But she wasn't trying to get all sprung out on X. She heard what her mama said, and despite the way X made her feel she had to keep her guard up. Who was she fooling, her guard was a wall of ice, dissolving by the seconds. She hugged him back, melted into his arms, and forgot where she was or what she was there for, until she heard Nia clearing her throat in the background.

"Hold up baby, there's somebody I want you to meet. Nia come here."

* * *

"Marisela says New York is the bomb! I can't wait to get there. I know I'll love it! Broadway, Time Square, the Empire State Building, I'm gonna see it all.

I'm already..." A child screamed in the background and she couldn't help thinking about Rashawn. This had been the third weekend in a row that she spent without him. Although she enjoyed her time with X, she missed her son. She turned her attention to the group of kids playing soccer in the middle of the field. Shantique didn't know a thing about soccer, but she thought it would be something Rashawn would like. The last time she had visited Centennial Park had been the summer of the Olympics, before he was born. She regretted that she never took the time to visit all of Atlanta's landmarks and go site seeing just like the tourists. I've got to bring my baby here, he would really enjoy it."

"You need to lick that," X said pointing at the double-dutch chocolate ice-cream cone Shantique was holding.

"You lick it.

"I rather lick you."

"You nasty."

X ran his tongue over her face and she screamed.

"Stop it X! So what do you think about New York?"

"New York's alright, colder than a muthafucka."

"It's not cold in the summer."

"Yeah it is, people cold, everybody rushing, pushing, bunch of cold muthafucka's, but the parties ain't too bad, the joints be jumping."

"Now why you want to blow my dream like that? I don't give a shit about the people. I'm talking about making it, the fashion world, seeing the sites and stuff."

"All baby, don't get all mad on me. I didn't mean anything by it. Anyway, as soon as your pretty ass hit that asphalt, the whole city will warm up just from seeing your smile. Niggas be speaking and shit, it will be crazy."

"You crazy."

X's smile faded. "I hear that shit more than I need to," he said standing up, "more than I want to. A nigga ain't trying to be crazy, a nigga just want to be normal."

"I'm sorry X. I didn't mean anything by it. I know you are not crazy, and I…"

"Baby, it's alright, my bad. Just been one of those weeks, the road stuff been kind of rough. It ain't you, it's me."

"What's the matter?"

"Nothing babe. Nothing to worry your pretty little head about. Look, I only have this one night before I have to go on the road again and this," he pointed at the park, the sky, "this is good! This makes me feel at peace, and you increase that peace by a thousand." He planted a kiss on her forehead. "I need you before, and after every road trip. I swear babe, you do it for me." X rubbed her arm and squeezed her gently. "This is really nice. It's what I like about Atlanta. So how old is your Shorty?"

Shantique was surprised by his question. She had never really talked much about Rashawn. As far as she was concerned Rashawn was her business, alone and what went on between her and X was between her and X. Her son hadn't had to deal with any other man but his father and she wanted to keep it that way. She didn't want Rashawn growing up like her, looking at all her mom's boyfriends and asking, "Is that my new daddy?" Only to be disappointed when they left. No, she wasn't going to go down that road with Rashawn. Rashawn has a father and a mother, although not together, they were raising their son together.

"Rashawn is four. He'll be five in September and starting school. He's big for his age, because his daddy is tall and I'm average."

"Four huh? I bet he's a hand full."

She nodded in agreement.

"I used to take care of my cousin's son, back home. It was cool though. Back then, we didn't have much, but we still had fun. Shit is funny like that. A nigga think he got to have paper to make him happy but as kids we didn't have shit. I remember how we would scrape up change from under couches, on the ground, wherever we could find it. My friend Walt's grandma's couch always paid off. Shit, we would get at least a dollar fifty or more whenever we went to her house. And no sooner than we would find it, me, Walt, and my little cousin Brandon will hit up the corner store for chips, pop, cookies, and all that we could carry. My mama would be mad as hell, telling me I shouldn't be feeding that boy all that junk and she would come home and fix us a big pot of chili, or soup, or stew. Mama fixed everything in that big, black cast iron pot and we would eat on it for days. That's why I ain't ate from nobody's big, black pot since."

He laughed to himself, then stared off into space, as if remembering something. Though, no matter how he tried to hide it, Shantique saw his pain. The pain X kept hidden under all his bravado, and thug shit. She saw through him, saw the child he used to be, the innocence before the pain.

X pulled out a cigarette and lit it, taking one long drag after another.

"Damn, I remember that shit like it was yesterday. Brandon and me running home, trying to make it in before the streetlights came on and mama waiting on the front porch with her belt. That woman could swing a belt better than anyone. That summer Brandon moved in with us permanently after my cousin, Brenda got picked up for hoeing. They only gave her a couple of months, but she never came back, just left him. We became his family, me and my mama."

"So you two grew up together? I guess he was more like a brother than a little cousin."

"Yeah, true dat. Brandon was my dog. We did everything together. When my first CD came out he toured with me and by the second CD, I made him my road manager. I always felt safe with Brandon around, you know ain't nothing like knowing that somebody has your back. Nigga's be tripping in the rap game. When you ain't got nothing everybody hustling, everybody down for you, but as soon as you hit the big-time, your ass is marked to be taken. Nigga's start hating on you, saying your shit ain't all that, want to call you out about all kinds of bullshit." He took his last drag, then flicked the cigarette butt to the ground. "But me and Brandon just let that shit roll off our backs, because they knew I wasn't hearing that shit. I come correct and Brandon had my back, because nobody wasn't going to mess with Brandon. Although I call him my little cousin, that nigga grew to be six feet two, two hundred and eight five pounds of pure muscle. Brandon lifted weights like I wrote rhymes," he laughed. "Says he was gonna do pro-wrestling. I even got him hooked up with this dude from the WWF."

X stood up and walked to the end of the sidewalk where he tapped out another cigarette and lit it.

Shantique could tell by his stance, the way he looked away from her that something was bothering X. "So, did he make it? The WWF?"

X shook his head, "Naw! A week before he was to start training he was found dead in his apartment from a gunshot wound. They tried to say it was suicide, but I know better."

"I'm sorry," Shantique said and she meant it. She wanted to be a comfort to X. She wanted him to know that she too had his back. X faced the street, but his gaze was off in a distance, far from the lights, the cars and the activity taking place on Spring Street. Shantique walked over to him wrapped her arms around his waist and squeezed real tight, the way her grandma would hug her when she was hurt or feeling bad. She could feel him tense up at her touch, but then he relaxed and let himself be held. He reached for her hands and held them tightly in front of him.

"It's been two years, but the case is still unsolved. You don't get no justice unless you pay for it, but I got somebody on the case. He paused. "Then Sammy came along and made everything right. Became my road dog, sort of like the brother I never had. He didn't take the place of Brandon, but having him around eased the pain for sure. Look here Shorty," he said turning to face her. He ran his fingers along her cheeks, and traced the outline of her jaw, "I didn't mean to bring you down, especially when you was all excited about going on your trip and things. I wasn't even meaning to go down that road."

Shantique kissed him softly on the lips, because she felt he needed it and because she wanted to. X had opened up to her today in a way she would have never believed. She felt his pain and his anger about the death of his cousin and she was taken by his honesty. As they stood in the darkness, amongst the stars and the moon, Shantique realized how much her and X were alike. They started out with nothing, her in Detroit and he in Chicago, and both of them suffered great losses at an early age. She lost her father, and he lost his cousin but no matter how hard they tried, that little bit of darkness, anger, pain and emptiness remained. They were two halves, trying to be whole.

CHAPTER 9

Martinette lifted the large pitcher and poured her second margarita. "Girl, I am feeling this. How long you been coming here? These Mexican's can make some margaritas! You here me!" she said lifting her glass for a toast. It was the perfect day for sitting out, and El Azteca's patio was filled to capacity. The mixed crowd of Yuppies, Buppies, Gay and Lesbian crowd all seemed to be enjoying the day and the very potent Margarita's El Azteca served. A few patrons ordered food, but the majority settled for a liquid diet.

"I hear ya girl," Shantique said refilling her glass. "These are some of the best margarita's I ever had. Come on Nikko get off the damn phone! This is girl's day out!"

Nikko listened to the recording one more time, but didn't leave a message. She closed her phone and reached for the nearly empty pitcher of Margarita's. "Damn, you could have left me some," she said pouring the remaining liquid in her glass and gulping it down. She waved to the waiter to bring another pitcher, but when he didn't come right away she rudely reprimanded him and asked for his manager.

"Nikko," Shantique asked, "What was that all about?"

"What? We are the patrons, the customer and he is the servant. All I want is good service. He should have filled that pitcher the moment he saw it was empty that's all."

"I hear ya," Martinette chimed in, slurping down the last of her glass. I could use another, rat now! You hear me!"

The waiter arrived with another large pitcher of peach margaritas and poured each of them a full glass. Shantique nursed her third glass, while Nikko and Martinette launched an all out glass for glass contest. From the look of it, Martinette was winning as always, because she could drink more than the three of them combined, but Nikko did her best to hang in there. "So Nikko where did you find this place?"

"Laron. Laron and me, we came here, to eat. We used to eat at Fellini's pizza all the time, but I got sick of pizza."

Shantique tapped Nikko on the shoulder and whispered, "I think you better slow up girl, cuz you slurring."

"I am not, slurring. Whateva, I am going to drink as much as you two if I feel like it, okay. Anyway, I staying at Kim's tonight."

"Okay, okay, check this muthafucka out," Martinette said way too loudly, then swung her wrist in front of them, nearly missing Nikko's chin. She was wearing a very expensive, diamond tennis bracelet. "Courtesy of my man, Ro. That ladies is 20 karats of flawless diamonds."

Nikko and Shantique were in awe and drew a collective breath before speaking. Shantique had been seeing X for as long as Martinette been dealing with Ro and she hadn't gotten anything like that.

"Damn, Marti that's gorgeous."

Nikko pushed her girlfriends arm out of her face. "Yeah, so what."

"Look don't hate sweetie. So what, ain't that a bitch!," Martinette mumbled under her breath.

Nikko averted her eyes and took another swallow from her margarita. "And, I ain't no Bitch."

"Girl, what is wrong with you? Didn't nobody call you a bitch!"

"Marti," Shantique said, trying to calm down her friend. Then she turned to Nikko. "Nikko, what's up girl?"

"Her ass is drunk, that's what's up? She handles her liquor, just like she handles her man!"

Nikko tried to stand up and nearly fell out of her chair. "What's that supposed to mean, bitch. Like I said, so what! We get tired of you always throwing your shit up in our face, "Ro gave me this, Ro gave me that, so what the Nigga is paying for all that pussy you dishing out."

Shantique and Martinette were both in shock. Nikko had never talked that way before, although Shantique may have thought the same, she would have never said it to Martinette's face. She knew how Martinette was. She liked to brag. She liked to make everyone think she was the shit all the time, but that's how she was.

Martinette started getting loud, cussing out Nikko, but Nikko just laughed. Either she was drunk out of her mind, or something else was wrong with her. Whatever it was, Shantique didn't like it. Shantique tried talking Martinette down, since as oddly as it seems was the calmer of the two, but Nikko wouldn't' stop and before she knew it, the entire situation had gotten out of hand.

"You ain't nothing but a hoe!" Nikko shouted.

"I'm a hoe," Marti said pointing at herself. "Me, you want to sit there and call me a hoe. You half-breed bitch and I thought you was my friend."

"Marti please," Shantique shouted.

"Naw, Shantique. You let her sit there and call me a hoe in front of all these people, just cause the bitch is jealous. Jealous that I got a real man, a man who appreciates me. A man who buys me things, not because I'm fucking him, but because he likes me. He likes me, you hear that Nikko. All this time you been knowing me, you been thinking like that. How about you Shantique, you think like your girl here? You been thinking... Marti's a hoe too. Well, I got your hoe! I didn't want to tell you this, but fuck it, since we talking about hoes. You wanna know who the hoe is Nikko? It's your boyfriend. Yeah that's right, your fucking little boy toy, Mister oh so fine, pretty boy Laron. Word on the street is that nigga is a bonafide hoe! Not only is he screwing everything up and down Peachtree Street, he swinging it both ways. Don't believe me; ask your limo friend. What's his name, Butter? Ask him, who's the biggest hoe in Hip-Hop!"

* * *

Shantique had an eye-popping headache, but it couldn't have compared to Nikko's wounded heart. She nearly had to carry her friend to her car and when Nikko handed over the keys, she realized that her friend was really out of it, cuz everybody knew

Shantique didn't drive. Martinette stomped away after her last outburst and without paying, so Shantique had to fork over the entire check. Nikko had been in and out of it since they had left the restaurant. Occasionally she would wake up and gag, then up and down the window went. Shantique feared Nikko was going to spray that shit all over the car. Luckily, they made it to her house just in time and for the next couple of hours, Nikko sat spread eagle on the floor hugging the bottom of a toilet bowl while spilling her guts. When it seemed her friend was all done, Shantique moved her from the bathroom to her bed and opened windows so Nikko could get some fresh air. Several times, she tried to wake Nikko up, but she wouldn't bulge. She wished her mom were there, because to be honest she was scared. No sooner than she had that thought, her mom knocked at her door.

"Shantique, why you got your door close? And what is that smell? Shantique, open this door!" she shouted. Shantique hadn't remembered locking the door, but she thought she might of done it to prevent her mom from knowing what was going on, at least that's what she wanted in the beginning, but now, she needed her.

Shantique unlocked her door and her mother gasped at the smell before her eyes rested on Nikko lying on the bed. "Hey Ma."

"Don't you hey ma me!" her mother said pushing her way past Shantique. "This girl done threw up all over your room. Why you got her lying on the bed Shantique?" Her mother placed her hand on Nikko's head and nudged her to wake up, but Nikko wouldn't move. "Shantique, we got to get this girl up. How much did she drink?"

"She had about three glasses of margaritas. That's not a lot, but Nikko don't usually drink that much."

"Well, how much did she throw up? Did you give her some water? She could be suffering from that alcohol poisoning. You ain't supposed to let them just sleep. Nikko, Nikko come on," she nudged and pulled at Nikko's limp arms. "All hell naw! Your ass is getting up, right now. Get up!" Nikko finally showed some signs of life by moaning. "Alright good, at least we know you alive. "Shantique, go downstairs and fill a bowl up with ice and bring the pitcher of water out of the fridge." Her mother removed Nikko's clothing. "Come on baby, we got to get you into the shower."

* * *

Shantique set across from her friend, while Nikko sipped the cup of coffee her mom had made for her. For the most part she was beginning to look like herself again, aside from that wet puppy look, the sweet girl she knew as Nikko was returning. Shantique had to admit her mom was great at taking care of people, especially drunks. She had a lot of history of nursing drunks; oddly enough most of them were her mom's suitors. Shantique couldn't remember if her dad drank or not, but she supposed he did too! Perhaps that's why her mom always found herself with the same kind of man, an unemployed drunk looking to prove his manhood.

"Shantique, I'm going to pick up Rashawn," her mom hollered from the door. "Y'all gonna be okay?"

"Yeah ma."

"Alright then, and Nikko finish all that coffee and drink some more water too! How's your head?"

"Its better, thanks Miss Robinson, for everything."

"You welcome sweetie, but we are going to have a real serious talk when I get back. Me, you and Shantique, all about the evils of drinking," Shantique's mother said exiting the apartment.

The silence between the two was uncanny and so unordinary. Her and Nikko could talk for hours, sometimes finishing each other's sentences, but now they sat like strangers. In many ways, Nikko seemed like a stranger to Shantique today. She had never seen Nikko act a fool, not even when she had been drinking. That role was usually played by Martinette. But this time Martinette had every right to go off on Nikko, even if it meant hurting her very good friend's feelings.

"I guess I should be thanking you too Shantique, you know for driving me here and…"

"It's cool, you would have done the same for me."

"Yeah you right. Shantique, I'm sorry about today with Martinette, the drinking too much. I don't know what got in to me."

"Nikko, you don't act like that, never. What's up girl? Is it Laron, your parents?"

"No, my parents are cool, hell they think I'm over Kim's right now, where I should be. Laron is alright, I guess."

"What do you mean, you guess?"

"I say I guess, because I haven't heard from him in a couple of weeks. Not a fucking word. I call and leave messages, but he never returns my calls. I'm through with him Shantique, especially after hearing what Martinette said. I don't want nothing to do with him anymore."

Shantique had known Nikko a long time, long enough to know that there something more going on between Laron and Nikko than just a few missed phones calls. Women don't fall all over themselves, cuss out their bestfriends just because a man didn't' call. That shit only happens when you've slept with him. And although she didn't want to bring the subject up, she knew it to be true. All she could do was to support her friend and allow her to share in her own time.

"Wait a minute Nikko, okay you haven't heard from him, maybe he's busy, you know when they are out on tour day in and day out, they have a lot to do. Don't believe Marti just yet. You know how Marti is, she will say some shit just to hurt you, even if it is only a rumor, Marti likes to have the last line."

"Yeah, I thought all about the road thing, but he could have returned my calls, if only to say, hey, I'm busy. You know I was real hesitant at first about dealing with Laron. A man that good looking has a lot of groupies, I knew that going in, but then he convinced me I was special and I thought we could have something real."

"Come on Nikko, you still can. You just gonna roll over and give up, cause he ain't called, or are you going to fight for your man?"

"Hell, I'm all fought out. Going up against Tyson-Marti is enough for me." They both laughed.

"Marti don't pull no punches. Damn, I really thought she was about to hit you upside the head with that pitcher of Margarita's and did you see the way everybody was looking at us!"

"Yeah, I'm not going back there anymore, at least no time soon."

"Me neither."

"You think I ought to call Marti and apologize?"

"Marti likes to be mad at somebody. I really think my girl got anger issues. Anyway, just give her a couple of days before you call. It won't do no good to call now, she won't talk to you or me for that matter."

"I'll call her next week." Nikko paused, "Shantique, if what she said wasn't true, why would she bring up Butter's name?"

"I don't know Nikko, perhaps you should ask her, or even better ask Butter."

CHAPTER 10

  Martinette checked her messages again. She had four new messages, two from Shantique, one from Nikko and one from her ex, Dwayne. Not one message from Ro. She tried calling him on his cell phone and when that didn't work she tried two-waying him. That was it! She thought and threw her cell phone across the room. "I ain't no trick." She was tired of being dismissed, by her so-called friends, by Ro. "Fuck them all," she said. Things been going downhill since the day her and Nikko got into it. She was spending less time with Ro, unlike when they first got together; the nigga was calling, sending flowers, and gifts, giving her money like crazy. Now she had to track a nigga down just to say hello. She believed all that bullshit about him getting ready for the playoffs, and how he had to concentrate on the game. Hell, she even believed him when he told her he was going to look for a house in Atlanta, some place where they could spend some time together, and a place she could fix up and call home. She believed all that crap, but where was he now? Martinette reached for her phone and dialed Ro's number again. She had a good mind to tell him where to go and when, but paused long enough to think things through and give him the benefit of doubt. She punched in the code to bypass the greeting and go straight to the voicemail, after the long beep, she recorded her message.

"Hey Ro, this me. Look, I thought we were going go do some sightseeing today, check out those houses we talked about, but baby I ain't heard from you. Call me sweetie, I'm at home."

*   *   *

Hours passed by, and still no word from Ro. Martinette pulled out the Grey Goose and made a pitcher of Apple martinis. Springtime in Atlanta was her favorite time of the year. The pear trees and dogwoods were in full bloom and the weather was off the chain, seventy-five degrees and no humidity, a day for sitting out. Marti took her pitcher and the April copy of Essence onto the deck where she could view the city skyline and blue skies while she enjoyed her favorite drink. She flipped through the Essence with Mariah Carey on the cover and daydreamed about the day she would grace its cover. Before long, she dozed off.

When she woke up, it was after six and still no word, no messages, no phone calls from Ro. She was pretty pissed and feeling the remnants from drinking an entire pitcher of margaritas, a little more than high and just one iota away from being drunk. She dialed Ro's number again and again she got his voicemail.

"You know what Ro," she said, "Fuck you! I ain't no trick, muthafucka! If you expect me to sit around and wait on your black ass to call, you got another thing coming. And if your ass is out there messing with some scrawny ass, chickenhead, hoodbooger, then stay where you are, cuz I don't mess around with spoiled meat. You here me! You fucking bastard!" She slammed the telephone down on the receiver. That was it! She was not the type to be used and just because this nigga had a lot of money, fuck him. Ballers were a dime a dozen and if she could hook up with him, she could hook up with another. It's too bad he couldn't see what he had. It wasn't like she didn't have shit, or didn't bring anything to the table. She was the shit! He said it himself every time they went somewhere; the nigga got his just do. Hell, she even cooked for a nigga, and that's something she hadn't done for anybody. Martinette didn't want to admit that she had fallen for Ro. For the first time in her life, she let someone in. She opened up her heart and now he was just doing what men do, walking over it. How could she be so stupid? Somehow, she had to turn this shit around. She knew she wasn't weak, and not desperate, so why was she sitting around waiting for him to call? For as long as she could remember, she had been on her own, taking care of herself, looking out for Marti and no one else.

    It was six o'clock and the weather was beautiful. It was time to get back her life. Get back to being Marti. She picked up the phone and started to dial Shantique, a day out with the girls would do her just fine, but then she remembered about their last outing, and the fact that they hadn't gotten together since. Although she really would love to see them, she wasn't in the mood for making up, apologizing for shit she didn't' do just because Nikko's ass was out of pocket. She quickly hung up and dialed another number instead. Why not, she thought, two can play the game.

    "Hello," a male voice answered.

    "What's up baby?" Marti replied.

"Who this?"

"Oh, now you gonna go and act all brand new on me? You know who this is."

"Yeah, but I'm surprised as hell Marti. I know I called you earlier, but I didn't expect you to call back."

"Why not? You know you will always be my baby."

"Oh yeah, so where is Ro?"

"Ro?"

"Yeah Ro, Marti. Word gets around. I know you two been hanging."

"We hang out, but it ain't like that. Like I got ties on him, or he got them on me."

"Word?"

"Word! So what's up Dwayne, you feel like doing something or what?"

"Hell yeah girl! You know I've been missing my sweet thing."

"Yeah, me too baby!"

"I'll pick you up around eight."

"Alright baby, I'll be here."

* * *

After having dinner at Bones in Buckhead, Dwayne and Martinette cruised Peachtree Street in his new powder blue, BMW 740I, in search of the perfect martini. Dwayne was unusually charming and fun to be with, not to mention fine. Although Martinette's taste in men rarely changed, she liked them tall, dark and balling. Dwayne was the exception. He was about 5'10", the color of caramel and out of touch with his black side. Dwayne Kent, was the biracial son, of an Italian mother and African father. He admitted to her, that she was the first and only sister he had ever dated. That information intrigued Martinette and she felt obligated to represent for all the sisters. She supposed she did a good job because Dwayne always came back for more.

"So what do you think of the car?" He asked.

Martinette rubbed her hands over the butter soft white leather seats. "It's nice, much better than that Range Rover you were driving. I'm glad up you got rid of it."

"I didn't get rid of it. It's parked at the house. That's my dog. My first big purchase since making the major leagues. She like family."

"She? I bet you actually have a name for her. What you call her, Rovine? Randi?" she said laughing.

"No, she's Ray-Ray. Don't' laugh. I'm not the only one naming their cars."

"Yeah, you right. I used to call my Toyota Corolla, Betsy because she was so old."

"You call her a girl's name. I thought you all named your cars after men."

"I don't. I had Betsy, and now I have Lexy."

"Lexy, that's cute."

Martinette turned her attention to the streets and the all the new buildings on Peachtree Street. It had been a while since she had driven downtown or Buckhead and a lot had changed. Peachtree Street from Five Points to Buckhead had been revitalized with new condos, lofts, restaurants, coffee shops, and even a brand new Koger and Lowes store. These new condo's weren't cheap either, but they sure were nice, just the kind of place she would like to live.

"I was thinking about getting me one of these lofts, you see those over there," he pointed out her window to a two story building that look like it used to be a warehouse. The price range was from the three hundred thousands. "They got everything in there, hardwood floors, sunken bedroom, Jacuzzi on the deck, plus it's not too far from the stadium. What do you think?"

"I don't know, they don't look like much from the outside, but for three hundred G's it's probably got all the bells and whistles."

"Yep, you right about the outside, but that' what I like about it. Nobody can really tell how you living, but when you inside, it's like damn!"

Dwayne had a nice smile, big and warm. The kind of smile you saw on small children before they learn how to pose and fake it. With all the changes, she was glad that his smile was still the same. Since she had last seen him, he had shaved his head and bulked up it all the right places. He even dressed better. Martinette was enjoying herself and to her surprise hadn't thought about calling Ro all that night. It wasn't that she hadn't had fun with Dwayne before, but sometimes, or as far as she could remember, most times his idea of a good time out was hanging at some sports bar. Tonight was different. The two them wound up at the Ritz Carlton Buckhead, where they sipped on chocolate martini's while listening to piano music. It wasn't her typical idea of a date, but it was fantastic. Martinette enjoyed the ambiance, the lavish surroundings, and the people, lots of rich white and black folks chilling

"Hey," Dwayne said. "What you thinking about?"

"Well, I was thinking that this is nice," Martinette said waving her hand in the air. "I like all of this, the furnishings, the music, the people."

"Yeah, the Ritz is nice. You should see my room. I've got the best view in the hotel."

"Really?" Martinette said, sitting straight up. She knew Dwayne made good money playing for the Braves but a suite in this place had to cost a grip. Dwayne had never been the kind of guy who splurged, not on clothes, cars or anything. Now he was taking her out to fine restaurants and living at the Ritz. Forget the past, all of a sudden he was looking better and better to her. She slurped the last of her martini, and ran her tongue along the rim, licking away the crushed chocolate that lined the glass. She didn't have to look at Dwayne to know he was eating it up. She had him right where she wanted. When she did look up, she found him staring at her breasts, like a newborn babe at feeding time. "Dwayne!"

"What? A man can look can't he?"

"I ain't saying that, but do you have to be so obvious?" All of a sudden, she remembered one of the other things she didn't like about Dwayne, his obsession with breasts. It wasn't just her breasts, it was any breasts. The two of them couldn't walk down a street, attend a function without him staring at some woman's breast. Subconsciously she guessed that's why she wore the low cut blouse exposing her cleavage. She tried changing the subject. "So what happened to your house?"

"I'm having it renovated." He pointed at her glass and asked, "You want another?"

"Yeah, these are the best."

Dwayne waved over the waiter and ordered two more martinis'. When they arrived cold and frosty, Martinette watered at the mouth.

"Ooh, these are so good!" She said before taking a sip. Martinette's head was swimming with vodka and ideas. *If she played her cards right, she could hold on to Ro and have Dwayne too! Like her mother used to say, "don't put all your eggs in one basket."* She thought, nodding her head to the pianist rendition of Marvin Gaye's "Let's get it on". "You know what," she said. "Why don't we have these in your room, where I can get a little more comfortable."

* * *

Martinette awoke to the sound of her phone vibrating on the nightstand. She checked the caller id, it was Ro. There was no way she was going to answer his call, not with Dwayne asleep next to her. But it was four o'clock in the morning and if she didn't answer Ro would be worried or suspicious. She eased out the bed, careful not to wake Dwayne and headed for the bathroom. The bathroom elaborately decorated in black marble with gold trimming. There were two wash basins and a shower big enough for four people at least. She started the shower and nervously dialed Ro's number. He answered after the second ring.

"Hey baby," she said.

"Where you at?"

He was angry and he had a right to be, especially if he knew where she was and with who. She wasn't about to let him know. She paused. "Damn baby, what's up with that? I'm at Shantique's. We were hanging out and I didn't feel like being home alone. Anyway, I should be asking you the same question."

"Martinette I've been calling you all night and all I got was your answering machine or your voicemail. I ain't heard from you since you left me that fucked up message early on."

"Oh, so you got my message."

"Yeah I got your message and I didn't appreciate it."

"Well, I didn't appreciate being stood up and I didn't appreciate not getting a call from you explaining why I was stood up," she said.

"Look, we really need to talk, cuz I got to tell you," he paused, "that message you left was way off base. I got a lot of things going on, trying to do some things for the betterment of my career and my life. And what I don't need is unnecessary drama."

Martinette could hear the seriousness in his voice. She almost panicked at the thought of losing Ro for good over some bullshit. Despite where she was and who she was with, she loved Ro. He is the best thing to happen to her and she enjoyed everything about him. There was no way she was going to let him just walk out of her life that easy. "Baby! I'm sorry. I just freaked out when you didn't call. I had all these plans to spend time with you and I know you busy. I know. Look, I want to talk about it too! I don't want to lose you Ro."

He was silent and for that moment, Martinette felt desperately ill down to the pit of her stomach. She couldn't tell if it was from their conversation or the four or five chocolate martini's she consumed the night before. She slumped to the floor and leaned her head against the gold-trimmed porcelain stool. Her heart was pounding and she got that warm salty taste in her mouth. She knew any moment now she was going to vomit all over that bathroom. But she had to fix it with Ro first. "Ro? You there?"

"Yeah, I'm still here. When you going back home?"

The shower was still running. "After I shower. I should be there in about twenty to thirty minutes." Martinette tried to remain calm but her head was spinning along with the room, and although she opened and closes them to stop the spin, it only seemed to spin faster. "Ro, I got to go."

"You okay?"

"Yeah, I'll see ya in thirty minutes, okay." She said hanging up, then leaned over the bowl and spilled a chocolate mess.

* * *

Dwayne lay butt naked across the bed and watched her dress. He didn't have much to say about her leaving. He didn't even ask her to stay, which was odd because he usually wanted to cuddle, but not this time.

"Damn girl! You still the best I've ever had. So when we gonna get together again? You know I'm going to be here for another month or so."

Martinette grabbed her purse, kissed Dwayne on the forehead and headed for the door.

"I'll let you know."

Dwayne slapped her on the butt as she passed by..

"I just bet you will. Tell Ro, I said Hello!"

What the fuck? She started to cuss him out, but she didn't, she knew how to hold water. Truth be told, she may need Dwayne again, ain't no since in burning bridges, at least not yet. Anyhow, if things go according to plan, she wouldn't have to deal with his ass again.

CHAPTER 11

Nikko dressed in pink leotards and tights then covered them with jeans and short sleeve T-shirt. She stuffed her ballet shoes in her purse next to her cell phone and her letter of invitation from the Atlanta Ballet. She could hear her mom downstairs cooking breakfast, oatmeal, wheat toast, eggs for her father and a pot of rice for her. It wasn't your normal breakfast, but it was what she had eaten nearly every morning since she could remember.

"Nikko, you up!" her mom said while she stirred the pot of oatmeal. Her dad looked up from his paper and smiled with his eyes first, then his mouth, like he had always done. Nikko hadn't planned to run into both of them this morning.

"Good morning Mom," she said kissing her mother on the cheek. Then wrapped her arms around her dad shoulders and kissed him as well, "Hi daddy."

"Hi Pumpkin. Where you off to so early this morning?" Her mother stopped stirring and turned to stare at her.

"To the library. I've got some more research to do."

"Oh, that's right you're still working on your application, right?"

Nikko's palms began to sweat. "Yes daddy. I still have a couple of weeks, but I'm almost finished."

"Well, I think Emory is an excellent school. It has one of the best medical schools in the country."

"I know dad, stop the selling, I'm convinced."

Nikko's mom placed a bowl of the hot oatmeal in front of her father and then rested her hand on his shoulders. "Nikko will make a fine doctor."

"That's what I've been saying all along. I'm just glad she got that dance stuff out of her head and is taking this college thing serious."

Nikko's mom eyes pleaded with her not to say anything and she didn't. She understood her father's preoccupation with her becoming a doctor although she didn't agree and she knew her mother would never defy him.

"I am dad, taking this college thing serious. I have to go."

"No breakfast?" her mother asked.

"No mom. I'll pick up something later."

"No junk food Nikko. Not good for you, all that burgers, and fries bad for health."

Nikko kissed them both and left and for many reasons she felt like she left half of her soul behind. If only they knew how much she wanted to dance. If only they could see her passion. But they would never see no matter how much she wanted.

It had been two weeks since Nikko had applied to the Atlanta Ballet Company. It was a longshot for sure, but it was what she wanted and had been preparing for all of her life. The years of training, practicing and performing had prepared her for this day, tryouts. This was one of the most exciting days of her life and yet she told no one, not her friends, her parents or Kim. This was something she needed to do alone and for herself. Her parents didn't want her to study dance, so what kind of support would they lend? Shantique had a new job and new boyfriend and not much time for Nikko, and well Martinette was an entirely different situation. She and Martinette hadn't spoken since that afternoon at Al Eztaca. As for Laron, she hadn't heard from him at all. Laron turned out to be like any other man, after he got what he wanted, he dropped her and it pissed her off that she could be used so easily, but that was behind her now. Her fate was in her hands. If she wanted to make it in this world, she didn't have to hook up with a baller to do it. She would do it on her own.

Everything was happening so fast and she didn't expect to be called in so soon, but the head director had said in so many words that her audition tape was the best they had seen. What a surprise, when she thought that her routines were far from traditional ballet, but instead incorporated modern ballet with hip-hop dancing. Her music was just as diverse, ranging from contemporary jazz, to classical, to Little John and the Eastside Boyz. She was proud of what she had done, proud that she represented all aspects of who she was and in the end, it paid off. The director explained to her that the company was evolving and how hip-hop played in that change.

She looked around her, catching an eye of one of the other four girls who were waiting to audition. Nikko smiled back and the girl looked away, pretending not to see her. Nikko could count the number of times that had happened to her. Especially when she was younger. It was never easy being different from everyone else. Her unique features, curly black hair, slanted eyes and olive skin drew stares from both white and black alike. She was the only Korean-Black kid in her school and they never let her forget it. The Black kids said she thought she was cute and unbeknownst to her when they would ask her that question she would answer honestly and imply, yes. They hated her. The White kids were even more confused by her mixed heritage, and just didn't feel comfortable associating with her at all, so must of her early years were spent alone and then there was dance. Dancing didn't rely on conversation, and it didn't rely on whether someone liked her or not. With dance she could choose to communicate or not, with dance she could be anyone she wanted.

The door opened and in walked one of the judges. Tall and lean, with a swan's neck and a dancer's body. Her dancing days had long past, and yet still she carried herself like a prima ballerina. She cleared her throat an announced in a scratchy voice, "Number two-thirty-two", Nikko Williams".

"That's me," Nikko said and headed towards the open door. This was it, she thought, time to put up or shut up.

* * *

Nikko followed the Prima Donna down a long hallway and into a small auditorium, what they called their rehearsal room. It was much smaller than the stage at the Fox, but bigger than she had expected. There were a total of five judges. Two of them she recognized from her brief stint as a dancer in The Nutcracker. The other three were executive board members and from their introductions alone, seemed to be extremely powerful people. The Prima Donna was well-renowned Russian dancer, Michelle Barishka. The entire panel interviewed her for more than five minutes. Each of them asking her a question. Most of the questions were general in nature, about dance, her history and her desire. Just when she thought all was going well, and the interview about to be over Michelle Barishka had one more question.

"Nikko, you are a very beautiful girl, and very intelligent."

"Thank you."

"I see from your application and from our records that you have been awarded a partial scholarship to attend a university. Why would you pass up this opportunity to educate yourself? Is education not important to you?"

Nikko hesitated before answering, and as well as she had done in her earlier interview she felt like she could blow it all if she didn't answer this one question to their satisfaction. "I want to go to college and I want to dance. I would love to go to college for dance, but that is not something I can do alone, especially since the scholarship is only a partial one. My parents, I'm afraid do not share my passion for dance, nor my dreams to be a dancer. They want me to be a doctor and will only finance my education if I major in medicine. My dad is from an older generation and my mom is a foreigner. To them, dancing is a past time, something you do when you are bored, or when you want to have fun and not a profession. I love my parents, and I respect their opinion, but this is my life to live and this is what I want to do. I want to dance."

* * *

Nikko was so hyped after her audition that she didn't want to just go home. She wanted to do something to celebrate. Although she wouldn't know for weeks whether she made it or not, she was just so happy she had went through with it. From the judges comments she stood a good chance and that was good enough for her. She reached into her bag for her cellphone and dialed Shantique's number.

"What's up girl?" Shantique answered.

"You Boo!"

"Naw, it's you Nikko, where you been? Every time I call your house, your mom's says you at the library."

Nikko laughs, "My excuse to get out of the house."

"Oh, so it's like that now. What happened to hanging out a Kims?"

"Had to give that a rest. Dad was getting suspicious. So what you got up tonight? "You feel like hanging out with your girl?"

"All Boo. I was supposed to attend this industry party with X tonight. Dirty South Records is throwing a party at Justins. Everybody's going to be there. Hey, why don't you come with us?"

"That's alright Shantique. I don't want to mess up y'all date."

"Girl, it ain't no date like that. Come on Nikko, it would be so good to hang out with you and I think Marti might be coming with Ro."

"Really? She still with Ro?"

"Marti aint' stupid, yo! That girl is like a leech when it comes to men and money." They both laughed.

"I hear ya. She must still be mad with me, because I ain't heard from her."

"She ain't mad no more. She just busy trying to hook Ro. Hell, we don't even talk a lot, but I did call her to find out if she was coming and she said that her and Ro would probably check it out. So see, it will be like old times, the three of us hanging out."

"Yeah, it does sound good. I just don't want to run into Laron, you know. We ain't really been talking."

"Girl, fuck Laron. There will be plenty of other guys for you to talk to, and anyway, it's girl's night!"

"Alright! I'll meet you at your house, but first I got to go find me something to wear."

Girl, you got to come by the store. I got just what you need."

"Word?"

"Word!"

"Alright, I'm there in fifteen."

CHAPTER 12

Limousines lined up and down Peachtree in front of Justins, blocking the street in both directions. The onlookers and security filled the rest of the street and sidewalks behind red, velvet ropes. Hollywood didn't have nothing on Atlanta with a celebrity list that included locals like, the Ying Yang twins, Ludicrous, Jermaine Dupri, Usher and a host of other hip-hop, NBA and NFL stars.

X was on the phone from the time they left Shantique's house until they arrived, but it didn't bother her as much this time because she had Nikko to hang out with.

"Shantique," Nikko hollered, "Girl ain't that the guy from Soul Food. What's his name?"

"Move, let me see," Shantique said peering out the tinted window of the limo. "Naw girl, that ain't him. He just looks like him. He's too short. You know Boris Kudjoe is over six feet. That dude can't be more than five-ten, at best."

"Yeah, you right, but he could..." she paused.

"What is it?"

Nikko couldn't take her eyes off of the tall, dark-skinned brother getting out of the limo in front of them. She couldn't be sure, but the brother looked like Butter.

"Hey, ain't that your friend, the limo driver?"

"Yeah, but he's not driving no limo. He's getting out of one."

"Girl, you no niggas be trying to profile. His boss probably let him have one for the evening. Whew! Niggas be tripping."

"Naw, it ain't like that Shantique. He is the boss."

"Say what?"

"I know, it surprised me too! Laron told me, he owns the limo company. He just drives for his friends some times. Damn! He looks good!"

"Yeah, even better now."

Nikko gives Shantique an evil stare.

"What did you expect? Girl, you know you wasn't even checking him before. Now, its like. Ooh, Ah, Butter. Please?"

"You know, you beginning to sound just like Martinette. By the way, you seen her lately?"

"No, but she's supposed to be here, with Ro."

The limo in front of them drove off and it was their turn to walk the red carpet. Nikko took the extra moments to refresh her makeup while Shantique sat between the two, trying to squash the feeling of impending doom that was settling in the pit of her stomach. The truth was, this was the first time her and X would be seen in public, amongst the media and a host of others as a couple. Alone they were good. Hell, they were better than good. She just didn't know if things would be different in the midst of his crew. X had a reputation for being a bad boy, a crazy ass nigga who could go berserk at any moment. But from what Shantique had seen of him, he was nothing like that, at least not with her. She hated that for the first time since they had been together she felt probably what most women felt in her position, the need to be validated. She never thought of herself as a groupie, hoochie, chickenhead, or any of the other derogatory names that labeled women hanging with stars. In their eyes she was a nobody; a no name, eye candy, a show piece, unworthy of press or respect. She had to deal with enough of that with Taye and now here she was again. It wasn't a pleasant thought. She had half a mind to leave. Tell X she would catch him later, but Nikko would trip out, especially after she had invited her and made her spend quite a bit of money on a new outfit. No matter what, she would have to go through with it. She reached for X's hand and he leaned over and kissed her on the cheek.

"You cool?" he asked.

"Yeah, just nervous."

He ran his fingers along her jawline and pulled her into one more kiss. "Look, all of this is for show. It don't' mean nothing to me, so if you want to leave, we can. It's your call."

"Oh my God! Oh my God!" Nikko screamed hysterically, "That's Ludacris!" "Ludacris is here! See right there, going in. Girl I love him. I used to listen to him on the radio. He was my favorite Deejay. Ooooh Shantique, thanks so much for inviting me. This is exactly what I need, a good party!"

X leaned over and whispered into Shantique's ear, "I guessed your girls' over Laron. It's a good thing, cuz I hear he's gonna be here."

"I don't know about all that, but we will see."

The limo driver opened the door and the night began with a symphony of screams and the chanting of X.

* * *

Justin's was particularly exquisite on this night. It must have been the throngs of megastars, the hyped media or the wall to wall showcase of some of the most beautiful people Shantique had ever seen. It was like looking at Essence Magazine, Esquire and Vogue models. Everybody was beautiful! And it was making her sick.

"Damn, I swear everybody in here looks like they stepped out of a magazine ad."

"Yeah baby," X said, "I feel you on that one. They ain't even moving or nothing, just posing. Shit is creepy. Come on, let's head to the back."

"Them mannequins," Nikko whispered, "ain't they?"

The trio followed their guide to the back of Justin's where an elaborate setup of champagne, food and more beautiful people partied. The trio agreed this group was a whole lot livelier than the earlier bunch. It was the kind of party where a VIP section didn't exist, because just about everybody were VIP's. The Deejay's were situated on each side of the room, with the velvet roped dance floor in the center. X steered them away from the partying crowd to a reserved table off to the corner. He popped the bottle of Cristal that was chilling at the table and poured all of them glasses.

"Here's to a fabulous night, with two fabulous ladies."

The three clinked glasses and enjoyed the revelry taking place before them. It was all good, and surprisingly Shantique was having a great time with X and Nikko. Since they had arrived X was there with her, feeding her strawberries and snuggling close. They were really a couple and she couldn't be happier.

"Babe, you see that nigga over there? The one with the black shirt and white kangol hat."

"Yeah, what about him?"

"That's rapper Baby E. They just added him to the label. Talking about me and him working on some cuts together, but I ain't feeling it."

"Why not? You do that all the time."

"I don't know, just something I'm feeling. Something up, and that nigga is dirty. Tell you the truth; I don't wanna have nothing to do with him."

"Well don't then. Shit, them niggas know who bringing in the money."

"Yeah they do," he kisses her on the cheek. "See that's why you may baby, cuz you be knowing what's up and you got your man's back."

"Look" Nikko said "all this lovey, dovey shit is making me ill, I'm about to be out."

"Naw, naw, don't you go nowhere." X said standing up. "Look here ma, I got to go handle some business. Anything y'all want just holla at the waiter with the purple sash, that's Benny. He's are personal waiter tonight. I'll be right back."

"Alright baby, handle yo bizness."

"Hey X!"

"Yeah, what's up Nikko?"

"I was wondering if you can bring me something back."

"Like what girl, I told you Benny gonna take care of y'all."

"What I want, Benny can't get."

"What you want?"

"Ludacris, okay!"

"Girl, you crazy. Look ma, I'll see ya in twenty. You," he points to Nikko, "be cool, and don't harass the guests."

"Whateva!"

Shantique watched X make his way across the floor to the rapper he had pointed out to her and another large man in a white suit. She recognized him from award shows and Vibe magazine as Sammy Pete, the CEO of Dirty South Records. He was notorious in the record industry, but he was also one of X's best friends and supporter. Him and X had made a lot of money together. X told her more than he could have ever imagined. Sammy was big too, about six foot eight and at least three hundred pounds, not the prettiest of nigga's but attractive to many a women, if you liked the strong, dangerous type. An ex-football player turned record producer and now the billion-dollar man.

The two of them poured more glasses of champagne and just about finished the bottle when Nikko spotted an old friend of theirs across the room. "Hey Shantique, there's Bling. Oh my God! It's Bling. Hey, hey!" she stood up and shouted, "Bling!":

"Nikko, what the hell wrong with you?. Sit your ass down!"

Shantique was embarrassed by Nikko's loud display, but more embarrassed that Nikko didn't realize that the man's name wasn't Bling, that was just the name they gave him.

"What? That's Bling. I like Bling."

"I like Bling too, but that's not his name."

"It's not. That's what we call him."

"Nikko damn girl, I know that but he don't know that."

"Oh shit, maybe he didn't hear me."

"He heard you alright because here he comes."

Bling was dressed in all white. White pants, white jacket, white hat and white shoes. He was what Shantique called "country clean". You could see Blings' smile from across the room glimmering and glistening in the lights. He seemed just as happy to see them. Bling made his way through the crowded floor, stopped at the end their table and bowed before them like a knight honoring his queens.

"Ladies, ladies, how are you doing? Don't' answer that, I already know. Fine, fine, super fine!" He took each of their hands and kissed them, then slid in the seat beside Nikko. "I remember you Nikki, right?"

"No, it's Nikko and this is Shantique."

"Yeah, Shantique and Nikko. Well looks like you girls have made it to the big time and it was all because of Bling."

Nikko and Shantique were surprised to hear him refer to himself as Bling.

"Yeah, thanks to you, that's what I go by now. It's catchy, flashy, and sweet, like me, Bling! I love it! So, let's see there's only two of you, somebody's missing."

"Not for long," Martinette said walking up with Ro. "What up my people?"

"Marti," Shantique said, "when did you get here?" She stood up, along with Nikko to hug Marti. "Girl, look at you, your hair! Gone Diva!"

Marti's hair looked like it was on fire from tip to head, it changed colors. From flaming red to a golden hue, each row a different color. It was wild, unusual, eccentric, but it looked good! Shantique had to give it to her, the girl could pull off some wild shit with her hair.

Marti twirled around to give them all a better look of her hair and her outfit. She wore a very tight fitting pale yellow halter dress that dipped so far down in the back if she bent over everyone would see the crack in her ass. When it came to fashion, J Lo didn't have nothing on Marti.

"Girl you know how I do. Hey Nikko! All come on girl, that shit is forgotten and forgiven. We girls got to stick together."

Marti gave Nikko a hug and the three of them squealed with delight.

"Bling, what's up dude? Long time no see. Ro, look it's Bling, you remember him don't you?"

Bling extended his hand to Ro.

"Yeah, what's up Bling?"

They shook hands.

"Alright then ladies, I'm out. Y'all take care now." Bling said standing up and leaving.

Ro took Marti by the arm. "That was rude. I'm gonna get me a drink and you need to chill."

"Yeah baby, that's exactly what I'm gonna do. Chill with my girls okay."

Shantique could tell that Ro wasn't too happy with how Martinette was acting. Something was definitely up. Martinette sat down between the two and poured a glass of champagne.

"It ain't nothing. His team didn't make the playoffs, blah blah this, blah blah that. You wouldn't think a big ass nigga like that would whine so much."

"Damn Marti, I thought everything was all good."

"It is. He's buying me a house in Fayette County. A ten bedroom, 5 bath house on 3 acres. Girl it's got everything, a basketball court, tennis court, swimming pool, even a fucking bowling alley. He loves me. He's just fucked up tonight."

"Oh, well you better be cool."

"Shit, I'm cool. So where your man X?"

"Talking business somewhere. Me and Nikko just been chilling and having a good time."

"Nikko why you all quiet over there? You still tripping about that thing. Girl, I told you, that shit is squashed. One thing I know for sure. You two are my girls. My girls' have my back when nobody else does." Martinette stopped mid-sentence and begun to look around the large room.

Shantique suspected she was searching for Ro and just like that she found him standing next to a very tall, honey colored, thin woman with hair down to her buttocks and smile so wide you could see all of her thirty-two teeth.

Martinette turned abruptly from the scene. "These muthafuckas ain't about shit, will fuck over you in a second. That's fine, because what he can do, I can do better. Fuck that muthafucka and his hoe. What else y'all got to drink over here besides champagne? This shit is weak. I need me a real drink. Waiter!" Marti called.

* * *

After their third shot of Tequila, the party seemed to pick up. Deejay Skin was off the chain spinning his blend of hip-hop and old school jams. People were dancing everywhere, on the floor, in the aisles and even on the tables. Martinette chose to demonstrate her dancing ability atop Justin's marble bar. Ro was furious with her. After awhile he left, but that didn't stop Marti from shaking her ass to a crowd of admirers. Nikko was on the dance floor with Bling and seemed to be having a pretty good time until she saw Laron roll up with his crew. Shantique could tell by the look on her face that Nikko wasn't especially happy to be seeing Laron, but still she left the dance floor with him. Nikko never really explained what had went down between her and Laron, but whatever it was it must have been pretty bad to make her turn down a fine ass man like Laron or his money. He was at the top of his game, next to Usher, the number two bestselling male artist. He had the money, the homes, the cars and plenty of women. Laron had everything and rumor was he would be starring in the next "Triple X" movie. From where Shantique stood, Laron wasn't a bad catch, so what was up with Nikko? Someone tapped Shantique on the shoulder. It was their personal waiter.

"You better check your girl. She's wilding out over there and security say's she's out of here if she doesn't chill."

Shantique looked over to the bar where a large, boisterous crowd, bellowed and screamed. In the middle of the crowd, front and center was Martinette cussing and screaming like she had lost her mind.

"Don't touch me. Did you hear me? I don't give a shit who you are. Fake, wannabee cop. Get off of me!" Martinette said swinging her arms and shoving Justin's security.

Their failed attempts to remove her from the bar, generated laughter amongst the onlookers. Some shouted disses, agreeing with Martinette, but the disses made the guards angry and they turned on the crowd as well. The atmosphere was hot, fiery temper's, mixed liquor and young heads was a riot waiting to happen. Shantique knew something had to be done before a real fight broke out and she didn't mean between Martinette and the security guards. Somewhere standing by there was a nigga ready to swing, or pop someone just for the hell of it. Martinette seemed unaffected by the change in mood around her. She kept right on disturbing the peace by kicking, swinging and cussing at anyone who came her way.

Shantique jumped up from her seat and ran to the bar but couldn't get any closer than three rows from the bar. She waved her hands in the air and hollered over the crowd. "Marti, girl what's up? Where's Ro?" She hoped bringing up Ro's name would calm her girl down. Bottom line she was hoping to get Martinette from a top that bar before Ro showed up. Martinette gave Shantique a blank faced stare as if she didn't recognize her. Shantique pushed further, trying to get closer to the bar when all hell broke loose. A couple of guys tried to bring Martinette down, grabbing by her legs and she went off, kicking and screaming, throwing beer bottles across the room like she was some kind of mad woman. No sooner than Shantique had reached the bar that she saw two security guards along with a handful of Atlanta police headed their way.

"Marti please", she said. "Get down girl, you about to get arrested. You hear me?"

"Shantique!"

When Shantique looked up, Martinette had fell head first. It was a good thing that there was a crowd of men around her or she would have knocked

Shantique to the ground, but the others were able to catch her fall. Martinette had passed out.

"Somebody call 9-1-1!" Shantique screamed.

The two Security guards and police kneeled down beside her.

"Alright Miss, come on move back. We got this now."

"No. I'm not going nowhere! This is my friend and I'm staying with her. What you need to do is get an ambulance here. "

The guard took offense to Shantique's tone and unleashed his set of handcuffs, along with his baton.

"I said you are either going to move out of the way or you will be going with your friend to jail. Now, for the last time, move."

Tears welled up in Shantique's eyes and streamed down her face. She couldn't believe what was happening. She turned to look around her, a hundred faces staring back at her but none of them she knew. Where was X, or Ro, or Nikko? Who was gonna help her now? She knew she couldn't leave Martinette with the police. She couldn't let her be arrested, but at the same time she didn't want to be arrested either. What would her mama think? What about Rashawn?

"Bitch, get the fuck up!" the Security Guard hollered, then grabbed Shantique's arm and snatched her up from the floor.

Shantique screamed, "No!"

"Get yo muthafuckin hands off of her!"

X pushed his way to the front and stood toe to toe with the guard. Things only escalated from their, when two Atlanta policemen stepped up next to the guard with their hands on their guns.

"Officer's I don't mean you no trouble, but this is my lady this nigga is man handling. You okay baby?" Shantique nodded her head. "Alright then, she say she okay and that's all good, but I still don't like the fact that you made my baby cry, held her on the ground like some kind of dog. As far as I can tell she didn't do nothing to deserve this type of treatment. So, all I want him to do is to let her go, now."

"You's one dumb muthafucka," the Security said, bolting around like he was about to hit somebody. Then he heard the clicks of 15 to 20 street soldiers standing behind him, all of them carrying heavy weaponry.

"Yeah," X said, "You hear me now. It ain't even got to go down like that. You hear me son. We can do this, or we can do that. It's your call son!"

The older of the two policemen stepped forward. "Look, I need to get this young lady to the hospital for observation. The rest of this mess you made," he said pointing at the guard. "Fix it! Young brothers put away your hardware, ain't nothing about to jump off tonight if I can help it and I mean's to help it. So everybody backup, go back to drinking, dancing whatever you was up to before this and we will be on our way."

"That's cool OG." X said waving his boys down. "I like the way you handle things. A young brother could learn a lot from a cool head like yours, Detective," he tried reading the name of the badge, "Monstar! Not the Zack Monstar of IU days?"

"Yeah, one and the same. Traded in my ball for a badge, how you like that?"

"From where I stand, not a bad call. You alright with me Detective Monstar."

"Alright X. The ambulance is here for your young lady's friend. You keep it cool."

Shantique stayed with Martinette while the paramedics checked her out when Ro arrived, Nikko right behind him. Ro was visibly upset seeing Martinette unconscious on the stretcher. Shantique didn't know if he had heard the truth, but if he hadn't she sure wasn't going to be the one to tell him. So much had happened in the last thirty minutes that Martinette's strip tease was the least of her worries.

Nikko stood by Shantique's side and hugged her around the waist. "You alright?"

"Yeah, thanks to X." She whispered, "Nikko, I can't do this shit no more. Marti wilding out," she looked around her, hoping Ro didn't hear her, "all of this. I can't do it."

"I know girl. I'm so sorry I wasn't here with you. I tried to make it back, but Laron kept me over in that corner with all his lies and bullshit about wanting me back. I almost halfway believed him until I got up to go to the bathroom and when I came back he had some chickenhead face down in his lap. That's when I left. I can't stand that muthafucka."

"Damn Nikko! Laron ain't about shit!"

"I know girl, but alls well that ends well, because I ran into Butter and we had a real good time talking. We were headed back to the table until some shit got started by this rapper wannabee and something about a deal gone bad. This nigga was talking about capping somebody for sure, so me and Butter chilled until Bling told us that Marti fell off the bar."

"Bling said she fell off the bar!" Shantique laughed. "I guess that's pretty much what happened."

"So," Nikko said smiling, "X came to your rescue? Must be nice to have hero."

"Whew, it is," Shantique said looking over at X. He had come to her rescue. Ro tapped her on the shoulder.

"The paramedics want to take Martinette to the hospital for observation. I'm going to ride with her."

"So, is everything okay?" Nikko asked.

"Yeah, they think, but they just want to check things out."

"You want us to go? We can meet you there?" Shantique asked.

"No, I got this. You already done enough tonight. Look, I don't know if Martinette told you but things been kind of messed up between us lately. I mean, that's why I wasn't here, wasn't around, but I should have been. You know what I'm saying."

"Ro, you ain't' got to apologize to us. What goes on between you and Marti is you and Marti's business. So, you sure you don't want us to come and keep you company?"

"Yeah, I'm sure. I'll give you a call tomorrow, let you know what's up with your girl, or she'll call you, I'm sure. Alright X, thanks man." The men give each other dap and handshakes.

"Hey," Nikko said, "I'm going to catch a ride with Butter. That's if y'all don't mind."

"Mind, Please! I haven't had a chance to be alone with my man all night. Good riddance! See ya!" Shantique hollers, then hugs her friend. "Alright girl, take care of yourself and I'll talk with you tomorrow. Hey Butter, no funny stuff now, get my girl home, safe!"

"I got this!" Butter says, "Did you forget I drive for a living. Later, X!"

X shakes Butter's hand, "Alright man, we'll talk later about that. You got some good ideas and you know I'm ready to make a move. So let's do this."

"X give me a couple of days to draw up some stuff and I'll give you a call. You gonna be in town?"

"Yeah man," he said looking at Shantique, "ain't no other place I'd rather be."

* * *

"So what you think Pdiddy gonna say about y'all messing up his restaurant? Can't take black folks nowhere!" X said laughing. "Man, I tell you, your girl is pretty wild!"

"Yeah, you telling me. Marti always been a little on the wild side, but tonight she was just straight showing out. Ro wasn't giving her any attention so she did what she had to do. And as far as Pdiddy goes, he probably used to shit jumping off in his restaurant. You know Bobby Brown's nephews got stabbed up in there not too long ago."

"I heard. It's a crying shame cuz they got some damn good soul food in there. Food so good, make you wanna cut somebody!" He laughs.

"Oh you a real comedian tonight, got all kind of jokes.

"I ain't got jokes, I got you! So I got joy, cutie!" He leans over kisses her soft on the lips. "I've been waiting to do that all night."

"So why didn't you?"

"Don't matter. I'm here now, where I wanna be." He holds her hand and looks off into the Atlanta city skyline. "For the first time in a long time things are going my way. I ain't doing business like I did before. I'm doing business smarter, taking control of my own destiny, and that feels good. I feel good," he said looking at her. "I got my baby by my side and the world is my oyster."

CHAPTER 13

Ro waited impatiently by the door, waiting for the doctors to finish up so he could get back to Martinette. He had never worried about anyone, less himself, the way he worried about his girl. He tried to shake away the memories of the night, but he couldn't, good, bad or ugly. He found himself back in the restaurant, grinding slowly against the marbled wall with some honey he didn't even know. She was beautiful, no doubt, one of the finer ones' but she wasn't Martinette. He knew the moment Martinette saw him things would get out of hand, but he didn't care, at least not then. A couple of nurses passed him by, giving him a second look and a smile, but neither of them stopped to say more. He pressed his face against the glass enclosure trying to see more, when the door suddenly opened.

"Ow!" Ro griped.

"Oh I am sorry young man," the doctor said, "I didn't see you there. You are welcome to come in now, if you like."

"So, she's okay Doc? She's all checked out?"

"Yeah, well yes, nothing that plenty of fluids and a few days of rest won't cure. Hangovers can be a monster."

"So what you're telling me doc? That my girl was just drunk and passed out last night, that's it?"

"Well, yes and no. Yes, she probably had more than her share of alcohol and that alone can have anyone passing out, and no there is more to it. But I'm afraid you will have to learn the rest from Miss Robinson."

* * *

Martinette had the strangest dream. She dreamed that someone was drilling a hole into the back of her head. It would have been funny if she hadn't actually felt the pain. With her eyes still closed she reached for her bottle of Advil that she kept in her nightstand but they weren't there, nor was her nightstand. She slumped back into the soft pillow, but squirmed in the hard bed, that wasn't her own. Where the hell was she? She tried opening her eyes, but even that was a struggle, until she loosened the eye boogers that glued each lid tightly together. After loosening one eye she was able to get a pretty clear view of her surroundings. The hospital was her first surprise. The next surprise was seeing Ro enter the room with a man in a white lab coat. Martinette quickly looked down to her arms and legs, she hadn't been restrained. Relief swept over her, *this wasn't one of those hospitals.*

The doctor introduced himself to her then proceeded to go over her chart. Martinette barely heard a word he said because she was so engrossed in Ro's behavior. He seemed overly concerned about her, holding her hand, smoothing her hair. If she wasn't mistaken, she thought she spotted a tear in his eye.

"Miss Robinson, like I told your friend here you should be in perfect condition after some much needed rest. Now there is something else I would like to talk to you about. And we should probably talk alone."

"Alone. Why? Is something wrong? I mean, if something is wrong, I want Ro here."

The doctor looked from Martinette to Ro, "alright then, it's your call Miss Robinson. It is normal for us to run routine blood tests, especially when a patient is admitted, such in your case....to determine blood, alcohol levels, and determine if a more aggressive treatment is required. Your levels were high, which is the reason for the way your feeling, but then something else showed up. Something we weren't expecting and in most cases, I guess congratulations are in order."

* * *

"Wow, what a view," Nikko said stepping out of her heels. "How do you sleep at night with all the lights?"

"That's what I have shades for." Butter said.

"What shades, I didn't see any."

Butter smirked, and then pushed a button on the side of the wall, letting down a series of shades turning the amber lighted room to blue black, but not for long. Three sconces on each side of the room lit up and the room was warm amber once again.

"Damn Butter, you got this placed hooked up. Electronic shades, mood lighting," she gave him a quizzical look, "what's up?"

Butter pushed the button again, sending the shades back and inviting the Atlanta City Skyline back in. "What are you talking about Nikko? I just like electronic stuff, gadgets, equipment. I'm an electronic addict. If I could push a button to do everything, I would."

"So this is how you spend your time?"

"Time, who's got time, I'm always working, and when I'm not working, I'm working on my next business venture, which is work too. You want something to drink?"

"You got some Chardonnay?"

"Kendall Jackson okay?"

"I love Kendall Jackson."

Nikko watched while Butter removed the cork and poured them both a glass of wine. He had surprised her in more ways than one, and to think that at first she had chosen Laron over him, all because she thought he was just somebody's chauffeur.

"So you are a classical dancer? I would have never believed it. Not that you don't have the perfect dancer's body, it's just that with you hanging with Laron and party. I thought Hip-Hop would be more your style."

"Hip-Hop is my style, but dance is my profession. I can do classic ballet, jazz, tap, modern, or a combination and it still can be Hip-Hop. I just chose to try out for the Atlanta Ballet. It's something I've always dreamed of, every since I performed as a child."

Butter hands Nikko a glass a wine, "I'm impressed." She gave him a quizzical look. "Really, I love the arts, especially ballet. Let me know when you are performing and I will be first in line."

"That's sweet, but first I have to get the job."

"You worried?"

She looked at him. That was the first time she thought about the possibility of not making it. Would she then continue on to school and study medicine like her parents wanted? "No."

"What's up? You seem preoccupied."

"I'm sorry, it's nothing."

"Have you seen the view from the patio? You should see this," he said opening the glass sliding doors. When Nikko hesitated, he asked, "You coming?"

Nikko reluctantly followed Butter out to the patio. According to him they were only 10 floors up, but for Nikko that was more than enough, since she was afraid of heights and had been since as long as she could remember. Nikko watched Butter move to the railing but she stood at the door.

"What's the matter? Come see this, from here, you can see the lights of Stone Mountain."

"Yeah, I saw that from the window."

"No you didn't. Nikko, what's up, are you scared?"

"Well, yes. I am."

He took Nikko's hand, pulled he gently towards him, and although she resisted, he didn't let go. "You can trust me. I would never let anything happen to you."

Nikko didn't understand why, but she believed him. In his eyes she saw what she had been looking for all her life, sincerity. A well pruned package, six-foot-two, dark chocolate wonder, with buttery soft skin that glowed, and the whitest teeth she had ever seen on a black man, that formed the warmest smile she had ever witnessed. Butter, Butter, Butter! Damn he was fine, and standing there, at that precise moment, in his black double-breasted suit, clean, smelling like a cool summer breeze, extending himself to her was enough to make her let alone come hither, but if she wasn't careful, she'd jump.

He wrapped his arms around her, and held her close. "You alright?"

She nodded afraid to say more, or else spill all her guts.

He laughed, "Who would have ever thought we end up here, together? I had my doubts, in fact, but I never lost hope. Laron was a fool, but I already knew that. I'm just glad that you were able to see that."

"Yeah, me too."

"Nikko, damn I know this is going to sound pretty crazy to you, and if it does just let me know, and I'll back off, I swear, but girl I have been wanting you since I first saw you. And there hasn't been a waking moment that you weren't on my mind."

"Wow!"

"You're surprised?"

"Yeah," she paused, "I am, but I like it."

"Good," he said pulling her into his arms. "Then I promise you lots of surprises. I mean, if it's okay with you."

"Butter, its better than okay."

*   *   *

The doctor had long since left, excused himself right after announcing to the both of them that Martinette was expecting. Not a word had passed between them since the news, a whole lot of breathing, maybe a few muttered curse words, but other than that nothing. Martinette's mind worked feverishly counting back days, months, periods, pills, when was the last time she took one? Pregnant, she thought, how did this happen? Damn, she could kick herself, just when everything was going so well with Ro. She glanced his way, but he was so immersed in his thoughts that he didn't look back. How did he feel about this, about his baby? Martinette reached down and rubbed her stomach. In all her years, this had never happened. Then it hit her the very date she forgot her pill and the tears swelled, she was an even bigger fuck-up. Soon her quiet tears became a sob. "I'm sorry Ro, it's all my fault. I never meant for this to happen."

Ro rushed to her side, "Baby, it's alright, we'll get through this."

"No Ro, I mean it's really my fault, I forgot to take my pills, and look what happened, I'm pregnant."

"Babe, look, we got time to talk about this. I'm not mad, really. Look at me." He turns her face toward him. "I might even be okay with this, I mean, that's if you are. No pressure or anything, but a baby, my baby," he began to choke on his words and Martinette could see tears in his eyes. "Let's just give it some thought first, alright?"

Martinette nodded in agreement. He pushed the hair away from her face and kissed her forehead. It was nice to have Ro so close. They hadn't been this close in weeks. Things were like they were in the beginning and she liked that. Maybe having this baby would be best, even if she wasn't sure if it was his.

* * *

The morning of Martinette's release from the hospital she was met by her two bestfriends and the love of her life. She could tell that they were more than surprised at her and Ro's behavior, especially after the events of the previous night.

"Baby, I was thinking we need to stop by IHOP and get you something to eat before we head home." Ro said, "I mean, that's if you're hungry, if not I can fix you something at the house."

It was too cute, him fussing over her like that. Shantique gave her a strange look, one that said "what's up?" While Nikko rolled her eyes in disgust, jealous again.

"That's okay baby, I'm fine, really. Hey, but you know what, I could use some water, the bottled kind, if you don't mind."

"Any particular kind? Dasani? Crystal Springs?"

"Ro, it doesn't matter."

"Alright then, I'll be right back."

Nikko and Shantique looked at each other and then at Martinette. But neither of them spoke until Ro was out the door and down the hall. Shantique was first to speak up.

"Alright spill it! What's up with you and Ro? Instead of being angry with you about last night, he's falling all over you like you got sugar drawls."

Nikko nods in agreement and Martinette laughs.

"I do!"

"Shut up Marti and tell us what's going on and what have you done with the real Ro."

"Listen up you two, that is the real Ro, my man, my lover and my baby's daddy."

"Your what?" Shantique almost shouts. "Marti, say it ain't true. You're not pregnant are you?"

"Wait a minute!" Nikko butts in, "everybody chill. This is too much! You are having a baby?"

Marti nods, "Yes to the both of you. I am pregnant, and I'm having Ro's baby. It's no joke. The doctor confirmed it last night. I didn't even know myself."

Nikko is talking so fast, Martinette could hardly understand her.

"Well how does Ro feel about it? I mean, what am I talking about, he's falling all over you, so it's okay with him, right?"

"You've seen him. He's okay with it. We're both okay with it."

Shantique is unusually quiet.

"Shantique, what's up girl? You're not happy for us?"

"Marti girl, having a baby ain't no joke. It can change your whole life. You hear what I'm saying."

"I know this. I'm ready. I got Ro by my side, plus my girls to help me out. And you being a mother and all, who better to have in my corner. I'm really going to need you two, to plan my wedding and my baby shower."

"Your wedding!" Nikko shouts, "He asked you to marry him too? This is too much!"

"I agree." Shantique interjects. "Have you even really thought about this? Just yesterday, you were saying F Ro this, F Ro that, now a day later, you having his baby and getting married. Just seem a little too rushed Marti."

"Rushed? I don't believe you two. My supposedly two bestfriends, who I thought would be happy for me, instead you do what you always do and hate on a siesta."

"Marti please, ain't neither one of us got reason to hate on you. We just looking out for you, like we always do. You not going sit there and tell me you're not rushing things. Had it been any Joe Blow off the street you be heading to the clinic so fast it would look like dust storm hit Peachtree Street. Who you think you fooling? I've known you since freshmen year in high school. You were the one who thought I was crazy for getting pregnant and having Rashawn. You were the one who said you were never having kids. Bullshit Marti, for you it's all about the money, not about Ro or the baby."

Martinette rose up out of her hospital bed. "I can't believe this shit! You know what? You two jealous bitches can just go fuck yourselves. I don't need you anyway. And just for your information, it's not about the money, but it is about the life I deserve, the one I should be living and I ain't gonna let nobody, not you or anybody else ruin it for me. So if you ain't with me, you against me, and since you against me, you bitches need to get stepping."

* * *

X met with his attorney and he was glad that he was able to accomplish one of the tasks he set out to do, the other would take more time, but time is not what he had. Getting out of his contract seemed grueling and at the helm of all his troubles was Sammy Pete. Sammy Pete, ex-football player, ex-con, ruled his empire by dominating the market and fear. He hired and managed groups that no other label will consider and turned these misfits of society into Hip-Hop Kings. Dirty South Records was his kingdom, it's where he ruled, no questions asked, until he met a nigga named X. X and Sammy met some years ago when X was shopping for a label that would let him have creative freedom. Sammy and Dirty South Records was his answer. Sammy came on strong. He could talk the talk and walk the walk. X was immediately taken by the giant man with the soft voice, who put fear of God into his subjects, but X was never scared. He considered Sammy a friend, a confidante and a business partner. That's how it began, but soon, after becoming millions of dollars richer, and 6 CD releases, their friendship would sour. X wanted out and Sammy refused to give it to him. He threatened him with suits, ownership of all his masters, and now bodily harm. The last was more than X could take, especially after he learned that Sammy may have had something to do with the death of his nephew. That was the last straw. X was now working with his 5th lawyer. His fifth because Sammy had scared away the other 4, nothing could be proved but X knew better, and although Sammy didn't know he had peeps on the inside as well and every now and then they let information slip. Sammy was the type of nigga you couldn't come correct with. He played dirty and in order to win his game, you had to play dirty too! X needed out of his contract and in order to do that Sammy had to be removed, by any means necessary. X flipped open his phone and placed a call. "Yo, I got that information you need."

* * *

"Nikko! Her mother called from downstairs. "There is a package for you."

She heard her mother climbing the stairs and heading for her door.

"Butter, I got to go. I'll call you later," she whispered into her phone. "Me too. Stop it! Okay, I love you too! Bye!"

Her door opened.

"Nikko! You are still in bed?" Her mother asked.

"Yes mommy. I'm tired."

"Here." She pushed a white envelope toward her. "This for you."

Nikko noticed the bright red lettering first and her stomach begin to knot up with anticipation.

"Thanks mommy."

"What's this Atlanta Ballet Nikko? This is dance, right?"

Nikko heard her mom but she wasn't listening, not now. This is what she had been waiting for week after week, since the audition two months ago. When she hadn't heard from them, she went ahead and enrolled in Georgia State just to keep her parents off her back. She pulled out the neatly typed letter and read it silently to herself.

Dear Miss Freeman,

We are so pleased to offer you a position with the Atlanta Ballet...."

"Yes!" Nikko screamed. "I did it, I did it mommy. I made it. Oh my God, I can't believe it," she said jumping on her bed."

"But Nikko," her mother said, "this is dance. This is not what your father wants for you. You are in college now. Georgia State a good school. You go to be doctor, remember, not dance."

"You have to be happy for me mommy. You have to be. Please, when are you all going to pay attention to what I want! I want to dance mommy" she cried. "It's what I've always..." she stopped mid-sentence when she looked up and saw her father standing in her doorway. "Daddy?"

It had been many of years since her father had been up to her room. A back injury left him nearly immobile, and simple things like climbing stairs only aggravated the problem. But there he was, standing there as clear as day, breathing heavily as if he had just climbed a mountain.

"Daddy, what are you doing?"

"Washington, no, it's not good for you on the stairs. You know this!" her mother fussed. "Come on," she stood up, "I'll take you back downstairs."

"No, I'm alright Min. I want to talk with Nikko."

"Daddy, I'm sorry, but it's what I want. I got accepted into the dance academy for the Atlanta Ballet. Not many girls do that, and I did on my first try. It's not that I don't' want to be a doctor, I just want to be a dancer more. I can finish school anytime, but I only have one chance...."

He stopped her, "say no more. I understand. Wipe those tears away. You know you and your mother are my heart and I can't stand breaking yours. I want you to be happy, but if things don't work out there, you have to promise me you will go back to school and be that doctor. In a couple of years I'm going to need you around."

"Oh daddy," she hugged him, "I promise and thank you. I love you so much!"

"I love you too, more than you know."

CHAPTER 14

Shantique looked at the already packed bags and then the stacked clothes still lying on her bed. There was no way she was going to fit all of this into two bags, at least not the bags she had owned since the eighth grade. The ones her mom bought her at Kmart when she took her first class trip to Canada.

"Ma!" she screamed. "You got a bigger bag. My stuff won't fit in these kiddy bags."

"That's because you're packing too much stuff Shantique," her mother said from her door. "Why you got take all of that? You're only in New York for three days, not a month. Damn girl!" She started picking pieces of clothing off the bed, "why you need 10 pair of shoes, or five evening outfits? I thought this was about work."

"It is, but then Marisela said we'll be attending the evening cocktail parties and stuff, you know networking. "

Her mom gave her a sly look.

"What you look at me like that for? That's how they do it in New York. It's all about who you know, who you rub elbows with. Now give me that." She takes back the five evening outfits. "I'm just going have to make them fit."

Her mother stood watching in amazement as Shantique dumped the suitcase out and refolded all her clothing again, then making it fit.

"See, I told you I could do it."

"Yeah well, you just better hope they don't charge you more because those suitcases are overweight."

"They don't do that do they?"

"Yes and you will pay if you want your luggage on that plane. Don't say I didn't warn you."

"Okay, I'll remove something; maybe I don't need these boots, or these shoes."

Her mother put away the outfits she removed. "How you feel about missing Rashawn's first day of school? You know he wants you to be there. But I ain't mad at you sweetie, in fact I'm real proud of you, all that you have accomplished, my baby going to New York, a buyer in training. Hell I wished I had got on your case a lot earlier."

"I know haven't been the model daughter, and getting pregnant and having Rashawn it's not what you planned but it all worked out. Things are working out for me mama, and soon things are going to get better, for all of us. This job, Rashawn starting school and X, I couldn't be happier."

"Wait a minute, hold up. I was talking about you and the job, not about you running behind that rapper."

"Mama, I'm not running behind X. X loves me and I love him."

"Whatever Sweetie, maybe it's love, I don't know. I'm just glad you got your priorities straight and realize that you have to make your own successes, and not depend on others. I ain't saying the boy don't care nothing for you, but baby love comes and go's. You loved Taye too, remember and look what happened there. You hear me?"

"Yeah mama, I hear you. But me and Taye were young and having Rashawn didn't help things. I've learned from my mistakes. This time will be different."

"That's good baby, good to hear. Now when you going to tell your son you won't be here for his first day of school?"

"I'll tell him tonight, right after we return from Underground."

* * *

"Play that beat again," X spoke to his sound technician Amari. "Alright, alright...yo, yo," he rapped. "Too many living in sin, yet I ain't here to complain, that Bush got my brothers and my sisters dying in vain." X stopped when he noticed the commotion taking place outside the sound booth. Although he couldn't hear them, he saw East Coast rappers, Def and Uzi manhandling his crew. X broke from the booth. "Yo, what's up son? Why you come up in here acting a fool and shit?"

"Ohhhh shit, if it ain't the snitch Bitch, X," Def spoke through grilled teeth. "I've come to give you a message bitch." He waved a glock in front of everyone and the small crew that gathered tripped over each other to get out of the way. "Right, Right," Def said nodding at the fear he caused. "Y'all feelin me." He pointed his weapon at X and said, "How about you nigga? You feelin me?"

X stopped short of busting Def in the head. This had been the second time he had bumped heads with him in the last month, first, at the industry party and now. He was beginning to think this nigga was crazy for real coming into his studio waving a gun, either that or he had a death wish. X sucked at his teeth, and then took a defiant stand against the wall. Def was full of theatrics, waving his gun, shouting and thinking he was scaring somebody, when in reality he only looked more like the fool he was. X decided he would hear him out, give his crew time to get their bearings and then bust him in the head. "Like I said, what you want nigga? Don't come in here talking that bullshit either or waving your glock. You know that shit is a dime a dozen. Every muthafucka in here got one of those on him," X raised his shirt revealing his piece, "I got two."

Def looked from X to Uzi, then lowered his gun. "You know nigga. Don't play me. You know all about Sammy going down. Yeah, that's right muthafuka. Sammy Pete got fingered by your bitch ass and he told me to tell you, sleep lightly." He laughed and gave Uzi dap. "That's it. I'm out, oh yeah, I like that verse you was spitting. Shit was tight! Too bad you ain't gonna get to record that muthafucka. Hey, maybe I'll use it on my album, if that's okay with you, I mean you can't spit no verse, if yo ass is dead, now can you?"

X didn't flinch. Sammy Pete was behind this, but unlike everybody else he wasn't scared of Sammy. He knew just like everyone else, Sammy being locked up didn't stop a thing. The man's hands reached farther than I-285. Sammy coming after him was what he expected. Sammy sending his fickled crew of wannabee rappers to do his dirty work, now that disappointed him. He should know better. X stepped to Def and Uzi, pulled his piece and jammed it into

Def's neck. "The difference between you and me son, is that I will use this." He pressed harder, twisting it into the boys flesh until it turned red. "You know why they call me Crazy son? You do know that, don't you? I mean everybody know that. Yo, Amari, you know that, don't you?" Amari nodded. "Yo Teak, Manny, Butter, y'all heard about that, right?" Everyone nodded. "So tell me son, how come you don't know."

"I don't know," Def cried.

"That's because your ass is green. You don't know shit! You just a puppet, Sammy's little bitch, ain't you?" The boy shook his head and X slapped him. "Be still! I could have killed you boy, you know how close I am to pulling this trigger. Just one little slip of my hand and bam! You are mush! You know what a bullet does when it enters your body, especially through the throat, or in your case the neck. Let me tell you son, it might not kill you, but it will destroy one of your most needed and major organs, your brain. Forgive me y'all, I forgot this nigga ain't got no brain, so it don't matter if I shoot him now, if I squeeze and pull the trigger and watch your brain hit the window, or the walls or even your nigga, Uzi."

Def started shaking. "Man, come on. I was just giving you a message."

"Yeah son, I hear you but you got to understand what you say and what you do go hand in hand. A nigga like you is new to the game, and me, I'm an old dog. All jokes aside, you don't pull your piece on a nigga unless you ready to shoot." X pushed Def to the side and waved his gun, "Get! And don't come around here no more, unless you ready to run with the big dogs."

Def and Uzi were out the door, while the other men laughed and joked about the incident, everyone except Butter.

"Yo X, you think it was wise to fuck with them boys like that? I mean no matter how you look at it, they are Sammy's boys, and we all know what Sammy can do."

X laughed, "Sammy Pete! That fat, baldhead, beefy muthafuckin wannabee gangster, ain't gonna do shit!" He thought of his nephew. "Yeah, Sammy's a bad nigga, but he can't do shit locked up, unless he got some magical power shit, like that magician, Blane, what's his name? That muthafucka can break out of anything," he paused. "Sammy is going to be gone for a long time, and I ain't even trying to hear that bullshit he talking. If he wasn't trying to hold me down on that non-existent contract, and trying to steal all of my masters, hell we would still be cool. Fuck! Alright hey, I ain't worried about it, don't you worry about it."

"I'm just saying X, you need to watch your back."

"I'm covered. You just get those contracts finished up Butter. We are about to make big time history!" He stopped to give daps to Omari and Butter, "and plenty of paper for everybody. Progress man, even Sammy Pete can't stop progress."

* * *

Martinette used her left hand to flip channels while her right hand reached for her third Krispy Crème donut. After stuffing it whole into her mouth, she licked the sticky sugar off her fingers and exhaled in complete satisfaction. There was nothing she loved more than Krispy Crème donuts, a bowl of Hagan Daaz ice cream and a Coke, its what she craved every morning since she learned she was pregnant. She threw the remote to the side, grabbed her cell phone on the bed and dialed Ro for the tenth time. After three rings, it went to voicemail again and Martinette threw the phone against the wall. "Shit!"

She should have known Ro wouldn't answer, especially after her first five messages. He didn't take to kindly to her cussing him out and she's pretty sure that her last message cursed him and his mother. That's just how it was between them; either things were very good or extremely bad. Ro wasn't the easiest person to live with, even though he wasn't there most of the time, which pissed her off more and more. It's like he didn't even want to come home, or see her for that matter. At first she could give a shit! Fine she thought, if he didn't want enjoy this beautiful home, then she would enjoy it without him. But how much could you do in a big, empty mansion? It wasn't like she was going to clean it, hell no, that's what Girva, the housekeeper was for. And she hadn't cooked for him in months, that's because he hadn't been there but six times in the last two months. Neither Shantique nor Nikko had been by to visit her, but she knew that was only because they were jealous. All she had was her baby and her brother, Calvin who she let stay in the basement until he found somewhere else to stay. He kept her company and it kept him off the street.

Martinette forced her hundred and sixty pound body off the bed and stood in front of her mirror for a good look. Although she had gained about twenty pounds, she didn't look as big as she felt. Pretty soon she would have start wearing those ugly maternity clothes, something she dreaded, but she had heard of a neat place in Buckhead, an up and coming boutique where they dressed most of the local celebrities. She would check them out this weekend. She had nothing better to do. In fact, she thought she would have more than an afternoon excursion, if Ro wanted to fuck around, then so would she. Hell, she thought, pregnant or not, two can play that game.

"Yo Marti!, Marti!"

"What Calvin!" Marti said opening her door. "Why you hollering? I ain't death. I can hear you. Damn!"

Marti's brother Calvin stood at the door, "well you been locked up in your room so long, I was wondering if you was alive baby girl. Damn, what you been doing in here?" He asked looking around the room. "You got enough food in here to feed the continent of Africa," he said through a snagga-toothed grin.

"Shut up! I got to eat sometime."

"Marti from the looks of it, you eating all the time and here I was downstairs fixing you a grilled cheese sandwich."

"Grilled cheese? The way mama used to make?"

"Better, with lots of butter and two slices of American cheese."

"Damn Calvin! You trying to fatten me up or what?"

"Babygirl, looks like you doing a pretty good job by your damn self. But hey," he laughed, "I ain't mad at ya. Baby's got to eat too!"

"Alright now, I'm about tired of your sorry ass jokes, just bring me my grilled cheese."

"Righto captain," he said saluting and heading back out the door.

"And don't forget to bring me something to drink."

*   *   *

"Remember when mama used to get buttered on Christmas Eve and try to make her sweet potato pies?" Calvin said laughing between bites of grilled cheese.

"Yeah, like the time she put paprika in the pies instead nutmeg. She didn't even tell us, and we were eating and like gasping for air because they were so hot."

"Those were the good old times. I miss mama. I know she wasn't perfect, but neither are we. It took a lot of hard times for me to finally realize that. But what I know now is worth a million dollars."

"Oh yeah, so what you know now?"

"I know that she would be so proud of you and the life you made for yourself. I know that you need to quit isolating yourself in your room and live your life again instead of living for that man. I know that you need your friends as much as they need you. And don't even try to lie about it, you miss them. What's up with you Marti, for as long as I can remember you been talking about Shantique and Nikko and now, since you hooked up with Ro they've disappeared and you don't talk about them no more."

Martinette looked away, put her grilled cheese sandwich onto her paper plate, "it ain't what you think. They abandoned me."

"Naw Marti, it's you and that fucked up attitude of yours. I don't know if it's the hormones or Ro, but you ain't easy to be around."

"Well then get the fuck on! Here I am trying to help your homeless ass and you calling me a bitch!"

"Nope, I ain't saying you a bitch, I'm saying you been acting like one. And me, it don't matter, I'm family. I'm gonna love you no matter. You my little sis and I only tell you this because it's the truth and you know it. Friends, real friends don't abandon their friends when they're in need. You three been hanging tight since high school. What's changed since then? Nothing but Ro, and this big ass house you can't do nothing with."

Martinette couldn't believe how the conversation had changed. The last thing she wanted to discuss was Shantique and Nikko. They were supposed to be her friends but they were the ones who thought she got pregnant just to trap Ro. Hell, she didn't even know she was pregnant until the doctor told her so. Yeah, she missed them, but she would be the last one to admit. Not even to her big brother. "Whateva! That's just how it is. I got new friends now."

"What new friends? You haven't been out the house in weeks."

"Well, I'm going out tonight."

"Really, where?"

"That's for me to know and you to find out."

* * *

Shantique sat on the concrete stair in front of her apartment filing away at her nails when Taye walked up from out of nowhere. He was looking every bit of good since the last time she saw him, wearing a white Sean Jean t-shirt and jeans. He smiled the same way he smiled at her the very first day they had met, with both dimples showing. She couldn't believe how his smile still made her weak at the knees.

"Hey," he said, "I see you still filing away at those nubs."

"I beg your pardon, these are nails not nubs. What are you doing here anyway? I thought you would be somewhere with your boys, planning your NBA signing after-party, or all hugged up with your new girl. What's her name Maria?"

"Naw, it ain't even like that. I'm just going to be chilling with my Mom, my uncle Jeff and some my cousins at the house afterwards."

"And Maria?" Just saying the girls name pissed her off. She still hadn't gotten over that incident, but she refused to let him see it.

He waved his hands in front of him, "that's been over. You can thank Martinette for that."

"Martinette, what she got to do with anything?"

"You saw, she nearly beat that girl to death, over some dumb shit. Man, I tell you, your girl got to chill."

"Well, she pretty much on ice right now."

"What you say, I don't believe it."

"Yeah, Marti carrying."

"She's pregnant?"

"That's right! Her and Ro gonna have a baby."

"Damn if that girl didn't hit the jackpot!"

"You stupid Taye!" she laughed. This seemed just like old times, when the two of them used to hangout at The Varsity, just shooting the shit with her friends and his.

"All, you know I'm telling the truth. That's all Marti been waiting on and just like that she got it. Having a baby by Rotundo Watson is like hitting the Mega-Millions jackpot."

"Yeah, I guess so, but I know everything ain't so lovely over there."

"What, she break a nail?"

"Shutup Taye! Marti's my friend and I'm worried about her, really. She done hooked up with Ro, got herself pregnant and now she can't even call nobody no more. She all shacked up in the mansion he bought her and ain't nobody heard from her since. She's changed."

"She ain't changed, she just doing what she always done, lying in wait for the kill."

Shantique rolled her eyes his way. Although there was a lot of truth to what Taye said she wasn't going to give him the satisfaction of knowing it. Nobody knew Marti like Shantique, and despite all of the money and the lavish surroundings Shantique knew something was wrong. "So," she said, trying to change the subject, "what's up with the surprise visit?"

"No surprise, your mama knew I was coming by. I wanted to see little man. You know, I am his daddy."

"Yeah, I'm reminded of that everyday."

"Oh, there you go."

"What? All kidding aside, he'll be happy to see you. It ain't like he get to see you all the time. Maybe when you get that big contract you can fly us in to see you every weekend."

"Us? What you mean us? The way I hear it, you pretty busy yourself with your own megastar, X. Damn! First there's Marti and now you, who Nikko dating, R. Kelly?"

"Shutup Taye! You can go upstairs now, I'm sure mama knows you here, she probably been standing at the window the whole time."

"Sounds to me like you avoiding the question. What's up between you and X?"

"We cool, but it's really not any of your business?"

"Yeah you right, but when it comes to my son, and who my son's mom is dating, don't get it twisted. It is and will always be my business."

"Oh there you go. Look Taye, you ain't had nothing to say to me besides hello, goodbye and where's Rashawn for the last two years, now you want to get all up in my face about who I'm seeing. This is bullshit!"

"Yeah, maybe, but it is what it is Shantique. That's my son, my blood and I have to care about what happens to him, who he's around, but you, I ain't gonna lie, I just care. Now with that said, I'm going to go check on my son."

CHAPTER 15

Shantique pulled her luggage behind her and tried her best to keep up with the fast moving crowd. She was about three feet behind Marisela when she lost site of her and then her phone rang.

"Hello, hey baby," she answered. "Yeah we just got in…ahh!" she screamed when someone ran over her foot with a huge rolling cart.

"Baby, you alright?" X asked over the phone.

"I will be, damn! People here are rude. He didn't even apologize or nothing. Oh shit!"

"I know you ain't letting nobody punk you! New York ain't for the weak ma, you got to man up, show them that other side, you hear me?"

"Yeah, I hear you," she said. But she really wished X was there with her. This was the first trip she had ever made in her life alone, without family. Yeah, she had Marisela, but Marisela fit in just fine, while she stood out and felt more foreign than most foreigners. All around her were people speaking different languages, very few black folks and she hadn't heard English since she left the plane. "Shit!"

"What's up babe?"

"I can't find Marisela. She was right in front of me, but I don't see her anymore."

"Well, you know what hotel you all are staying in, right?"

"Its starts with a W, the Wardor, Waldorf or something like that."

"The Waldorf Astoria."

"That's it." Her phone beeped, indicating another caller. "Hold up baby, I think that's Marisela." She clicked over to the other line. "Hello." Marisela spoke fast and in Spanish. "Marisela, I can't understand you."

"Oh, oh sorry Titi, where are you? I have the cab waiting. Hurry Titi!"

"I'm still in the concourse. How far down are you?"

"Come outside, I will wave you down."

"Okay, I'm coming now." She clicked back over to X. "Hey baby, that was Marisela, she's getting us a cab. I got to go, but I'll call you when I get to the hotel."

"Alright babygirl, ring me when you are settled."

She hung up and joined the hundreds of travelers outside and into the wet, chilly weather of New York.

* * *

After X hung up from talking with Shantique, he received another call, the ID registered "Private number". "Yo" he answered.

The connection was bad, but he recognized the voice the moment the caller spoke. "We need to talk."

"Sammy, Mighty fine time for that. First, you send your boys, now you wanna talk?"

"Time is right, X. Look, I ain't got a whole lotta minutes to waste. You know how it is. So here's the deal, I need you to pay me a visit. We talk face to face, and get this mess cleared up."

X moved the phone from his right ear to his left. It didn't make the connection any clearer. He heard what Sammy said the first time, he just wasn't sure what his response would be. "Yeah man, I hear you. So when's visiting hours?"

"You can come tomorrow. Anytime between nine and five, my times up. So, I'll talk with you tomorrow, Son."

The call disconnected. X was frozen with the phone to his ear. Although he didn't want to see Sammy, didn't want anything else to do with him, he guess he owed him this last visit. If he was sure of anything, it was that it would be the last time he would see Sammy Pete in the flesh.

* * *

Shantique unpacked her bags quickly, moving clothes from the bed to the closet. She only had a few minutes before she was to meet Marisela in the lobby and off they went to the fashion district. She dialed her mother's phone one more time, hoping she would catch her before she headed to work. Her mother picked up.

"Hey Mommy!"

"Shantique! How you doing baby?"

"I'm fine, just tired, from all this rushing here and there. How's my baby? Did he make it to school okay?"

"Rashawn is fine. You should have seen him in his uniform, carrying his new book bag. He was adorable. Anyway, I took pictures, so you can see them when you get back. So, how is New York?"

"Cold and dreary."

"Is that it?"

"Yep, so far all I've seen is the airport and the hotel. I did see the city driving in, but we got in late you know. Marisela and I are going to the fashion district this morning."

"The fashion district, well you go girl. I'm so proud of you Shantique. I really am. Now don't you worry about anything here, me and little man going to be fine. You just take care your business and do a good job."

"I will mommy. Give Rashawn a big hug and kiss for me and I will call you later on tonight."

"Alright Sweetie, I love you."

"Love you too mommy!"

* * *

After a full day in the fashion district, Shantique was mentally and physically worn out, whereas Marisela seemed to be running at full speed.

"Okay Titi, we have about thirty minutes to change and then we go to the most fabulous restaurant in the entire city. You are going to love it!"

Shantique stopped to pull off her shoes the moment they got off the elevator. For the first time in her life, she despised shoes and vowed to go barefoot for as long as possible. "I don't know Marisela, I'm beat!"

Marisela turned to look at her. "You young kids. You should be full of energy. Instead you let an old woman like me run you around and wear you out."

"You're like no old woman I know," Shantique said tiptoeing behind her. She wanted to complain to Marisela about her feet, her back and her head, but why bother; the woman wasn't hearing any of her excuses.

"Titi, if you want to make it in this business, you got to have drive. Tired or not, you are coming with me tonight. It is important that you meet some of my contacts, just in case you have to do business when I'm away. Go take a fifteen minute cat nap, soak your feet and be ready to go at six-thirty, alright?"

Shantique didn't want to agree, but she had no choice. She couldn't remember anything she had done in life being harder than this. Yeah she had plenty of energy when it came chasing Rashawn, partying and hanging out with her friends, but this was altogether different and more demanding than she had imagined. That glamorous vision she had about being a big-time buyer went "poof", vanished sometime around three pm leaving her with a grim reality—being a buyer was hell! "Alright, Marisela, I'll be ready."

Her room was down the hall and around the corner from Marisela's, a normally short distance that seemed like a mile. Shantique didn't know how she was going to pep up for another four to six hours of networking or whatever Marisela would have her doing. She could barely open her door, let alone think about the night ahead. She fiddled with the key card until the light turned green then opened her door to welcoming surprised. Her room was filled with dozens and dozens of pale pink roses. "Oh my God,"

Shantique said moving from bouquet to bouquet, smelling, touching, bathing in the sweet scent. She counted twenty-four vases total, and one card with a special message, that read, *"2 months, 10 days and 4 hours that is the time I've been blessed to spend with you. It's not an eternity, but it's an eternity for me. Miss you, X"*

    She dialed his number, but got his voicemail. "Aw damn X, where you at? I mean, I ain't checking on you or nothing, a girl just likes to know where her man is, that's all. Okay well, hey I just wanted to say thank you sooooo much! The flowers are beautiful! But why so many? I ain't mad or nothing, but that's a lot of money. You know me, always trying to save a dollar and don't say I'm being cheap, because I'm not, I'm just frugal, that means I'm smart about my money. Okay boo, I know you must be busy, so I'm gonna holla at you later, alright. I miss you too and thanks for this."

*   *   *

    Several hours and 3 bars later, Shantique sat shoeless, sipping on her second cup of coffee. Marisela had her all over New York and as much as she loved the nightlife, she wasn't used to the running here and there, dealing with icy stares, that posed the question, who was she, and what was she doing there? She saw the way those gay boys looked at her, as if to measure her existence, and the women, well they looked too, but there's were a look very much close to lust, which didn't make her feel anymore comfortable. Shantique surmised she had a lot to get used to, a lot to learn and it wasn't all about the business of fashion. Someone screamed, but Shantique didn't bulge, she could tell that it was a scream of pleasure, not of pain. She watched Marisela entertain herself and friends of her boyfriend, Yuri in the lobby of the Astoria. Yuri positioned himself at the bar, several seats down from her, and closest to the television which played ESPN. As far as Shantique could make out, Yuri was the kind of guy who preferred his party's private, and he seemed to shy away from a crowd—total opposite of Marisela. Marisela embraced the nightlife, wrapping herself around it and twirling in it's revelry like an Olympic ribbon dancer. She was spirited, sassy—an expert closer of deals. There was no doubt about it, Marisela knew her business and Shantique would be the first to admit that she had a lot to learn from her, not only about the fashion business, but how to smile and fake it when she wanted to cuss a muthafucka out, now that's a true talent. Yuri stood up to ask the bartender to turn up the volume of the TV. She hadn't paid much attention to the broadcast earlier, but then she heard Taye's name and moved next to Yuri to get a better view.

"You like basketball?" Yuri asked after noticing her taking an interest in the broadcast.

"Yeah, I do, but it's more personal than that."

He gave her a strange look. The question she knew he would ask pursed on his lips.

"I know him," she said pointing at the television, "Taye Anderson."

"Oh," he smiled, "Yes, Taye Anderson. He is very good player! I predict he will go in first round. You think?"

Shantique didn't know what to think, all at once she felt so happy and proud for Taye, so much so, she thought that she was about to burst or cry. She could feel Yuri's eyes on her.

"I'm sorry, this makes you sad?" he asked.

"Oh no," she said wiping her eyes. I just got something in my eye. I'm okay." But was she really? What was that all about? She couldn't still have feelings for Taye, after all this time. How could she? She loved X now. She almost said it out loud, to convince herself. *I love X now.*

CHAPTER 16

Martinette swelled with pride and an incredible sense of accomplishment when she heard her baby's' heart beat for the first time.

"Babe, did you hear that?" She asked without looking. Had she been looking she would have seen the blank faced stare and part grimace that Ro wore. "Babe," Martinette called, searching for Ro and finding him facing the window as if what was taking place in that room had nothing to do with him. "What's up babe?" It was a question meant only for Ro, but it seemed to peak the interest of all of those in the room, the nurse assistant, the doctor and Ro's agent, Manny. She couldn't figure out what Manny was doing there, but didn't question Ro about it, since the two seemed to be really close.

"Nothing," Ro said.

Martinette was about to respond to Ro's nonchalant attitude when Dr. Washington interrupted.

"Sounds like a healthy baby to me. In a couple of weeks we'll be able to get you a picture."

"Wow! You hear that baby, we gonna have a live picture of our baby."

Ro said nothing.

"Okay well," Dr, Washington said, "I am going to get the receptionist to schedule your next appointment and then I'll be right back in to see you." He patted Martinette on the shoulder then exited the room, along with the nurse's assistant, followed by Manny, who made up some excuse about an urgent phone call.

Martinette could barely contain her anger. "So, what is it now Ro? Every time I see you, you got a fucking problem. I would think you would be happy about hearing your baby's heartbeat, be happy about having a healthy child, but no, you come in here with another chip the size of an oak tree on your shoulder."

"Martinette shut the fuck up!"

Martinette was stunned. Ro had never spoken to her like that, not even when she cussed him out forty different ways. For a moment she was speechless, but that only lasted for a moment. "All hell no! You shut the fuck up!" She jumped off the bed, nearly tripping on the sheets to get in Ro's face. "What the hell is wrong with you Ro?"

Ro turned away from her, and paced the floor in front of the door. Now Martinette was really scared. She had never seen him this way, couldn't understand why he was treating her so harsh.

"Marti, I want," he paused, "I need you to take a paternity test."

Martinette couldn't believe what she was hearing. "What? You saying you don't trust me now Ro? This isn't your baby?" She laughed and slapped her thighs. "You got to be kidding me, halfway through my pregnancy you questioning me. Now I done heard it all brother. I think you need to leave."

"I'm serious Marti. You and I are going to take a paternity test. It's only fair."

Martinette looked at Ro like she wanted to kill him. She couldn't believe what he was asking her, especially now.

"No," she said. "I'm not taking it."

"What?" he asked.

"You heard me, Hell NO," she hollered. "I'm not taking no fucking paternity test. You heard that, didn't you?"

"Marti, please?" He begged.

"Why? Why now Ro? You could have asked me that the very first time you found out I was pregnant. What, the league don't want you having no children now? It's Manny, isn't it? That muthafucka so afraid of losing his grip on you, he would have you question me about the paternity of your baby? Fuck Manny and fuck you very much!"

"I'll get it, whether you agree to it or not. I'll get the paternity test Marti. You can't stop me."

"You know what Ro, you're right, I can't. You are almighty Ro, Mr. Muthafuckin basketball, and me, I'm just little old Martinette, oh you know that Ho, that Bitch, who got fucked by Ro. I ain't got a leg to stand own, but I tell you what, when the truth comes out, and everybody knows how you fucked over your baby's momma, when your son or daughter find out how you had to have a fucking test to prove you was their daddy before you accepted them. When the world learns what a simple ass punk you are, then justice will be mine. Now, please get the fuck out of my face."

* * *

Martinette had put on a good front in Ro's presence but the truth was she was shaken to the core. Here she was pregnant, and alone, the one thing she promised herself she would never wind up as, a single mother. As much as she tried to avoid following in her mothers footsteps, once again, she had taken one giant step and landed flat in the middle of her mothers existence. With no job, and no means of support, how was she going to handle the note on that house, or the car? She broke down in tears. She couldn't do it all by herself, not now. She needed Ro to take care of her, and her baby. And having a paternity test right now would be like her committing financial suicide. Martinette wiped away her tears and began to dress herself. She was 99% sure that the baby was Ro's, but then again it was that 1% that frightened her. She shook her head in disgust, how could she be so stupid, so careless. She needed more time, time to put together a plan B. The paternity would prove proof positive who the father of her baby was, and if it wasn't Ro, then it could only be one other person, Dwayne.

* * *

Nikko finished her routine on point, receiving applause from the entire room.

"Good job Nikko", her dance lead, Susan screamed from the sidelines, before grabbing her by the shoulders and squeezing her tight. "You keep working out like that, you'll be headlining before you know it."

Nikko was all smiles. She had worked hard on that routine, day and night for the last week and all the practice paid off today. "Thanks Susan, I couldn't have done it without you."

Susan swung her long blond hair behind her, something she did on occasion, but especially when she was about to make a serious statement. "Listen hear, not everybody makes the dance company on their first try, or perform in the first production. But you did both! That's something to be really proud of Nikko."

"Thanks Susan."

"Thank me later, after you get that headliner spot," she said winking. "I've got to go. Don't forget to get your physical and have the paperwork back to me by next week."

"I won't Susan. I'll see ya next week."

Nikko packed up her bag and headed to her car, when she heard her phone ring from deep inside her purse. "Damn," she cursed, searching inside her purse to retrieve the ringing phone, but she was too late, it stopped ringing. By the time she found her phone, she noticed she had 3 missed calls, all from a private number, with no listing or message. In fact, the calls were from a number she didn't recognize at all. Her phone rang again and this time she immediately recognized the number.

"What's up Shantique? If it isn't Miss Fashion herself, how long you've been back in town?"

"Hey Boo! I got back last week and let me tell you it was a trip! What you doing?"

"I just finished practice." Nikko said getting into her car. "So tell me about your trip? Did you get to meet a lot models and stars? You know New York is full of stars."

"Yeah, but it's not what you think. It was cool, but I was glad to get home. You heard from Marti?"

"No, you?"

"No, I tried calling her a couple of times and I even left her messages but she didn't call back. I don't know Nikko, I'm kind of worried about her and I miss us. I miss hanging out like we used too!"

"I hear you Shantique, I miss you too! And Marti with her crazy ass!"

"We really need to get together, a girls night out or something. I need to talk."

Nikko noticed a change in Shantique's' voice, something bordering on sadness. "Is everything okay Shantique?"

"Yeah, everything is great. I got a good job, a beautiful son, who just started pre-k, and a good man. What more can I ask for?"

"Well, that's exactly what I was thinking, but you don't' sound so happy about it. Look, I'm about to head home, how about I stop by your place and pick you up? I'm craving one of those DQ freezes anyway, and you know the one by your house make them the best."

"Cool, mama and Rashawn are out visiting my grandma, so I got the place to myself."

"What about X? Y'all not hanging out?"

"No, he said something about visiting a friend."

"Alright then, well I'll shower and be right over." The moment Nikko hung up, the phone rang again. "Hey Butter!" she answered.

"And how are you today?"

"I'm just wonderful! I just finished practicing and I did so good that the lead dancer told me before long I would be a headliner. Now how's that for a first practice?"

"I'd say that was pretty damn good, young lady and worthy of a celebration. You feel up to doing something tonight?"

As much as Nikko wanted to spend time with Butter, she felt like her friend needed her more. "All sweetie, I don't know about tonight. I promised Shantique that I would stop and visit and it's already after six. I hope you don't mind. Tomorrow?"

"Tomorrow is fine. I am still at the studio trying to put together some tracks for X. So, it's all good, this way I can have them finished and we can have the whole day tomorrow and I can plan something extra special for my girl."

"Extra special! What did you have in mind?"

"It's a surprise."

"A surprise?"

"You like surprises, don't you?"

"Yeah, I guess, most of them."

"I promise you, you will like the one I have planned for you. So what time should I pick you up?"

Nikko thought, there was no way he would be able to pick her up from the house, not with her mom and dad around.

"You don't have to pick me up. I'll meet you, just give me directions."

"I can't, it's a surprise, I told you. Be ready around 4pm. I will call and give you directions."

"Butter what's up, why you being all mysterious?"

"Because I can, and I like it."

"Yeah, I kinda like it too!"

"I knew it, see you ain't fooling nobody. Tell your girl Shantique I said hello and I'll holla at you later on."

Nikko hung up her phone feeling warm all over. It had been awhile since her and Shantique talked, and she had so much to share with her about dancing, but more importantly about Butter and how she had fallen for this man, in all honesty— she was sprung!

* * *

X checked his messages for the third time, and Shantique hadn't called, which was odd. He had gotten so used to speaking to her 3 to 4 times a day, and today she hadn't called at all. X didn't know what to make of it, but with what he was facing, he would surely put whatever was going on with Shantique on the backburner.

Less than 30 miles from Milledgeville, X let down his window and lit up a cigarette, pulling on it so hard that the smoke burned his throat. It was crazy to be this nervous, this anxious, but then again he was meeting with Sammy Pete—probably for the last time. He was getting close the sign for GA State Penitentiary was just up ahead. This was his destination, where his old friend and producer Sammy Pete resided. After all the talk, this is where it all ended, with him facing Sammy, behind bars because, if truth be told, he had helped to put him there. There was no other way to put it, it is what it is, and Sammy being the man he claimed to be would understand the situation and the bind he put X in. But Sammy was at most times a chameleon, a Broadway actor in a ghetto get up. He was never who you thought he was, not even when you've seen him at his worst. Him calling X to the pen for a meeting could mean a lot of things. Maybe he wanted to make amends, smooth things out between them, or maybe he wanted to cuss him out in person. X would have chosen the latter, if Sammy hadn't sent his would be henchmen to threaten him. It was a dumb thing to do, and the act itself solely disappointed X, but who was he to be sensitive. He alone had sent Sammy up for 10 years, and no matter how close they once were, Sammy would never forgive him for that. So, in the end, it was a game time. Sammy called the meeting, now it was X's turn to move.

* * *

X had never spent one day in jail, that was a phenomenal task, taking into account all he had been through growing up on the hard streets of Ohio. He was lucky at best that he didn't get caught up in the game early, but then again he was smart and chose to use his skills as a rapper to finance his habits and living. X dressed down for the meet, not wanting to draw any unwanted attention to himself or his fame. He even rented a toned down, Hyundai for the drive up. You never knew who would be watching, so to be inconspicuous had become a way a life for him. He pulled up to the gates of GA Pen, where guards waited in booths with guns and no smiles. His good sense told him to back up, turn around, forget about Sammy, but his heart took charge and urged him on. What he had to say to Sammy, he had to say in person. He owed him that much, afterall he was once his friend.

After X was stripped of everything but the clothes he wore, he sat down on a cold, hard, plastic chair and stared into a barred, double-paned window waiting for his old friend and producer to appear.

Sammy was led into the small room by two guards, one large oversized version of Vin Diesel, the actor, and the other a small, but balky black man who looked liked he spent most of his time lifting weights. The small one whispered something into to Sammy's ear, then proceeded to undue his chains. Sammy seemed unaffected by the guards, or anything else for that matter. He smiled and winked at X, like he always did, then sat before him.

"It's good to see you man."

"You too! Just not in this place. How they treating you?"

"Like an inmate," he paused and winked, "with perks."

"Yeah, I hear ya." X heard Sammy but was having a difficult time believing him. What's a nigga got to be happy about being in jail? Sammy wasn't the type. Sammy was weed friendly. Only after puffing on 2-3 joints was he able to be sociable at all, other times he was just mad.

"So, what's up with the new style? Looks like you gone all schoolboy on me?"

"Naw, just toned it down for the visit."

"Yeah well, word on the street is you starting up your own business, you and that limo driver, what's his name?"

"Butter." X had feared that this was the reason Sammy was on the attack. Sammy didn't like losing money. And losing X was as close as it came to losing his wealth. "True dat, we trying to do a little something."

"That's cool. I always liked that in you, creative minds think a like."

"Thanks man."

"You ain't got to thank me. I should be thanking you."

X didn't know what Sammy meant by that, even sitting face to face with the man, Sammy had a way of hiding his true feelings.

"Look X, I don't have a lotta time, so I'm gonna get right to the point. Somebody dropped a dime on me about that robbery thing. I ain't saying it was you, I'm just saying only the closest to me knew about that…you're like a brother to me man, blood. If you say it wasn't you, it's squashed, just like that.

"Is that why you sent your boys after me?" X jumped up from his seat, knocking the chair to the ground. "What the fuck!"

Two guards approached. "Everything alright over here?"

"Yeah it's cool," Sammy said, waving them away, but the guard wouldn't budge. "Its cool." He said again, more sternly. The guard retreated back to his station. "X, have a seat."

X picked up the plastic chair and sat. He would hear Sammy out.

"Sending Uzi was wrong. I should have spoke with you first, but with all that was going on, me losing the business, this jail thing…I wasn't thinking right. You know I thought this might have been about your nephew."

"What about him?"

"You two were close, I know and you think I had something to do with his death. Maybe this is your way of getting back at me. We're alike, you and I. Family means everything to us. We are loyal by creed, it's something we live and die by. It's what keeps us going."

"Two minutes", the guard yelled.
"So, what you saying Sammy?"
"All I'm saying is, we straight. What's done is done."

CHAPTER 17

Nikko stuffed her hands in her jacket and struggled to keep warm while Shantique seemed unaffected by the chill or anything else. Nikko had been running her mouth uninterrupted, aside for an occasional "uh hum, and I hear you's" from Shantique, not exactly what she was looking for when it came to discussing the love of her life.

"Shantique, did you hear a word I said?"

"Yeah, you're sprung."

"That's not what I said. Girl, what is up with you? Everything okay with you and X?"

"Yeah, we're cool."

"You're cool? Just the other week, X was all you could talk about, now you're just cool. I know you better than that, what's really up?"

"Nothing girl, really, it's not about X."

"Then who? Rashawn, your mama?"

Shantique took a deep breath and exhaled a small white cloud. "It's about me," she paused, "and Taye."

Nikko jumped up and faced her friend. "Taye? All hell naw, you and Taye didn't...?"

"No, we didn't do anything, but talk, and the funny thing is we weren't even talking like that, about us or anything. It's just I realized how much I still care for him, and I don't know. I just want to do the right thing by Rashawn and X. I mean, wouldn't it better for Rashawn to grow up with his father?"

"Wait a minute girl, I hear you talking but you're not making much sense. When did you and Taye talk about getting back together? I thought he had a girlfriend, and you, you're dating X."

"We didn't, I mean we haven't. But I felt something between us, and I know he felt it too. AHHHH!" she said grabbing her head. "I don't know what I'm saying. Just forget it."

"No finish. What's going on?"

"It's just that things are getting serious with X, and I need to be sure about Taye before I go any further."

"What do you mean serious? He give you a ring? Ask you to marry him?"

"No. He asked me to move in with him."

"Oh, that is serious. So, what did you say? Did you tell him about Taye?"

Shantique cut her eyes at Nikko. "What do you think? Damn Nikko, I ain't stupid."

"You can't keep stringing him along."

"I'm not. I'm going to figure this thing out with Taye, and one way or the other, I'll be ringing in the New Year with only one. Now, lets change the subject, when you gonna let Butter hit that?"

"Damn, Shantique, why you all up in my bizness?"

"Cuz I can. So, what's up? He ain't man enough for you?"

"Oh, he is plenty man enough, but we just taking our time, getting to know one another."

"He's one of those," Shantique makes a gesture, "gentleman kind."

"And, so what? I ain't heard nothing about you and X hitting the sheets." Shantique grinned.

"No you didn't? And you didn't tell nobody! You are not my girl! Does Martinette know?"

"I haven't spoken to Martinette in months."

"Me neither. Every time I've tried, she's not home or no one answers. She can't still be mad at us?"

"Probably not, but you know how stubborn she can be. She'll come around soon, in her own time. She's got Ro and her brother looking after her, so I guess she's okay."

"Yeah well, I don't know about Ro."

"What you mean?"

"I mean, I ran into her brother a couple of weeks ago downtown, and when I asked about Marti and Ro, he said he hadn't seen Ro in months."

"What?" Damn, I know she is freaking out."

"Yep."

"Maybe we should give her a call. It can't hurt."

"Yeah, I miss the three of us. Things haven't been the same." Nikko's phone rings and she answers. "Hey baby what's up? No!" She screamed.

"What's up Nikko?"

Nikko's lack of response and tear-filled eyes scared Shantique. "Nikko!"

"Laron is dead."

* * *

Laron's death sent shockwaves through the entire Hip-Hop community and in many ways it turned Nikko's world inside out. There had not been one waking moment that she hadn't pondered, thought and religiously sought out answers to why and how a twenty-two year old man in excellent health would suddenly and unexpectedly die. The answer came sooner than she expected. Butter was the first to share his suspicions, but then a phone call from Laron's sister pretty much drove the nail in the coffin.

"Hello, Is this Nikko?" the caller asked.

Nikko said nothing, looked at her phone and tried to identify the caller by the number, but couldn't.

"Hello?"

"Yes, this is Nikko."

"Nikko, good, I thought I had the wrong number or something. We've been trying to reach you."

WE, Nikko thought, who was WE? Who was she? "Really?"

"Yeah, my mama called several times when Laron was in the hospital, but she said she couldn't reach you."

"Laron? This is about Laron?"

"I'm sorry, I should have introduced myself. My names Brianna, I'm Laron's older sister."

There was another pause and Nikko could hear her sniffling in the background. This was about Laron. Laron's death, or life, or whatever, she didn't know and she wasn't sure she was entirely ready to talk with Brianna.

"I'm sorry to hear about Laron. My condolences to your family."

"Thank you Nikko, we really appreciate it, but that's not the reason I'm calling. Laron's autopsy revealed he was HIV positive. Nikko," she paused, "you need to get tested."

* * *

Martinette stood in front of the full-length mirror examining her body once more. There was no other way to see it, she was fat! Her butt and hips were twice their normal size no matter which way she turned. The outfit she wore concealed her swollen middle, but the rest of her spread so far, east and west that she had trouble maneuvering. But that wasn't going to stop her from going out and having a good time. She had been stuck in the house for weeks, waiting on Ro to call, come by, but he had done neither and she knew why. The times she did talk with him all he could talk about was the baby and her taking a paternity test. Martinette refused again and again and when that didn't work she cussed him out for good measure. Eventually Ro stopped calling altogether. She didn't worry, though, as soon as her baby was born Ro would come around and things would be back to normal. The phone rang.

"Marti", her brother hollered from below. "Get the phone."

Speak of the Devil, she thought. He would call now, just when she was trying to get out and get her groove on. "Who is it?" she hollered back.

"Marti!" her brother hollered again.

"Who is it?"

"I don't know, your girl, Shantique or Nikko, I think. You gonna get the phone or what?"

Damn! She hadn't heard from Shantique or Nikko in weeks. Why would they be calling her now? "Hello."

"Hey Marti, its Shantique."

"Yeah, I know."

"Marti, I know you not still mad, so cut the shit."

"How you know I'm not still mad at you heifers, the way you treat me. I got a good mind to stay mad at y'all asses for the rest of my life."

"Yeah, but you're not."

Martinette was more than happy to hear from Shantique but she didn't want to show it. "So, why you calling me now?"

"Marti, look, if you don't wanna talk, its cool. Me and Nikko were gonna call you the other day," she paused, "but then that stuff came up about Laron."

"I heard about that. How's Nikko doing?"

"She's okay. I mean, it wasn't like they were still seeing each other."

"I sure hope not. I tried to tell her about him, but she jumps down my throat. So she's alright then?"

"Yeah, I talked with her yesterday; anyway she got Butter looking after her."

"Butter. The limo driver?"

"Butter. The Limo business owner."

"What you talking about Shantique? I know who Butter is. He drove us to the concert."

"Yeah, but did you know he owns the limo he drove us in and a whole lot more?"

"No shit?"

"No shit! They have been hanging real tight since Justin's."

"Well, I'm happy for Nikko. She deserves a good man."

"Who don't?"

"I hear ya girlfriend!"

"So what's up with you, Ro and baby makes three?"

Silence.

"Marti?"

"Yeah, I'm still here. We're fine. I'm just getting sick and tired of being sick and tired, if you know what I mean. Girl, I should have listened to you, being pregnant ain't no joke!"

"I told you. You over the morning sickness yet?"

"Yeah, pretty much, now if I could get over all this damn eating and peeing I'd be fine."

Shantique laughed. "Girl you are crazy! And I miss you!"

"I miss you too Boo! We got to hook up real soon, cuz I'm about to lose my mind in this house with nobody to talk to but Calvin. You know he think he some kind of doctor or something always trying to tell me what to eat and what not to eat and shit, just cuz he eating healthy don't mean I have too!"

"I hear ya girl. I was hoping we could get together this weekend, that's if you free?"

"Free, shit yeah I'm free, I ain't see Ro in over a month. He stays on the road, or at least that's what he's telling me."

"Marti, he's a pro-basketball player and one that's in demand. Don't worry he knows where home is."

"I ain't so sure Shantique. I'm not even sure if I know where home is."

"You really think it's that bad girl? He loves you Marti. He told me so."

"Yeah well, he told me to, but saying something and acting on it is two different things. Anyway it goes, I'm alright. You know Marti always lands on her feet and it won't be any different this time around. It's never the man that makes Marti, Marti makes the man."

"Well alright then, you gonna put that on the front of your car?"

"Shut up Shantique, you stupid."

"No I ain't. Look about this weekend; I was just thinking they probably will have Laron's funeral on Saturday, so getting together might be out of the question."

"Oh yeah, well I'll meet you all at the funeral then. Shit girl, everybody and their mama gonna be there. I wouldn't miss it for the world."

"Marti, it's not a show, it's a funeral."

"Yeah, tell that to the chickenheads that show up wearing black band-aids. Like I said, I wouldn't miss it for the world, anyways I'm there to show support for my girl."

"Alright then, I'll call you with the information. You gonna need a ride?"

"Yeah, you riding with X?"

"True."

"Then I'm riding with the first family, cuz I know X ain't riding in nothing short of a Hummer Limo."

CHAPTER 18

Nikko worried about everything the day of Laron's funeral...her hair, her dress, the way it fell below her knees, how she truly felt about his passing, but not the most important thing, or what should have seemed important to her, her own health and the risks she had taken. She looked behind her and saw waves and waves of people, some walking, some running to get a place in line....a Sea of black. Butter stood by her side, looking handsome and strong. She would need his strength before the day ended. She saw no sign of Shantique or Martinette, although both promised to be there, with her, for support, although she didn't really feel that support is what she needed, a good doctor and a cure for AIDS would have been helpful, even better than that, if anyone of them could turn back the hands of time, she would be indebted to them for the rest of her natural life. She smiled unexpectedly at the thought. Butter gave her a confused look.

"You alright?" he asked.

"Yeah," she said turning away from him. She was so far from being alright in any form or fashion. How could she? With Laron dead and her not knowing if she too might be joining him. Not knowing was killing her, but knowing would surely put her in the grave. Butter had been especially nice, and she knew he knew about Laron, but he hadn't mentioned a word to her. Maybe he thought that her and Laron never had sex, or maybe he thought her smart enough to use a condom. If so, he was wrong on both accounts.

"Nikko, what's up? You can talk to me."

"Nothing, I was just wondering about Shantique and Martinette. It's going to be hard to find them in this crowd."

"Not too hard, not if you got X as your lead man." He pointed in front of them. And standing at the top of the stairs to the church were Shantique, Martinette and X. X waved them over.

Nikko was too glad to see them, and nearly tripped over herself to get up the stairs. She hadn't seen Martinette in almost a month, and was pleasantly surprised to see the additional hump protruding from her mid-section. She looked beautiful, glowing, and pretty much the same, except for the basketball size belly.

"Hey girl," Martinette said, "You okay sweetie?"

She had already adopted that motherly tone, and used it well on Nikko. It was hard to believe Martinette was a mother-to-be, but seeing Martinette in the flesh, made a believer out her.

"Marti girl, you look great!"

Marti blushed then rubbed her swollen belly. If Nikko hadn't seen it with her own eyes, she wouldn't have believed. Martinette actually cared for someone other than herself.

"Yeah, he don't let me get much sleep, and I can't stand up for shit, but it's all good. Me and junior been getting real acquainted." Then she blabbed out loud to everyone, in typical Martinette fashion, "Oooh shit! Excuse me, I gotta pee."

Shantique reached for Nikko and hugged her tightly, "Girl, we just about gave up on you."

Nikko fought back tears. Shantique always brought out the crybaby in her. "I didn't see you all anywhere. Thanks for coming." She turned to see Butter and X taking a backseat to their conversation and emotional exchange. They were both really good men, who cared about them. "I see you brought X along."

"Yeah, he insisted on coming, and I'm glad he did." Her eyes shifted between the two men and back to Nikko. "I know what I told you, but X is good to me, you know what I mean?"

"I do," Nikko said, holding on to Shantique. There was so much she wanted to tell her, and would have, hadn't Butter been there, but it wasn't the right time.

"You alright? You shaking girl."

"Yeah, I'm okay."

Shantique looked at her, "No you ain't. What's up Nikko? Girl we've been through too much for you to be holding out on me now."

Nikko looked over to where Butter and X stood, they weren't watching the two of them, but then Butter looked up and gave her a concerned look. She tried smiling to let him know everything was okay, and he nodded and continue to carry on his conversation with X. "I can't talk now Shantique, but I do need to talk with you, afterwards."

"Yeah, you, me and Marti gonna go somewhere and have a real talk, like we used to do, alright?"

She nodded, just as the usher informed them that the service was about to begin. Shantique, X and Martinette entered the church, followed by Nikko and

Butter to pay their last respects to Laron 'The Lover' James.

* * *

Nikko breathed deep, but it didn't seem to do any good, her stomach still turned over and over and her chest tightened with each breath. The Wayside Clinic was small, discreet, and pretty much unnoticeable amongst the various offices inside the multi-conglomerate building that sat across from the shopping mall she normally visited.

Since this wasn't the type of thing she would ask someone to give her a referral on, she performed her research on the internet. She liked that they were private, relatively unknown, and obscure to most of the public. It had been exactly 65.5 minutes since she had arrived and signed in at the front desk before anyone had seen her, a doctor, nurse, not even the receptionist had spoken more than three words to her, "sign in here". Obscure was right. She cradled her head between her legs, wishing, hoping, praying for this to be over, but on second thought, wishing away precious moments of her life might be too ambitious.

The electronic waterfall was soothing, but also annoying. At any other time she would have enjoyed it, even lavished in the drip and swish of the running water, but today all she could think about was that water and a vacuum the size of a portable hairdryer would probably make the same sound and yet have unequally morbid effects.

"Miss Nikko," and she paused, "O-Kem-I" the receptionist said slowly as if not knowing what else to say or how to say it. Nikko had already stood up and approached the window as her name was spoken. She had decided to use her mother's maiden name on the form, trying to be discreet, hidden, undetected and yet she felt as if the entire world knew who she was, even if the waiting room was only occupied by herself and another lady who hadn't given her a second glance. The receptionist then handed her a clipboard with a list of questions.

"Fill this out and the nurse will be out to get you."

Nikko looked over the questionnaire and nearly ran out of the clinic. Every single question inquired about her sex life, sexual behavior, and sexual preference. How in the world could her visit be considered confidential when she was giving them a diary about how many times she fucked and with who? What was the reason she was here, in this dreaded place about to be stuck, probed or God knows what else, only to be told that she would soon die. She shook her head trying to wave away her thoughts and the nausea, but it did little to clear her head or settle her stomach. How could she sleep with a man unprotected? She was a smart girl, going to college, dancer, daughter, friend. She had known better all her life. Wasn't it in fifth grade that she was first taught about birth control, condoms, HIV, AIDS? How could she be so stupid, as to sleep with—no FUCK Laron without a condom? She twisted in her seat and looked around as if someone other than her could hear her thoughts. *Lord, if I get out of this...I promise to never be so stupid again. I promise.* She smiled, and almost laughed out loud. It was so totally absurd for her to be praying, when she never prayed. Would God even listen? Would Buddha? That's who her mom prayed to. She turned her attention back to the clipboard. *Have you had sex with someone who has had sex with the same sex in the last year?* Nikko had seen this question before. It was the same thing they asked when you went in to get a Pap smear, or birth control. How many times had she laughed and thought *how absurd,* and checked NO without hesitating. This time she hesitated.

"Miss Okemi," the nurse called.

Nikko looked up from her clipboard and was met with a warm smile. It was so unexpected after her earlier exchanges with the limited staff. She had come to think that everyone wore icy glares and had cold hearts. Nikko thought it must be a requirement for working in a place like this, where everyone comes to find out if they will go on another day, or if today will be there last.

"Miss Okemi," the nurse said again, and when no one else looked up, she turned her attention to Nikko. "Miss Okemi," she beckoned.

Nikko stood and with all the strength and courage she could muster, she dragged herself to and through the door, but taking a moment, just a moment to look back at the life she once knew.

* * *

Martinette moved the pot of rice from the stove, and then checked on the cornbread she had baking in the oven. She was a good cook. There was no doubt about it. She retrieved a fork from the drawer and stirred the pot of greens on the stove. Everything was as it should be, now all that was missing was Ro. Despite his late arrival, Martinette was in a surprisingly good mood. She hummed and cooked, stirring this, and poking that, as if she had spent her entire life in the kitchen, when in fact, she rarely cooked a thing. For the first time since she had moved to the house, she sat the table with her newly purchased china, with wine goblets and all. Although she wouldn't be partaking of any liquor, she thought it a nice accompaniment to the dinner she had prepared.

She dropped her fork and bent down to pick it up, when she caught sight of her protruding belly. Two months ago it would have been impossible for her to stand in front of a stove cooking, with the nausea, and her infrequent bouts with dizziness, her fondness for food or anything else had dissipated. But now, she could do it all, and the one thing she loved more than sleeping was eating.

The doorbell rang, and she started to holler for her brother to get it, but then remembered he had taken off earlier to visit an old girlfriend. Martinette waddled to the door as fast as she could, which really wasn't fast at all, barely a skip. But even at a skip, her heart beat fast, and before she reached the door, she had to stop to catch her breath. The bell rang again, and almost simultaneously the baby kicked, and nudged inside of her. She rubbed the spot where its little foot protruded.

"I guess you know your daddy's here."

Martinette opened the door and as happy as she was to see Ro standing in front of her with flowers and a smile, she couldn't help but feel betrayed when she saw who he brought with him.

"Martinette. Damn! Look at you.....you"

Martinette interrupted. "Ro, what is Harvey doing here?"

Ro looked from Martinette to Harvey. "Hey man, can you give us a few moments? Harvey spoke to Martinette and then returned to the car.

"So, how you doing?" Ro asked.

"I'm fine, at least a minute ago, before you showed up with your guard dog I was fine. What the fuck is going on Ro?"

"Look Marti, don't start. It's not what you think...okay?"

"Then what the hell is it Ro? You told me we were spending some time together, quality time. I spent all day cooking and shit and you show up with that muthafucka!"

"Marti, come on let's go inside. We can talk about it there."

Martinette didn't like the smell of things, despite the fine aroma coming from the kitchen, it smelled like shit. She walked towards the kitchen with Ro following behind.

"Damn, did your ass get bigger?"

She turned and looked at him like he was stupid. "Does it look bigger?"

"Yep!" he said, eyeing her from top to bottom. "I like what you did with you hair. You look good Marti. Pregnancy becomes you."

"Well," she said looking him up and down, feasting on his fine, fit physique, tan suit and tan shoes. She hadn't seen him looking better. "It looks like it fits you too!"

"Girl, you crazy. Ummm, it sure smells good in here. What you cooking?"

Him asking about her cooking made her feel good. That was probably the one thing any of them other Tricks couldn't do, make a man a meal. But she could, in fact, besides the great sex; she thought that Ro hung around more for the food. "I got some stewed oxtails, mac and cheese, collard greens, rice and cornbread. And for dessert, I made peach cobbler."

"My God girl, you put your foot in it this time."

Martinette smiled and reached for the oven mitt to remove the cornbread. "Well, it's been awhile since I've cooked for my baby and I just wanted to do something special for you."

"Not many women these days would go through the trouble of making a home cooked meal."

Martinette placed the pan of cornbread on the stove, placed her hands on her voluptuous hips and said, "I'm not like any woman. You should know that by now Ro."

"Oh, I do, Marti."

If she wasn't mistaken she could have swore she heard sarcasm in his voice, although it came out soothingly sweet, his eyes said something different, putting her once again in a defensive mode. "So, why is it you had to have Harvey tag along?"

Ro moved from the kitchen island to her side. He was a giant of a man, both in heart and appearance, a big teddy bear most of the time, but both on and off the court he could easily transition into the grizzly that men feared. "I wanted," he paused, "we wanted to speak to you about the baby."

"The baby? You say that like he's some object, a ball or something. It's our baby Ro!" she shouted, then rubbed her stomach as if to emphasize the point. "You don't give a shit about us! I mean how many times have you asked about me, or our baby for that matter? You know he's kicking now. He got legs already as long as my forearm. He likes when I eat ice cream and Oreo cookies. That's when he does the most kicking, between every spoonful. And he likes when I sing to him, even though I'm not the best singer, it's my voice Ro that he will remember when he comes into the world. What will he think about you? Hell, what will he know about you? I'll tell you, not a gottdamn thing, because you are not around!"

"Marti! It's not like that. I think about you and the baby all the time. It's just some things…"

"What things Ro?"

"Some legal matters have to be taken care of….Harvey said."

"I don't give a fuck about what Harvey says, you hear me. All Harvey is concerned about is your fucking money and his fucking wallet, nothing more, nothing less, and if you don't pay attention to your on fucking money he's gonna rob you blind. Mark my words."

The silence between, the tension in the air was thick enough to cut and place between two slices of bread. Marti had turned the heat off her food nearly an hour ago but the kitchen still felt like hell, in more ways than one. Ro stripped out of his suit jacket, and excused himself to the restroom, leaving Marti sweating over a hot stove. She couldn't believe it. Is this what she will be reduced to, a kept woman, barefoot, pregnant, sweating over another uneatened dinner, while her man went out and caroused with other women. "F@#$ NO!"

She grabbed Ro's jacket, searched his pockets and smiled when her fingers wrapped around his wallet. It was thick and worn. You would think a man of his caliber would have purchased another one by now, but still he held onto his weathered Oleg Cassini wallet, like an amulet. The first thing she noticed was that it was full of bills, hundreds, fifties, no twenties or tens. She took out two hundred dollar bills, then on second thought, removed two more. *Baby needs a new pair of shoes.* She tried stuffing everything back in its place when a business card fell to the floor. Now that's the last thing she wanted to happen, since that would mean she would have to bend down and pick it up. She struggled to bend down, holding on to the table to steady herself and picking up the card. She read, *Carissa Santiago? Who the fuck was Carissa Santiago?* She reread the card, memorized the phone number and message, *tonight, 8pm at Visions. See you there Babe!* Oh hell no! Her blood was boiling. She heard the toilet flush and slipped Ro's wallet back into his jacket. Martinette tried her best to be calm and not cut off his balls just yet. There could be some other reasonable explanation for the meeting. She knew pro players always drew a crowd of hoochies, and women were always slipping cards into their hands and pockets with seductive messages and phone numbers. But this one wasn't found in his jacket. It was in his wallet, which meant this was one call he was intending on returning, one meeting he was intent on making, and when he did...

"What's up babe?" Ro asked.

Martinette turned around so fast she almost slipped and fell, but Ro was at her side within seconds to catch her fall. "You okay?" he asked.

"Yeah, I'm fine. A little clumsy with all this weight, but I'll be fine. So, you staying for dinner? Why don't you go ahead an invite Harvey in, I got plenty."

"You sure. You don't mind?"

"No, I don't mind, but I'm not discussing anything about the baby. And if he decides to mention anything about a paternity test," she picked up a spatula, "I will slap him into next week."

"I don't really think you want to be hitting no lawyer."

"Oh, is that what he's calling himself now…I was thinking more like skeezer."

Ro gave her a concerned look. "On second thought, would you mind just fixing me a plate; I've got to run….got some business to take care of before I fly out."

"Fly out! Damn Ro, you just got here."

"I know, but I've got to get ready for NBA weekend, you know meet with the press, attend a few charitable events…stuff like that."

"So when's your flight?"

"Around eight."

Martinette had to do everything she could to resist going off on him right then and there, but she did. "Oh, so I guess you better get going then," she said handing him a foil wrapped paper plate.

"Ummm, smells real good. Thanks baby! Look if you need anything while I'm away, just give Harvey a call."

Yeah, I wish. "Well, come to think of it. I could use a little cash to tide me over. I mean, I am growing out of everything."

"Say no more," he said pulling out his wallet and handing her four one hundred dollar bills. "Buy what you need, and if it's not enough, just call Harvey, he can write you a check."

Martinette accepted the money through clinched teeth. Harvey had more access to Ro than she did. He had his hand in everything, but especially Ro's pocket. When was Ro going to learn, that Harvey was robbing him blind. "Thanks Baby," Marti said, pecking him on the cheek. It was so wifey like, the peck on the cheek, the foiled wrapped plate, the man leaving, smiling, and the damn cheating. It was enough to send spasms throughout Martinette's entire body, the baby felt it too, and delivered a quick jab to the kidney that had her doubling over.

"You alright?" Ro asked looking down at her stomach. "Was that the baby?"

Martinette was almost stunned by his excitement. That was the first time Ro had shown any concern for their baby. She decided to milk it while she could. "Yeah", she whined, "he's a big kicker."

"I saw that. Your entire middle shifted. Damn," he said, then pausing. "Can I touch it, I mean him, I mean..."

"Go head Ro. He is just as much yours as he is mine. Come here," she said pulling his arm. "Now be gentle." She had Ro just where she wanted him, he rubbed and poked until their baby responded with a jab of his own, amusing both Ro and Martinette. "I told you he was a big boy."

"He sure is. It's hard to believe something so small and yet so big can be living in their like that." Ro seemed genuinely touched.

"Well you just wait till he's here. He is going to be all over his daddy."

All of sudden Ro's mood changed, and the room felt a lot cooler. He grabbed his jacket from the chair, swinging it over his arm, kissed her on the forehead and said, "I gotta go."

"Ro, what's the matter?"

"Nothing, I just have to go. "I'll call you tomorrow, alright, and thanks for the plate." Without even glancing back he was gone.

Once the door closed behind him, Martinette grabbed the phone and dialed. "Hey, you know I can really need a night out on the town, how about you?"

CHAPTER 19

"So, I was thinking," X continued, "that me, you and little man could do something tonight, see a movie, get some food."

Shantique glanced over at her mother, who seemed to be doing more listening than dusting. "Sounds good to me, what time?"

"Say around six or so? I've got to meet up with Butter to go over some Dirty South business and then I'll be free for the rest of evening."

"Me too!" she said, watching her mother dust over the same spot since she picked up the phone. "Oh yeah, Marti called me and wanted us to meet her and Ro out tonight. I kind of told her yeah, since I had no other plans."

"Sure Shorty, I'm game for a night out, but what about Little man?"

"I'll work on that. You just get your business taken care of and call me when you're done. And why don't you tell Butter too! Maybe him and Nikko would like to meet us."

"Sweet! I'll do that. Alright baby, I'm heading onto the interstate now, I'll ring you when I'm done."

Shantique flipped her cell phone off. "Ma, what you doing?"

"Huh? Dusting, what it look like I'm doing?"

"To be honest, it looked like you were eavesdropping on my phone call?"

Shantique's mom stopped what she was doing, placing her hands on her hips, "and if I was, so what. It's my damn house and if I want to listen to my daughters phone call, and so be it, I will. Now what you got going on so secret that I can't listen. That's the million dollar question."

"Nothing Ma! It's just rude that's all."

"Rude my ass! What's rude is your ass; out all time of nights with that boy...oh excuse me I mean man. When your ass should be home, raising your child. That's rude."

Shantique could tell that she was going to have a hell of a time convincing her mom to baby-sit tonight. "Mom, why you got a problem with X? He's been nothing but a gentleman around you and you still want to be going off."

"Yeah, yeah I know, but I don't know him and I still don't think I want to know him," her mother said, coming around to sit on the couch beside her daughter. "I can't stand them baggy pants he wears and to tell you the truth he looks like some street thug. Shantique, I know you all into who he is, some big time rapper with a lot of dough, but he reminds me too much of the hustlers I grew up with, and I just want more for you. Can't a mother be concerned?"

"Mama, he ain't like that, and you know it. So what's the real deal? Just a few weeks ago, you were saying you thought he was okay, and now you flipping the switch on me and telling me he some kind of thug and you don't know about him."

Her mother looked away, and then back at Shantique. Her mother had tears in her eyes. "I am a lousy liar," she said wiping a tear, "I know."

"What is it Ma?"

"Shantique, I've worked too hard and too long to have you throw your life down the drain over any man. That whole situation with you and Taye nearly sent me to the hospital. Taye broke your heart, and it broke my heart to see you like that. I don't think I can go through that again," she patted Shantique's knee. "I overheard you telling your friend, Nikko that X asked you to move in with him, and you were going to say yes. That messed me up, real good. I just don't want you going out and making foolish mistakes because of no man. And what about Rashawn? You gonna put that boy in the middle of this, not knowing what the end results will be? You got to put you and Rashawn first Shantique, or else you'll end up just like me. And I'll be damn, if I'm gonna sit around and watch you destroy your chances at a better life!"

"Mama." Shantique didn't really know what else to say, or how she could convince her mother otherwise that she wasn't making a fool out of herself. All she really knew was that she did love X, and he loved her. She also knew that her hooking up with him was not about his money or his fame. For the first time in her life she saw things so clear, that at times she felt like she had experienced some weird spiritual cleansing. It was kind of funny, her mom was always telling her to be responsible, that she was no longer a child, and yet when she starts acting like a grownup, her mom sang a different tune. What her mom didn't know was that she had her had on straight, and although X had it all, she wasn't even looking for him to take her where she wanted to go. She would get there on her own. She had a good job, a burgeoning career, a fine son and a man who loved her. She was betting a thousand. "Look, I'm haven't made up my mind yet, but I am seriously considering it. I love X, Ma. Not like I loved Taye, but better. I mean, with Taye, love was all new, and we didn't know what to do with it, but with X, it's like I've found my better half. It just feels right with him, but I don't want you over here getting all sick over it."

"Shantique, your mama is a big girl, even though, at times like this I may freak out. Just let me go on the record for saying its something I don't think you should do, but if you decide to leave, to move in with X, then I'll be here for you in anyway that I can, cause I'm your mama, and will always be your mama, wrong or right, you can always count on me."

Shantique hugged her mother tight. There closeness wasn't something you could count on between mothers and daughters, but through the years they had forged a friendship that traveled well beyond the boundaries of mother, daughterhood. Her mother was her bestfriend, her counselor, her disciplinarian, her shoulder to cry on, her bid whist partner, and the best damn grandma she could have asked for. Through her mother's trials and tribulations, she had learned overtime what and who to avoid, right from wrong, and when the areas in her life were shaded grey, it was her mother who came along with her broad swipe of wisdom to color it right. "Mama, don't worry, okay, I promise you everything is going to be alright. Remember what you and grandma always say, "Your mama didn't raise no fools."

"You right about that Shantique now don't be one."

* * *

Nikko wrestled for three days before getting her nerves up to call the hotline number to find out the results from her test, although she wanted more than anything to know. She couldn't bring herself to dial those ten digits; instead she walked around pretending that everything was alright. Around her family, the dance company, even with her friends she tried to keep up the appearance that all was well, while that went over pretty good with most everyone, Shantique was the only one to question her about herself.

"What's up with you?"

"Huh? What you mean?"

"I mean, you acting different. Is it Laron?"

Nikko could feel Shantique staring at her from the side, while she pretended to be engrossed in the latest Vibe magazine. Shantique only knew the half of it, or at least she never opened up that she knew more. Out of all people she could have figured it out. She was the only person Nikko told that she slept with Laron, but had she told her that they hadn't used protection? "I just have a lot things on my mind, you know."

"Girl, I know what you mean. Did I tell you my mom asked me about moving in with X?"

"She did?"

"Yeah. I almost freaked out. But I just told her the truth."

"What she say?"

"Nothing really, just that she wanted me to be careful, and a lot of stuff about not making mistakes, not falling for no man. Pretty much the same talk she gave to me when I was dating Taye."

"Speaking of Taye, you talked to him about moving in with X?"

"No, not yet. That's one conversation I'm not looking forward to."

"He ain't gonna like no one else raising his son, men are like that."

"I know, but it's just something he's gonna have to get used to. I can't really be concerned with what everyone else thinks. I'm grown, and from now on I make my own decisions."

"Wow!"

"What?"

"Spoken like a true adult."

"Shut up girl! You stupid."

"Just listen to yourself...if I didn't know any better I would think you were your mother."

"Aw hell naw!" The two of them laughed. "I talked with Marti earlier, she wants us to meet her out tonight. You game?"

"I don't know. I'm supposed to be hooking up with Butter tonight."

"X was gonna ask Butter if you two wanted to meet us at Visions later on. It would be just like old times, me and X, you and Butter, and Marti and Ro. Come on girl, I sure could use some fun and from the way you looking you could too!"

"I'll think about it, okay! It would be fun to hang out with old friends. Seems like all I be doing is working out and studying."

"See, that's a good reason to go out and let your hair down, do some regular dancing, instead of all that ballet stuff."

"Girl shutup you don't know what you are talking about."

"Sure I do, you all be pli – aying and tip-toeing all across that floor. I saw The Nutcracker!"

"Shantique, shut up! You killing me!"

"Not until you say yes."

"Alright, I will meet you guys at Visions."

"Eight o' clock and don't be late."

* * *

Nikko pulled over, parked in the back of a Kroger store on Ponce De Leon Ave. It wasn't the preferred place for her to find out about her fate, but it was doable, and far from the stress of hearing the news in her home or amongst her closest friends. She dialed the numbers, slowly, deliberating while keeping an eye on the passerby shoppers. Friday's at Kroger's seemed more like a club scene than casual shopping. People came and went dressed in all types of get-ups, from business casual to the more elaborate, club chic, the place was a potpourri of style. The digital voice on the other end asked her for her code, and she punched it in slowly as well, then waited for a reply. She switched her phone from her left to her right hand, since her left hand had become wet, and cramped. And that wasn't all of it, her heart was beating a mile a minute. If she didn't get her answer soon, she was sure to have a stroke.

The digital voice said, "We have received your test results, and your results are...."

Nikko held her breath.

"...negative."

* * *

X pulled into the former warehouse turned Dirty South Studio, in a part of what people were calling the revitalization of Atlanta. Mechanicsville was once known for its poor and working class. The area just south of the central business district, bordered by I-20 to the north, the I-75/I-85 connector to the east, and the Norfolk Southern rail yard to the west and south. The white men who worked the railroad and the locomotive repairmen were known as "mechanics", thus the area came to be known as Mechanicsville and one of the only places a black family in the early 1930's could work and live amongst other ethnicities, free of Jim Crow. X had learned all of this information from Butter, who in his own right was a history buff as well as a skilled producer.

"Yo man, you early," Butter said when X entered the studio.

"I'm a man on a mission, brother," X said while slapping hands with his friend. "So, you holding everything down in here? Where's everyone else?"

Butter closed the door to the studio, and then motioned X back towards the sound room. "They'll be here soon enough, but I'm glad they're not here now, cuz there's something I need to speak with you about. In private."

"What's up man?"

"How did everything go down between you and Sammy Pete, I mean are y'all straight?"

"As straight as we're going to be? So where is this coming from, you heard something different? People been talking?"

"Man, you know how it is. And yes, word is, Sammy's just lying and waiting for you to try and take over Dirty South."

"Yeah, well, what else he gonna do? Shit! Fifteen years upstate, all that nigga got to do is wait. He think I was just gonna sit around and wait for his ass to get out to hand me my contract back? That's bullshit! Sammy knows better. Our contract is non and void. A done deal! You and I both know that if it wasn't for me, Dirty South wouldn't be shit!"

"I hear ya man, and you're within your legal right to purchase whatever business you want. I'm just saying, there's gonna be some beef. Sammy ain't never been a straight shooter. If this deal goes down, he's coming after you, and if he's gunning for you he's gunning for me too!"

X rocked back in his seat taking in everything Butter had to say. Butter kept it real and he liked that, but it was too late in the game for them to be back tracking. No doubt, Sammy had a long reach, even from the Pen, he could reach out and touch them at a moments notice, but he thought he squashed that on his last visit. Sammy was all smiles when they parted, even if they didn't part as friends, word was bond and Sammy gave his word that day.

"X, what you wanna do?"

"Do the deal son. My irons in the fire, you know what I'm saying. Ain't no turning back now."

"Word?"

"Word man!"

"Alright then," Butter said, "looks like we're in business."

* * *

Butter cranked up his Lincoln Navigator and sat for awhile, languishing in the moment. This would be the biggest thing he had ever done, signing and partnering with X was like a dream come true. Sure, he thought the limo business was good, brought in a steady cash flow, but it was nothing compared to what he could do in the music business, and having X on the label was like winning the lottery. Things just couldn't get any better. He scored a major deal and he had found the girl of his dreams all in one month. The Gods must be smiling down on him, except there was one or two cracks, Laron's death for one and Sammy's threat.

X gave too much credence to Sammy's word. Butter thought differently. Like Sammy, he too came from the streets, raised in the streets, hell he could even say he got his PHD in the streets. That's why he knew in his gut that Sammy Pete wasn't going to go away quietly, no matter what X thought. All of sudden, he began to feel anxious, like he was being watched or something. Butter looked around, and the scene was pretty much the same, quiet, almost too quiet. There were only a few cars parked outside the studio, and he recognized two of them, but the third car, a black Range Rover, with dark tinted windows puzzled him. It had been parked there since he left the studio, but he couldn't remember if it was out there when X had arrived, and didn't know if any of the sound crew drove a Rover or not. He stared at the car, the dark windows, but couldn't tell if anyone was inside or not. Maybe his paranoia was getting the best of him, could be Dirk's, or Mark's car, could be nothing, he thought. He put his car in drive and starts to drive off, that's when he hears the Rovers engine start up. He whipped around and their headlights were on too! *What's up with that?* Butter pulled out of the driveway, and so did the Rover. Traffic was light, so he was able to make his turn onto Dekalb Drive, a usually busy intersection with no problems, all awhile checking his rear mirror for signs of the Range Rover. And as he suspected the Range Rover was behind him still. Butter reached for the phone to call X, when it rang. He answered.

"What's up?"

"Hey baby!"

"Nikko, what's up baby?"

"Nothing really, you busy?"

"Naw, just leaving the studio." He made a left turn at Clairmont and the Rover followed. Butter wiped a bead of sweat from his forehead.

"You sound funny. You alright?"

"Yeah, yeah, baby, sorry about that, just got some things on my mind. How you doing?"

"I'm fine. In fact I'm better than fine."

"Well I already know that. Tell me something new?" Butter continued on Clairmont, and as far as he could tell, the Rover was behind him up until he made a right turn on Decatur Street, and then they were gone and Butter felt an ounce of relief.

"You funny. Now you sound more like yourself."

He wiped a bead of sweat from his brow and contemplated what next to do. "Yeah well, it be like that sometime. You know what I mean."

"Yeah, I do. So, we hooking up tonight?"

"It's your call baby. We can do the couple thing or maybe we can do something solo, you know just you and I."

"I think I can work that out, but I did promise Shantique that we would hook up with her and X, and Martinette's coming out too."

"It's all good baby, whatever you want to do, I'm cool with it."

"Well to tell you the truth, I want to be with you."

Butter smiled instinctively. "Yeah?"

"I was thinking about stopping by your place first, you know, so we can chill out, alone," she paused. "I know I haven't been myself lately Butter, but I want to make it up to you."

"I think I would like that Nikko. I like that a lot. But check this out, not at my place, I've got a better idea. Just ring me when you are heading out and I'll give you directions."

"What are you up to?"

"Nothing, really, just trust me, you will love it."

"Alright then baby, I'll call you around five or so."

Butter hung up feeling pretty good about him and Nikko's date and forgetting all about calling X.

* * *

Sammy Pete made his way to the phones amidst a sea of admirers and haters alike. They parted on each side of him allowing him to pass by without even a whisper. Even if they wanted to say something, they wouldn't, not with the protection he had. Sammy managed to do what no other nigga had, by surrounding himself with The Nation, a group of brothers who studied the word of Elijah Muhammad, and a group of street thugs, calling them selves The Fifth Ave Crew. They were some of the biggest, meanest dudes he had ever seen, and they meant business and business is what Sammy knew best. From the moment he stepped foot inside, he knew his street credits wouldn't be enough to insure his safety. In the pen, there were always bigger and badder dudes, and some of them would whup his ass just for hell of it. Just like in the real world, money talks, so if it wasn't for his money and his fame, he would be just like any other inmate, prey.

The phones were all being used, but with just a look, one poor guy nearly lost an eye for not hanging up when he was asked to. Sammy didn't flinch at the unnecessary violence. He never showed any emotion, at least none that could be read on his face, because they were always watching him, waiting for him to show some signs of weakness. Sammy took his time punching in the numbers.

"Yo son, it's me." He said. "So, you get that information?"

The caller said, "Sammy what's up man?"

"Look, I ain't got all day nigga, did you get the information"

"Yeah man, look it went down like you said, everything. So what you want us to do?"

Sammy slammed the receiver against the wall, adding one more dent to the already cracked phone. An inmate hollered from behind.

"Yo man, don't fuck up the phone. We only got two!"

Sammy turned around and stared at him, and the man sank back in line.

"Sammy, Sammy!"

"Yeah, I heard you," Sammy said, covering the phone with his hands. "Then it's a done deal, right?"

"Word."

The caller hung up and Sammy held onto the ear piece long after the dial tone returned, wondering if he would one day regret his decision.

* * *

"Shantique!" her mother hollered from the stairs. "I'm heading over to mama's." When Shantique didn't answer she hollered again. "Shantique!"

"Yeah Ma," Shantique said stepping around the corner, and looking down the stairs.

"Oh, look, I'm going over to mama's for...wait you going somewhere? All hell naw, Shantique, I told you I was visiting your grandma today. What you gonna do with Rashawn?"

"Mama, it's okay. Rashawn is going with me, and X. We're going to Underground to hang out."

Her mother gave her a strange look, "Oh, so y'all a family now? You, X and Rashawn?"

"Mama, what's up? I thought we already talked about this. Why you tripping again?"

"Shantique, I'm not tripping. Okay look, I was wrong. It's just...it takes time to get used to."

"Mama, it's cool, really. X is cool, and Rashawn will be fine."

"Oh, I know he will, cuz anything happen to my baby, X will live up to his name. He will be X'ed out of here."

The doorbell rang.

"Mama, that's X, be nice."
Her mother opened the door.
"Hello X."
"Miss ...," he paused.
"Eva. Come on in."
"Thanks. For a moment there I thought you were her sister. I see where Shantique gets her good looks from."

"Don't bother trying to charm me boy, all I want to know is what your intentions are with my daughter and my grandson?"

"Ma!" Shantique yells. "What you doing?"

"Shantique, go get dressed!"

"But Ma?"

Her mother gave her a look that was hard to defy, and although she was already dressed, she moved out of the hallway and back into her room, just to give them some semblance of privacy. But there was no way she was gonna close that door, at least not until she heard what her mother and X had to say.

"Look Miss Eva, I have only the best intentions for your daughter and I respect and appreciate you asking. I know we haven't really had any kind of discussions, and you probably don't know me the way you should, but all that can change, at least I hope so."

"Sit down X."

X took a seat on the couch, and Shantique mother sat directly in front of him.

"I know who you are. You are a big time rapper, hip hop star, with lots of money, and cars and it looks to me like you can have any woman you want. I'm pretty sure women throw themselves at you everyday for what you have and who you are. What I want to know is why Shantique? And wait, don't answer that yet, because I want you to think long and hard before you do. You see, I know why Shantique, because I know my baby, and I know what she has to offer this world, not a man X, but the entire world. "

Shantique leaned so close to the door with her ear pinned in between, she nearly fell through. It was a good thing Rashawn was sleep or he would have surely blown her cover, her thighs began to ache from squatting, but she didn't want to move now.

"Miss Eva, you are so right about Shantique, but so wrong about me. Why Shantique? Because Shantique is not only beautiful on the outside, she is truly beautiful on the inside. Shantique is like a rose in the cement, strong and beautiful, captivating and indestructible. I'm no playa Miss Eva. I truly want to settle down, and I would really like to do it with Shantique. All my life I wanted a family, a real family, with mom's and pops together, kids...you know the whole picket fence dream...but my circumstances growing up were different. Look, I love your daughter and all I want to do is make her happy."

"Well damn, X. I didn't think you had it in you, but I was wrong. Shantique you can come downstairs now."

"Huh?" Shantique stuck her head out the door.

"Oh just quit it! I know you've been listening the entire time. X," she said turning to back to him, "thank you for being honest and forthright. I wish my daughter would be the same, but sometimes...."

"Sometimes what?" Shantique asked.

"Oh, is there something you didn't hear?"

"Ma, what's up?" Shantique said, taking a seat next to X. And she couldn't hide the smirk on her face or the joy she was feeling. She knew her mom hadn't totally accepted X, but she had accepted their relationship, so that was a good start as far as she was concerned. "So," she turned to X, "You and ma getting acquainted?"

X smiled, "You can say that."

"Yes, you surely can, but it's a good thing Shantique. Don't you forget that!"

"So, where's little man?"

Her mother stood up, "I'll get him. You two sit here."

Shantique looked up and her mother gave her a surprised nod of approval. And she nodded in return, silently mouthing her thanks.

"You know, your mom's is pretty cool. I like her. She reminds me of mommy."

"Mommy? You call your mom, mommy."

"Yeah, and?"

"Nothing, I just never heard a grown man, call his mother, mommy."

"Mommy, ma, same thing, different region," he said pulling her closer to him. "Pretty soon, I'll be calling you mommy."

"Say what. All hell naw, I'm not having no more babies, anytime soon."

"I didn't mean it like that Ma. See what I mean, Ma, Mommy, is a term of endearment. It means you special to me, as dear to me as my Ma, or Mommy, that's how I feel about you."

"Oh yeah." Shantique leaned in and gave him a kiss on the lips, and he returned the kiss.

"Yeah!"

"Uh Huh," her mother interrupted. "Rashawn is dressed and ready to go."

"Mommy," he said.

"Hey baby, come here. You all ready to go play some games and get something to eat." Rashawn nodded his head, but kept looking at X. "Rashawn, you know Mr. X, say hello."

"Hi!"

"How you doing Little man?"

"Fine."

"You ready to go race some cars, and ride some motorcycles, cuz I'm sure am, and I'm the best car racer in the world."

Rashawns' eyes lit up. "I'm the best in the world!"

"Well not until you beat me. You think you can beat me?"

"I don't know," he said burying his head in him mother's chest.

"I think you can and I'm going to show you how. You want to learn how to go real fast?"

Rashawn nodded.

"Come here," X said patting his lap.

Rashawn moved towards him and he lifted and placed him on his lap.

"First, you have to trust me. You trust me?"

Rashawn nodded.

"Now when you want to go real fast, all you have to do is press down like this on the pedal, and when you want to slow up, you just pull the gear like this. But you are gonna have to keep your foot on the pedal if you want to beat me, you hear?"

"Yes."

"You think you can do that?"

"Yes, but I'm scared."

"Oh, you don't have to be scared with me Little Man. I promise you," He said looking at Shantique, "your mom, and your grandma, I won't ever let any harm come to you. That means, that I will protect you with my life, and believe me, that's a lot."

"It is?"

"Yeah, it sure is."

Shantique was touched by X's exchange with Rashawn, so much so, she was moved to tears. It obviously had an affect on her mom as well, because she was quick to excuse herself to the kitchen, but not before Shantique caught her wiping her eyes. It was a beautiful moment, and one Shantique would recall and embrace during her hardest times.

CHAPTER 20

Nikko did something she hadn't done in a while; she took a long, hot bath with candles and scented oils that reminded her of an ocean breeze. It was the first time she actually felt relaxed in months. The bath did her good, but it was the news she received about her test that finally put her mind at ease. She poured more oil into the water and turned the faucet to hot to warm up the water while Eric Benet serenaded her into perfect bliss. In just one hour she was to meet up with Butter and she couldn't wait. Although she had told him nothing about her test, she suspected that he knew more than what he lead her to believe. It wasn't anything he said, or did, but there was something. She would tell him the truth tonight. That's the promise she made to God when she found out her results were negative. It was a promise she would keep. God had every right to ignore her prayers and pleas for help since she rarely prayed and only remember attending church once, that was when one of her cousins were being christened. Her dad said he was Baptist and she had seen him read the bible daily, but religion was never a topic of discussion in their house. So Nikko thought she would make one more promise to God and that is to get to know him better.

*   *   *

Nikko pulled out of her driveway when her phone rang. It was Butter.

"Hey Butter, I was just leaving."

"Good, but I don't want you to come to here."

"You don't." Nikko started to worry. "What's up?"

"There's somewhere I want you to meet me. It's not too far from here."

"Well, where is it? You have the address?"

"Its better I give you the directions."

"Alright then."

"Okay, you take Ponce De Leon Ave to Highland and make a left turn at the light. Go two more traffic lights…hold up baby, I got another call."

It was just starting to get dusk, and although Nikko loved driving, driving through unfamiliar neighborhoods at night made her nervous. She was ready to tell Butter to just meet her somewhere and pick her up. He clicked back on.

"Sorry about that baby. So where you at?"

"I just turned on Highland. So where is this place? Does it have a name?"

"Yeah, oh hold up baby."

Damn, he did it again. Nikko passed through the two lights and didn't know what to do since Butter hadn't given her any more directions. She started to pull over to the side of the road but traffic was moving so that she just continued to drive while looking for a gas station or nearby parking lot.

"Sorry baby."

"Butter, I already passed through the two lights, now I'm lost. Could you please give me an address?"

"Don't have to, you're doing fine."

She was getting pissed now. "No I'm not doing fine. How can I be doing fine and I don't know where the hell I'm going."

"Turn right."

"What do you mean turn right? Where?"

"At the next street, it should be Peachtree Hills, make a right turn and follow the driveway to the end."

Nikko followed Butter's directions but she wasn't happy about it. Not at all, in fact she thought she had a good mind to hang up the phone and go back home. The long driveway led her up to a Victorian styled house, or church, she really couldn't tell which, but if it was a church there was no sign.

"So where to now?" she asked dryly.

"No where, you're here. Get out the car and walk up to the door."

"Butter, what are you up to? Whose house is this?"

"You'll see, come on, and get out."

"Where are you? Are you watching me?"

"Maybe."

"Oh, now that's sneaky. Okay, I'm at the door."

"Open it."

Nikko turned the knob and it opened into a dark room lit with candles. "Butter where are you?"

"Right here," he said closing the door behind her.

"What is this?"

"It's a surprise. Come on, walk with me."

He took her by the hand and walked her down a long, dark hallway. She wanted to ask him to turn on some lights, but the whole dark house thing was beginning to creep her out. But up ahead she could see some lights and more.....she saw a stage.

"Butter what is this? What is a stage doing in a house? Oh my God it's an entire theatre." Nikko couldn't believe her eyes. The room they had entered was actually a small theatre, with chairs for about 150 people. It looked like a mini Fox Theatre. And sitting on the stage was a table for two, with candles and flowers and their own personal butler to serve them. "Butter!"

"You like it!"

"Oh my God, how did you do this?"

"A friend owed me a favor, and he's a real theatre buff, turned half of his house into a theatre. I told him about your dancing and he said that you could use his stage anytime you wanted."

"Use his stage. You're kidding to dance for who?"

"To dance for me or for yourself, whatever you like Nikko. Here you can dream, but if only for one night, live the dream. Come on, let me show you," he said taking her by the hand. "It's got a sound system, lights, scenery, everything, just like a real stage."

"I see, and the butler?"

"Naw, that's just for tonight, can't dance on an empty stomach."

Nikko was in awe of this man, that he would go to such lengths to please her brought tears to her eyes.

"Thank you, Butter!"

"No," he said grabbing her hands and bringing them up to his lips.

"Thank you. Thank you for being who you are, the strong and yet tender woman, courageous and beautiful too! I know what you have been going through and I wanted so much to be there for you, but you wouldn't let me, not at least in the way that I wanted to. I hope that I can change that. I hope that you can begin to trust me and know that I'm not like Laron. I'm not out to hurt you, or use you, I just want to enjoy getting to know you. Oh yeah, I forgot, SURPRISE!"

* * *

Underground was busier than usual, but not as busy as a Saturday afternoon, still Shantique was excited about spending the evening with her two favorite men, Rashawn and X. In the short time they had been together, X managed to wrap Rashawn around his fingers with the promise of games and horseback rides and a few tickles, air lifts and shadowboxing that had her son more hyper than she had ever seen.

"X, X, lift me up again," Rashawn screamed.

"Alright, Little man, if you think you can handle it?"

"I can. I ain't scared."

Shantique was amused at her son, pretending to be bigger and braver than he was and it made her heart jump at the idea that he was actually enjoying his time with the two of them.

"Hold up Rashawn, you don't need to be doing all that lifting."

"Mommy, I'm okay."

"Yeah, but you need to calm yourself down boy. You gonna wear X out."

X grabbed Shantique around the waist and squeezed, "its okay baby, I can handle little man."

She smiled, appreciative of his gesture. He was really good with Rashawn.

After an hour of video games, the three of them sat down to a dinner of beef patties, stewed chicken and rice and peas, at X's favorite Jamaican restaurant.

"That was good!" X said wiping his mouth with the line napkin.

"Mommy can I have some more patty?" Rashawn blurted out.

"You like these, huh?"

"Yes. Mommy can you make these at home?"

X gave her an inquisitive look, "yeah mommy, can you make these?"

Shantique shot him a look that made him think twice, "no baby, but we can buy you and X some when you want them. Mommy can make you other things, like chicken fingers and fries."

"I like chicken fingers and fries." Said Rashawn.

"I know baby. Now what do you like X?"

"Mommy, I like whatever you cooking," he slaps her thighs under the table, "or not cooking and that's no lie."

"I guess you like your meals hot," she teased back.

"Like fire baby. Burn me."

"I don't like hot mommy. Hot burns my tongue." Rashawn interjected.

"I know Sweetie, but when you are older, you may like it too!" She smiled and winked at X.

"You know, this was good. Really good. I hope you are thinking about taking me up on my offer?" He asked.

Shantique had been thinking about his offer all week. Moving in with X was a big deal, and she was glad that she let it slip in the conversation with her mom, because that was her biggest obstacle, convincing her mom that it was what she wanted and the right thing to do.

"I've been thinking."

"That's not telling me nothing Shantique. So what's it gonna be? I want you with me, as much as you can, 24-7, and I want to get to know little man, really. I'm serious girl. I love you!" He whispered to her.

Shantique grabbed a hold to his hand and squeezed tight, for her words escaped her and her emotions were in toil. She wanted to believe X more than anything, but life her taught her something different, to be cautious, to not jump at the first opportunity, even when it seemed perfect. It wasn't until Rashawn spoke up that she considered the real possibility of the three of them building a life together.

"Mommy, can I live with you and X?" he asked.

Shantique was unaware that Rashawn had been listening or even understood what was going on, but she knew she had to answer him and X, who showed more patience than she could ever muster.

"Yeah baby. You go where I go, no matter what. You sure you want to live with me and X? You don't mind leaving grandma?

"Un huh! Grandma says you got to learn re-spon-si-bility. And I told her I would help mommy." The three of them laughed.

"That's a pretty big word their fella." X said, patting Rashawn on the shoulder.

"My grandma taught me."

"That's good Rashawn, but when you start school you are gonna learn all kind of words, some big, and some not so big. But it's important that you know what they mean, and when to use them. I'm proud of you baby," Shantique said, hugging her son. "You are such a big boy and I don't mind at all you helping, in fact," she said looking at X, "I could use a lot more help."

"So?" X asked. "Does that mean that you are taking me up on my offer?"

Shantique nodded and X smiled. Just like that they had made a commitment to be more than just casual friends, more than just lovers, tonight they chose to be a family, her, X and Rashawn.

*   *   *

"Hey, hey, can you hear me?" Martinette hollered into her cellphone amidst the loud music and chatter. "Shantique, when y'all coming?"

"What? Martinette, girl I can't hear you, so I guess you're at the club. Listen, we are just about to leave Underground, gonna drop off Rashawn then head on back, so It's gonna be about another hour before we arrive. You heard from Nikko?"

"Naw, I tried calling her, but it just went to voicemail. So y'all be here in an hour or so?"

"Yeah," Shantique hollered back. "We'll see you then."

"Okay girl, well, Ro hasn't gotten here yet either, so I'm gonna hang out in the VIP section until y'all arrive. Call me when you get here, okay?

"Alright girl, we will, and don't you be drinking nothing. Your brother with you?"

"Naw, I don't need no babysitter and I ain't drinking, can't stand the stuff right around now. Just hurry y'all asses up, okay. It ain't right to make a pregnant woman wait."

Shantique laughed, "Okay girl, hold it down. We'll see you soon. Bye."

"Bye Nigga!" Martinette closed her flip phone and made her way through the sparse crowd until she reached the VIP section. The large comfortable looking couches and low lighting was just what she needed. As much as she wanted to get out the house, being in a crowd on the dance level was giving her headache. It was enough to deal with the stares, but when the men starting acting like pure animals lusting at her middle and her enhance backside, she felt like she was about two minutes from cussing a nigga out.

"Can I get you something to drink," the scantily dressed waitress asked.

"Yeah, Perrier with lime, and don't drop it in, put it on the side please," Martinette said turning her attention back to the dance floor. When she looked up again the waitress was still there. Martinette gave her a look, as if to ask what?

"You sure you need to be in here girl. I mean you look like that load is gonna drop any moment now?"

Martinette could feel her temperature rising and tried her best not to go all out on the girl, but her hormones were raging, and she wouldn't have set foot in their in the first place had it been for Ro trying to step out on her. The last thing she wanted was to be out in the open looking 20 lbs heavier and have thin, sickly looking bitches, and hard up freaky muthafuckas trying to pass judgment on how why she was in a club, nearly eight months pregnant and alone.

"What did you say?"

"I'm just saying...."

"I tell you what, don't you worry about me and why I'm here. Do your damn job and get me my drink, and don't open the bottle till you get here bitch, cuz I don't trust your skank ass as far as I can throw you."

"Fuck you!"

"Naw fuck you, you skinny, chicken bone bitch!" Martinette hollered after her. How dare she question her? It wasn't long after that the manager of the club apologized personally for his employee's behavior and offered Martinette drinks on the house. Any other night, the offer would have been grand, but tonight, while she was drinking Perrier, that shit stunk to high heaven.

Martinettes' phone rang.

"Yeah," she answered.

"Marti, where you at?" Her brother asked.

"I'm out, why?"

"Out where? I know you don't have your ass up in no club girl. What's up with you?"

"Look Calvin, I'm not for your shit right now, but if you want to know I'm meeting Ro, and my girls. Why you calling me any damn way?"

"Girl, I'm just checking up on you. I came home and the house was empty, just looking out for my little sis, that's all."

"Well, like I told you when you moved in, I'm a grown ass woman, and I can take care of myself."

"Yeah you right. So I see you been cooking. Girl, them greens is off the chain, and that cornbread, girl you would make your mama proud."

Martinette couldn't help but smile. "Yeah, I put my foot in that shit. You should have seen Ro slobbering over my food. Did you taste the oxtails?"

"Yeah, that shit is banging too! That nigga don't eat much, cuz there's got be enough here left to last us through the weekend."

"Well, he took a plate, but I'm not even going there. Look, I got another call coming in bro, so I'll see you back home later." She said hanging up her phone. The last thing she wanted to hear was her brother dissing Ro. Calvin was good for a lot of things. He was a good brother, but he didn't stand a candle to Ro, and what could do for her, no matter how he felt about him. He thought that Ro was just another playa, and that could be true, but in the end it was her decision to hang with Ro, and despite what Calvin thought it wasn't all about the money. She wanted her child to grow up with a father. She wanted what she never had, a family.

Martinette sipped on her Perrier, when she heard the crowd road below her. She stood up to look and saw clearly, Ro had entered the place wearing an off-white fedora, white suit and white shoes. If she hadn't known better she would of thought she was in an 70's flick, and he was trying out for Superfly, the only exception he wasn't even as pretty as Ron O' Neal back in the day. She moved back, out of sight, afraid that he would see her, and that's the last thing she wanted, since her prime mission for being there was to spy on him and his doings, and to find out who he was gearing up to meet.

Her stomached bubbled, burped and baby Ro shifted positions causing her to reclaim her seat, and rethink her reason for being there. How in the hell did she let herself become so consumed with this man? How and when did she fall? She downed her water, while she fought back tears, hoping and for the love of

God praying that he was alone, because if he wasn't she didn't know what she would do. Once the crowd settled down and everything seemed to return to normal, Martinette peeked once more over the railing. Ro was signing autographs, shaking hands, and giving hugs, just like any normal celeb would do on a night out. She scanned right to left, front to back, but noticed no particular woman in his presence, and she smiled, satisfied that her man was honoring their relationship. Martinette sat back and thought about their relationship, the beginning, the middle, and now...what seemed like the end, but she didn't want it to end. For the first time in her life, she realized that she was in love with Ro, the man, not his money, not his fame, but him and she wanted more than anything to share a life with him and their baby. She wiped an escaped tear from her eye and dialed Shantique's number.

"Marti, what's up girl?"

"Where y'all at?"

"We're still at Underground, but we should be leaving soon."

"Girl, I'm thinking about leaving...I don't know, I'm not feeling it here, my feet hurt, and baby Ro is kicking up a storm, so I'm thinking about canceling this event until another time."

"Well, I hear ya girl. Ro gonna bring you home?" Shantique asked.

"No," she paused. "I don't know Shantique. He may want to stay; I just know I have to go." Martinette said breaking into tears.

"Marti, you alright?"

"Yeah, girl, it's my damn hormones, girl they have me crying like a bitch, but I'm okay. In fact, I'm better than okay. I don't need to be here. This shit is so in the past. I need to be home and if Ro knows better, he'll go with me, if not, well; I just got to do what's right for me and the baby." She was about to hang up the phone and proceed to the exit when she heard a loud roar from the crowd below. Shantique stood up. "Hey, let me call you back," she said hanging up the phone. She leaned over the railing and got a glimpse of Ro making his way through the sparse crowd. He shook hands, gave dap, and hugs to the ladies, but as far as she could tell, he was alone, besides his bodyguards. Martinette watched a few more moments, and Ro acted like the perfect gentleman, finally settling himself down against the long marble bar, surrounded by his bodyguards and autograph seekers. She had seen enough, and grabbed her purse and Perrier and hurried downstairs to be with her man. She didn't know what she was thinking. First off there wasn't a woman in there that could hold a candle to her, even in her present state, and secondly Ro loved her. She was just being overly emotional and protective, that was it, she thought as she made her way down the winding staircase. She would be a fool to lose Ro over some bullshit, like jealousy. He had always been good to her and she just wanted to return the favor ten-fold, and let him know how important he was to her. That thought stopped her in her tracks. If Ro saw her there, he would think she was spying on him, and that would make him angry. And the last thing she wanted was to make him angry at her, so she needed to find another way out of the club, where Ro wouldn't see her, or know she was there. She returned to her spot in the VIP section and reluctantly called over the waitress she had cussed out previously. It took 3 waves, and 2 excuse me's before the waitress would even acknowledge her, but she finally did and approached Martinette with caution.

"Hi, I'm sorry, what's your name?"

"Fontiqua" she said bluntly.

"Fon who?"

"Fon-Ti-Qwa!"

Martinette tried not to laugh, but a smile and a giggle escaped her.

"Okay, girl, look. I'm real sorry about earlier. It's these damn hormones, the baby," she said rubbing her stomach, "got me all off key. I didn't mean nothing bout what I said, and I hope you can forgive me for going off on you. I should know better, hell back in the day, I was a waitress just like you."

"You was? Girl, I was like she tripping, going off on me like that. I had a good mine to say fuck this job."

"I know, you right, but listen to an old pro. You got what it takes to soothe any savage beast, including me. Just keep flaunting that fine body of yours and smiling, and I guarantee you, you gonna make more tips than you can handle." Little by little Martinette warmed up the very cold, Fon-Ti-Qwa, and five minutes later they were acting like best of friends.

"Listen, all you have to do is go down the stairs, and then take a right, the exit door is to your left. You don't even have to go by the bar or anything, and I promise you, nobody will see ya. I'm a walk you down myself, and I swear if anybody even looks our way, I'm a give them the bizness."

Martinette had to laugh at Fon-Ti-Qwa's toughness. This was indeed a girl beyond her young years, and she could see a lot of herself in Fon-Ti-Qwa.

"Alright then, let's go girl. Cuz I got to get out of here, like yesterday."

Fon-Ti-Qwa led the way, while Martinette followed behind, wishing she was invisible, and hiding behind a woman too skinny to hide a broom, let alone an nearly 8 month pregnant woman. But still she followed, hoping that Ro was so caught up with his fans that he wouldn't recognize her. But that was a whole lot of wishful thinking on her part.

She had nearly made it to the last step without incident, following so closely behind Fon-Ti-Qwa that they appeared seamed together by some invisible thread. At the last step Fon-Ti-Qwa pointed to the exit door, reminding Martinette how close her escape was, just a step away. She chanced one more look at Ro over in the corner, entertaining his fans and all of a sudden she had been somehow transformed into a dream state, or more likely a nightmare. She turned to check out Ro, and what she witnessed next could be perceived as a series of ghastly pictures, the truth whether she wanted to accept it or not, or what she really came to see, Ro fucking with another woman. The woman was tall, probably about 5'11" or more, light skinned, or white, with straight black hair. At first she appeared like any other fan, groupie, gold-digger type, hanging close, flaunting cleavage she probably had to buy on discount, wearing the most revealing cut of a dress any designer could have imagined, and smiling that welcoming, come hither grin that had all the men drooling. She was Martinette before pregnancy, but minus the ample back part, although her ass stuck out like a sore thumb, Martinette attributed that to her pose, more than natural esthetics. She leaned over to Ro, wrapping her arms around his neck, as if they were meant to be there then kissed him in the mouth, a tongue kiss at that. He didn't pull away, call for his bodyguards, or anything, in fact, Martinette would later remember watching Ro wrap his huge hands around her tiny waist and pulling her into him, as if she was liquid water. The two of them making lemonade, right in front of her was enough to make her angry as a starved pit bull and sick as a dog. She could feel the salty taste consume her mouth, and swallowed hard to relieve it, but to no avail she was about to puke something stupid, and she hoped it would be all over Ro and his girl. Martinette tried her best to maintain her composure until she reached Ro and his bitch, because when she got close enough she was going to slap the spit out of his mouth and beat his bitch down to a vanilla pulp, at least that's what she thought she would do, but her body had other plans.

 First came the loud whistle, and then the tunneling sound, Fon-Ti-Qwa turned to her and said something, but Martinette couldn't hear a word of it, between the music and her sudden death ear, everything was muffled, except her heart, which begged and pleaded for her to reach Ro, and find out what the hell was going on, and so she did, or least she thought she did. She had all intentions of giving Ro the riot act, slapping his wannabe bitch, and telling him where to go, when baby Ro delivered a hellified punch to her abdomen, which sent her sinking into the stairwell, grasping at the rails.

 "Hey, you okay?" Fon-Ti-Qwa shouted.

 But the ringing was too loud, for Martinette to answer, so she nodded slowly, and tried to right herself and do what she came there to do. She felt the urge to pee really bad, which had her shifting back and forth between kicking somebody's ass and relieving herself, because she damn sure wasn't gonna pee on herself in front of everybody. Hell to the NAW! Martinette moved forward and could feel her body releasing fluid as she moved, a whole lotta fluid. She stopped to examine herself and found a large pool of water swimming around her feet. She panicked. What the fuck now? No sooner than she has asked, the world around her faded to black and she rested in that darkness, wet pants and all.

CHAPTER 21

Sammy Pete pounded his bag, unaware of the pain, or anything else. He pounded so hard, his bones jumped in unison, riveting and springing to the impact. He had never punched so hard, and for so long, but he needed this now, more than anything.

It was the only thing that kept him sane.

"Everything is worked out, no slip-ups," he said through jagged breaths.

"Yeah man, I got my boys on it now. It goes down just like you said."

Sammy paused, sweat dripped from his body and pooled onto the floor. "Keep it clean, no witnesses, and no survivors."

"We got it man. Like I said, it's all taken care of, tonight, just like you wanted. It's gonna be sweet!" His soldier laughed, which was stunted by the swift kick to the groin Sammy delivered, sending his man toppling over onto the map.

"Ain't shit funny! He is, was my brother and even in death, he deserves respect." Sammy crossed his chest, kneeled to the ground and recited the 23rd Psalm, "The Lord is my shepherd...I shall not want."

* * *

"So," X said, "you thought about where you wanna live?"

Shantique grabbed a napkin and wiped Rashawn's mouth which was covered with ice cream. "Naw, I mean, I like Buckhead, and Midtown, but not really. Where you wanna stay?"

"Baby, wherever you are and that's on the real. But if I had to make a choice, I'm kind of loving Midtown right now."

"Yeah, me too! I seen some slamming townhouses on Ponce, and that wouldn't be too far from work either."

"I hear ya." X's cell phone buzzed. "Hold up baby. Hello," he answered.

"X, what's up man?"

"Hey Butter, what you up to dude? I was just thinking about you. So, you and your girl gonna hook up with us tonight?"

"Yeah man, no doubt, we just chilling right now, but we're planning on heading to the club, I say I about an hour." Nikko giggled in the background. "Or maybe an hour an a half."

"Alright dude, whatever, handled your bizness. We still got to drop off little man, so it will probably be at least an hour down the line for us as well."

"Look X, man I been meaning to call you earlier, cuz I experienced something stupid the other day that I thought you should know about."

"What's up man?"

"Well, I don't to raise your radar or anything, but the other day when I was leaving the studio, I could swear I was being followed. The dude watched me from the time I left the studio, until I spotted him a few streets down and man, I ain't shitting you, the shit has me uneasy. I could swear it was some of Sammy's crew."

"Sammy's crew! You mean that nigga I corrected!"

"Yeah man, one and the same. I didn't get a good look, but he had that same wire-fired hairstyle and stupid grin. All I'm saying is be careful man. Watch your back. I don't think Sammy is being straight with us."

X tried not to express his anger at Butter's revelations, or to spurn any excitement. "I hear ya man. Will do, no doubt, and you do the same."

"Look X, he was driving a Black, Cadillac Escalade, license plates said some shit like, 'SLICK'."

"Alright dude. It's cool, alright, we about to roll out now. So we'll catch up with you later at the club."

Shantique watched X's mood change in just an instant and she was about to ask him what's up when her phone rang. "Hello!" She answered.

"Shantique, its Ro! Look, I think Martinette is about to have the baby. The ambulance is taking her to Crawford Long right now."

"Ro, you lying, what happened?" Shantique nearly shouted into the phone. "Let me speak to Marti."

"You can't I told you she's on the way to the hospital. The ambulance just drove off, and I'm following behind. I just wanted to let you know, cuz I know how tight you all are and you would want to be there."

"Okay, we're on our way," Shantique said looking at X, who had inched so close to her, wrapping his arms around her waist, supporting her both physically and emotionally. "Marti went into labor at the club. She's on her way to the hospital and..."

"Hold up," X interrupted. "Breathe baby, she's gonna be okay. Marti and the first or last woman to go into labor at no club. Why you so upset?"

"I don't know, just something, something don't feel right X. You looked the same way a few minutes ago, while you were talking with Butter, and then this thing with Marti...I don't know got me feeling sick in my stomach."

X looked surprised.

"No, I'm not pregnant, I mean spiritually sick. I can't really explain it; I just know how I feel."

"Alright Ma, I hear ya. Look, let's round up Little man, and head on over to the hospital, while you visiting with your girl, helping her to bring her own little shorty into the world, I can drop off Little man."

"Thanks X."

"No thanks required. This is what I do...and you know, like I told you a thousand times before, I would do anything for you and yours. So, you ready to roll?"

"Yeah."

X turned to Rashawn, who was busy coloring, oblivious to their conversation or the excitement and said, "How bout you Little man, you ready to roll?"

"Yep!"

"Okay then, hop up here," X pointed at his back. "Just for being so patient, I'm gonna give you a horseback ride all the way to the car. And let me warn you, this isn't no ordinary horseback ride boy. When you hitch a ride here, you riding the black stallion, champion of horses, so you got to know how to control him, cuz he don't let just anybody ride him."

"What's a black stallion?"

"A thoroughbred, born to race, bred to win. You game? You think you can handle it?"

"Un huh!" Rashawn said nodding. "But I don't want to fall."

"Oh you ain't got to worry about that, if he likes you, and I think he does, he won't ever let you fall. See he's a loyal horse and he takes care of his own. Come on, hop on up here."

Shantique was once again touched by X's actions, especially with regard to Rashawn and her son seemed to be loving it. She had wished a long time ago that her and Taye could have experienced the same. *Damn! Why was she thinking of Taye at this moment?* That was the strangest thing no matter how far they were apart, somehow they were always connected, by Rashawn. She hoped Taye would be happy for her and her decision, because, she had made her decision to live with X, and make a family with her and Rashawn. She was happy with her decision a minute ago, but now, something was itching at her, like a grey cloud passing over, maybe she thought, it was Taye. While X busied himself with Rashawn, she excused herself to the restroom and called his cell. When he didn't answer, she called his home, but no on answered there either. She called her mom.

"Hey ma, how you doing?"

"I'm fine. Y'all enjoying your night out?"

"Yeah, but we just got a call that Marti was sent to the hospital. Ro thinks she's gone into labor. We're heading there now."

"Really? Isn't early?"

"At least a month."

"Damn baby, well call me if you need me. I wasn't doing nothing, just about to run up to the store and play some numbers."

"Alright ma, look have you heard from Taye?"

"No baby, you know this is draft night. I suspect he's in New York with his family. What? Something wrong with Rashawn?"

"No ma, Rashawn's fine, I just thought he may have called and all, you know to speak with Rashawn."

"Well baby, he probably will once he's drafted. If he does, I'll have him call you on your cell, okay?"

"Okay Ma, well, look I gotta go."

"You alright Shantique? You don't sound right."

"Yeah, I'm good ma. I gotta go. I love you."

"Love you too baby, kiss my baby boy for me. Oh, that's right y'all bringing him home. Well tell him Grandma made some cookies just for him."

"I will ma. See ya soon." Shantique said, hanging up her cell. Everything seemed to be okay with Taye as well, so what was really bothering her? She met back up with X and Rashawn.

"You ready babe," X said riding Rashawn on his back.

"Wheeeee mommy, this is fun!" Rashawn screamed.

"I know baby, but don't you wear X out now."

"I won't mommy. I'm riding black stallion, and he's the strongest. The three of them headed to the car.

* * *

Nikko was frustrated, but concerned about the welfare of her friend, Martinette. She just wished the night didn't have to end the way it did. Her and Butter were having such a nice time, before they got the call from Ro, saying that Marti had gone into labor. Although they had planned on joining their friends for a night out at the club, she didn't expect to be spending it in a hospital.

"So what did Ro say, exactly," she prompted Butter.

"He said your girl was about to have the baby. Said she was transported to Crawford Long. We should be there in minutes. What's up?" Butter said, sneaking a glance at her.

"Nothing, just worried that's all. So, Shantique and X gonna meet us there?"

"Yeah, X said they were leaving Underground about 10 minutes ago. They should be there already. What's up baby? You seem like something is bothering you."

"Naw, I'm good. I just wish that we weren't always caught up in Marti's drama. You know I love my girl, but it seems every time things are going right for me, she does something to ruin it."

"Damn baby, she couldn't predict the baby coming, so what you saying?"

"That's stupid. I know she didn't plan this. But Marti has a way of invading your life in the most inopportune times."

"I hear ya baby, but for you and me, there will be plenty of more times. You can count on that." He said leaning over to kiss her and at the same time a car swiveled in their path, causing Butter to break hard. "Damn, that fool almost hit me." Butter tried to straighten out his car, when the same car turned around and rammed him. "Muthafuck!"

"Butter, what's going on?"

"I don't know, but this muthafucka don't know who he messing with," Butter said reaching into his glove compartment for his glock.

Nikko grabbed his hand, "what you doing?"

"Protecting us."

No sooner than he spoke, a barrage of bullets riddled the car, leaving them hostage and unprotected.

* * *

While the threat of yet another storm lingered in the distance, everyone seemed pleased with the Northern breeze that whipped around their bodies, reminding them of maybe an early fall. Shantique enjoyed the wind, but she especially enjoyed watching X with Rashawn. Rashawn was laughing so loud, she thought first to quiet him, but she came to her senses and relished in his joy.

"Go, Go," Rashawn shouted, pretending to whip Black Stallion, and sending X into a frenzy of movement, up and down, back and forth, which thrilled it's young rider, causing giggles and laughter far louder than Shantique could remember.

"Don't hurt him now Rashawn," Shantique teased. We want to save Black Stallion for another day."

"I won't mommy." He giggled more. "This is fun!" he screamed.

X didn't let up on the fun, and seemed to enjoy it as much as Rashawn. He took a moment to glance over at Shantique and she winked in approval. At that moment, he felt on top of the world and finally felt safe and loved. This is what he always wanted, a family to call his own.

"I was thinking," he said. "That maybe, after we dropped little man off, we could stop by and take a look at some of those condos on Ponce."

"You think there still open?"

"Can't do nothing but see."

"Alright then, after we check on Marti, I'm game. We can grab up some Krispy Kreme on the way...I'm so craving some of those donuts."

X didn't respond, his attention was drawn to a certain black car that had been following them slowly up Washington Ave.

"X?"

The car was creeping up near them and slowed to a stop at the traffic light.

"Yeah baby."

"You want to pick up some Krispy Crème?"

When the light turned green the car should have proceeded across or turned, but it waited at the stop light amidst the blowing of horns behind it. X slowed himself, waiting.

"Why you stopping, the garage is just across the street."

"I know baby, it's just my knees gave out, and I was giving them a rest," he lied.

"Rashawn, give X a rest." Shantique said reaching for her son, but he pulled away and held on tighter to X's neck. "Put him down X, I'll carry him." She motioned.

"Naw baby," X said watching the car, "I'm fine. You alright little man?"

"Un huh, I'm sleepy too."

"I know, but soon will be at your grandma's and you can sleep there." X said moving slowly around the corner. The car was still parked at the light, unmoving, despite the traffic. The windows were tinted dark, so he couldn't see who was in the car, but he didn't really need to—his gut warned him moments ago. "Shantique, come on baby, you need to step up," he said waving her to his side.

"Okay, but why you walking so fast."

"How soon we forget. Didn't I tell you I was the black stallion?"

"Oh X, come on now. I'm not Rashawn." She glanced up and Rashawn had laid his head on X's back. "Shhh!" she whispered. "That boy is knocked out."

"No wonder, I thought it was me, getting old or something, cuz Little man was starting to wear me out." They had just reached the corner and X looked over to his left and spotted the same car sitting at the corner. "Shantique, take little man and head to the car. I'll meet you there."

"Why?" Shantique looked at him strange. "What's up?"

"Listen," he said more sternly, "Please do what I say, okay. It's all good girl. I just got some bizness to take care of."

X handed Rashawn to Shantique, when someone shouted his name.

"Yo! X, is that you man? Hell yeah," the voice said, "That's Crazy Ass X!"

X didn't have to turn around to see where the noise was coming from and he didn't want to until Shantique was safe.

"Who's that?" Shantique asked.

"Nobody, just go. Go now Shantique!"

Yo X! What nigga, you don't know nobody no more! Turn your punk ass around."

"Go!"

The car revved its engine and jumped the curve. X and Shantique only had seconds to get out of its way. They were trapped. One side of them stood a brick wall, on the other, the car with four guns pointed in their direction. X pushed Shantique and Rashawn to the ground, covering them with his body, like a human shield. Their only viable escape was getting to the garage, which was just around the corner, no less than ten steps easy. X raised up to get a better look and became an easy target, taking a bullet to the shoulder. He slumped back to the ground next to Shantique, blood streaming down his arm.

"Oh my God X," Shantique screamed "What we gonna do?"

X struggled with the pain, but he remained cool for all of their sakes.

"We got to get out of here," he said calmly, removing his shirt, and wrapping it around his arm and across his shoulder. "Pull on it tight."

The bullets never let up. X counted about twenty-four shots in all. These dudes had plenty of fire power, so he couldn't count on them running out of bullets.

"But the police should be here soon. Somebody had to hear the gunfire." Shantique said sheltering Rashawn under her arms.

"Can't wait on them either."

"What you mean we can't wait? What we gonna do X?" Shantique started to cry.

"Shantique, look at me. I ain't gonna let nothing happen to you and little man, okay. You trust me?"

Shantique nodded.

"Okay then, when I say go, you and little man head for the garage door."

"No, X no. They'll shoot us.'

"Listen, it's only about five steps away. Y'all gonna crawl, down on all fours and I'm gonna draw the attention away with this," he said removing a small caliber pistol from a strap around his ankle.

"X, no, they got four guns, you just got that one. Baby, I can't"

"Yes you can."

The gunfire stopped.

"Little man, you okay?"

Rashawn nodded.

"Alright then, I want you to go with your mama. I want you to move fast, crawl like you never crawled before, like a race, and keep your head down. Okay?"

"Okay," Rashawn whispered back.

"It's time, they probably reloading."

He looked at Shantique whose eyes were filled with tears, and he wiped them as soon as they fell.

"Come on baby girl. Be strong for me, alright. Please," he said grabbing her face and kissing her. "Go," he whispered.

"X. I'm scared," she whispered, covering Rashawn's ears.

"Me too baby, but this may be our only chance. If they get out of the car, we're dead."

"What about you?"

"I'll be right behind you."

"X, don't let them hurt my baby."

"I won't, now go. Go!"

Shantique got on all fours and crawled as fast as she could, holding Rashawn under her. No sooner than she had made it four steps than the shooting started again. She screamed and stopped.

X returned fire and shouted, "Go! Keep going Shantique!"

She kept moving and made it just inside of the garage door. She turned around to see X dragging himself across the concrete. They were gonna make it.

"Come on X! You're almost here."

He struggled around the corner and made it inside the garage door, along with her and Rashawn. She was all smiles, and so was Rashawn, but then they heard the opening of car doors.

* * *

The doors to the emergency room of Crawford Long Hospital burst open, wheeling a screaming Martinette.

"Oh Shit! It's coming, the baby's coming!" She hollered.

Ro followed behind the rolling contraption, afraid to get too close, since Martinette had cursed him out and tried to swing on him, at least five times since she departed the ambulance.

"Ro, where the fuck are you?" She screamed even louder, twisting her head around, trying to find him. The pain she was feeling was beyond pain, in fact she felt like she was dying. "Get my brother. Where's Calvin? Where's Shantique? Where's Nikko?" Where the fuck was everyone? Another pain ran up her back, causing her to twist into some weird form, reminding her of the acrobats she saw on Circ De Solei. She never even knew her body could bend like that. Martinette held her breath, afraid to breathe, although that's the one thing they taught her in birthing classes, breathe.

"Breathe Marti, breathe!" Ro hollered from behind her.

What the hell was he hollering for, she thought and as soon as this damn ax stop swinging into her body, she was gonna get off this cart, they called a cot and whoop his ass, all seven foot of him. At least that's what she was thinking until she felt something protruding from her kitty kat. Martinette reached into her pants and screamed. "Get me a doctor, the baby is here, between my legs!"

No sooner had she spoke a doctor walked up. Martinette wanted to cuss his ass out to, but for a moment the pain had subsided and she took that moment to breathe and rest. After confirming her situation with both the attendants and Ro, he ordered a nurse to find her a room and finally took the time to check on her.

"Alright now," he paused checking the chart, "Martinette is it?"

"Yes," she struggled to speak. That's when Ro finally found the nerve to stand by her side.

We are gonna get you a room right now. I'm going to have a nurse check to see how far you are dilated though, and I'm afraid we might have to perform the inspection out here. Is that okay with you?"

Martinette bit her tongue, trying to repress what she really wanted to tell the doctor and simply nodded in agreement.

"Good. Nurse, can I get an extra sheet so that we can check her dilation?"

Martinette was do another big bang of pain at any moment, so she decided not to waste her time on the doctor, the nurse, or their examination. Talking took up energy, and as far as she could tell, she needed every breath just to get through this. And just before the pain hit, she had a moment of clarity.

"Where my drugs? I'm supposed to get something for this pain?"

"And you will, but you may not need it. Your water has burst, and it appears the baby is near delivery. This could be a natural delivery, if you want?"

"I don't. Dammit I want the drugs and I want them now. What the fuck is wrong with you people? Ro, tell them to get me my drugs. I can't take this shit no more! Oh shit," she screamed, "here it comes again!"

The nurse arrived with the extra sheet and as soon as it was draped over Martinette's body everything shifted into gear. They rushed her down the hall, in a room and the doctor was hollered commands as loud as she was screaming, but still Martinette wished, prayed and begged for the drugs. It was drugs or death, and her faith was lingering more towards death at that point. Then all of a sudden everyone was quiet. Too quiet. Martinette looked up and caught them whispering.

"What's up?"

The doctor turned to her and said, "I think we may have a problem."

* * *

Ro stepped out of the room and into the buzzing hallway filled with white coats, sick people, and others like him, who had no real reason to be there, except for support. But support was the last thing he could give. He felt squeamish, and lightheaded. The doctor announced that the baby was breached. They were talking about cutting Martinette open, performing a c-section. That was enough to send him to the hall. He started walking, head down counting the many squares, trying not to look at anyone, or anything. To be truthful, sick people made him sick, and if he didn't get out of there soon, he felt like he would pass out right there, but instead he ran into an unexpected friend.

"Ro, where's Marti?" Nikko asked.

"What happened to you?"

"We, me and Butter were in an accident. Somebody shot at us and tried to run us off the road."

"Say what! Is Butter okay?"

"Yeah, Butter's at the police station giving them a report now. So how's Marti? What are doing out here? Did she have the baby?"

"No, not yet. They just found out that the baby is breached. They're gonna have to perform a c-section. So right now, she's in a lot of pain, but they're giving her meds now, readying her for surgery."

"So why are you out here Ro? Shouldn't you be with Marti?"

"Yeah, and I am. I just needed some air."

"Oh. You one of those types."

"What you saying?"

"You know what I'm saying. Anyway, have you seen Shantique or X around?"

"No. Nobody but you so far. I've got to give Marti's brother a call to let him know. I'll do that while I'm outside. I can't get no good signal in here."

"Well, alright then, I'll follow you. I need to call Shantique and see where they're at?"

Once the two of them made it outside, Ro made his call to Martinette's brother, Calvin, who needed a ride to the hospital.

"I can go pick him up," Ro said.

"No Ro, you need to be here with Marti, in fact you should probably be getting back."

"Yeah, you right."

"I'll call Shantique and X, if they haven't left already, maybe they can pick up Calvin, if not I'll have Butter go get him."

"That's cool. Boy, it's been some kind of night."

"You telling me. After them fools shot up Butter's car, and nearly landed us in a ditch, man I thought my life was over, you know the whole flash thing. It really happens."

Just then an ambulance came speeding around the corner, landing at the emergency door. Nikko and Ro, were just a short distance from the door, and couldn't help but be caught up in all the excitement. The doors to the ambulance flew opened, and two paramedics, removed two cots, from its back. A baby was crying, moaning, "Mommy, mommy", but the person on the other cot never moved.

Nikko overheard the paramedic telling the attending physician that he had three gunshot victims, one more on its way.

"That's a damn shame," she said. "Did you hear that, that's a baby over there?" She struggled to see the other victim, but couldn't.

"Mommy, I want my mommy!" the baby cried.

"Oh that's a shame, that must be his mother the doctors are working on. That poor..." Nikko stopped mid sentence. "Oh my God," she took off running.

"Hey where you going?" Ro asked. "Nikko, what's up?" He tried to stop her, but Nikko kept running and screaming until she reached the ambulance.

"Oh my God, Rashawn! Rashawn, what happened?"

Two attendants prevented her from coming any closer.

"I'm sorry ma'am but you're gonna have to stand back."

"No, you don't understand I know him. He's my bestfriends son. Where's Shantique?" Nikko screamed. She looked at the other cot, covered and blood, the same one the doctors worked feverishly over.

"Ma'am please, stand back, we just want to check him out, and then if it's okay, you can see him."

Rashawn stopped crying once he saw Nikko, and let the doctors check him. It turned out he only had a few nicks and scratches, which they cleaned and placed bandages on.

After which, they let Nikko hold him. "Hey little man, you okay?"

Rashawn nodded, and sucked his thumb, something Nikko had seen him do since he was one year's old. She wanted to ask him about his mom, but she didn't want to upset him anymore.

"I'm gonna take care of you until mommy's better, okay."

He nodded again.

Ro hadn't left yet, and she understood why. They were both paralyzed with fear, hoping against all odds that Shantique and X were okay.

A doctor yelled out, "Okay, we got him stable. Take him to surgical room 1." When they all stepped away, they saw that it was X on the gurney and not Shantique. Shantique must be the third victim.

The second ambulance arrived. Nikko didn't know what to do. Should she remain outside with Rashawn, not knowing what condition she would be in, or should she go inside. She turned to Ro, who seemed to sense what she was going through.

"Hey, let me take Little man inside, find him some cookies or something. Anyways, it will be good practice for me."

"Thank you," she said handing Rashawn over to Ro. Who didn't put up a fuss at all.

Once Ro was gone, Nikko stepped closer to the landing and waited for the doors to the ambulance to open. She wished Butter was there with her, she needed his strength. He was on his way, that's what he told her when they last spoke, right before she saw Rashawn. Then she realized that Butter hadn't heard yet, about what happened to X and Shantique. She dialed his number quickly.

"Hey baby," he answered, "you alright?"

"Yeah, where you at?"

"I'm just picked up Calvin and we are on our way to the hospital now. I should be there in about fifteen minutes tops. What's up with you, Marti didn't have the baby yet?"

"Butter, X and Shantique's been shot."

"What! Damn! I told X, I told him I thought something was up. So what do you know? Are they okay?"

"I don't know, they wheeled X off to surgery, and the ambulance just arrived with Shantique. I'm waiting on them," she paused when the doors to the ambulance opened. "Oh Butter," she cried. Nikko couldn't talk from the sobs that escaped her. Seeing Shantique covered in blood, and lying so still she couldn't tell if she was dead or alive was more than she could take. The moment they exited the vehicle, two doctors accosted the gurney and wheeled her away, running through the halls. Things were really bad. Nikko wanted to go inside, but couldn't, afraid she wouldn't be able to keep it together when she saw Rashawn, but she was sure that Ro probably needed some relief, and also time to check on Marti and the baby.

But Ro wasn't in the lobby of the hospital and she could see why. Almost every inch of space was filled with reporters, policemen and some groupies. Out of the three, the wildest of the bunch were the reporters, approaching anyone Black it seemed and asking them if they knew anything about the shooting, or X. Nikko slipped around the corner unnoticed. This was the last place Ro would be, she thought. And decided to head back to Marti's room when she saw Shantique's mom running through the emergency room doors. She followed, but was stopped at the door by some orderly.

"You can't go in there, for family only."

"But, I am family. That's my aunt, my cousin in there."

"Nope, she ain't even suppose to be there, so you definitely not going in."

Nikko wanted to argue with the guy, but didn't. She would find Ro first and get Rashawn, and then the three of them would talk with Shantique's mom.

* * *

Shantique's mom entered the all-white room, so brightly lit and pristine, it was like a scene out of some movie, and this room was heaven. It's funny what you begin to think about when you are about to lose your mind in worry. Since she received the phone call that her daughter and grandson had been injured in a shooting, she didn't quite know where she was half the time. Her mind moved in warp speed, and her body followed only because it had to, because it was the mind that ran the body, but her emotions were ready to run a coup. She searched each room, more like cavities, open to the public, but walled on each side. There was so much activity, so much clinging, banging and beeping going on in there she couldn't here her self speak, which might have been a good thing, since her thoughts were jumbled, and frantic and as close to crazy that she was ever gonna get. In fact, she thought if she didn't pull herself together, right here and now, they would be escorting her to a more comfortable place, somewhere with lots of padding.

"Shantique," she whispered at first, afraid to shout, afraid she may hear the desperation in her voice, and hearing it, she would recognize it for what it was, fear. Her eyes led her to a table, in a room full of doctors and nurses, working feverishly, hanging things, and talking so fast, she could barely understand them. She was drawn to that room, that particular room with the blue walls, and white floors, the blue curtain that swung back and forth, moving in out and out, allowing her a view every now and then. There was blood on the floor, she hadn't noticed at first, but now she could clearly see it pooling at the base of the bed, and the doctors white coat and smudged on the curtains. So much blood, she thought. Where did it all come from?

And then she saw her baby, Shantique, lying still, too still, and she saw, all that blood belonged to Shantique, and she screamed. "Shantique!"

* * *

Shantique sat straight up, hearing her mother's voice, while a nurse tried to press her body back down.

"Please miss, you have to be still. We're almost through stitching you up."

Shantique ignored the warning. "Wait, hold up. Ma!" she called out. "Ma, I'm okay. I'm okay."

Her mother came running into the room. Her eyes were filled with tears, and she looked at Shantique with disbelief, as if she was a ghost.

"My baby," she cried. "You're okay."

"Yes mama, I'm okay. I had a flesh wound and some cuts. Don't cry."

"Oh baby, wait," she said, looking around the room. "Where's Rashawn?"

"He's fine mama. He's with Ro, Martinette's boyfriend. They gonna let me see him, once they finish cleaning me up."

The nurse finished the last stitch, then wrapped gauze and bandaged Shantique's wound.

"You sure you okay?" Her mom asked again, holding her hand, and wiping sweat from her brow. "I was just so scared baby."

"I know mama. I'm still scared for X."

"How is X?"

"I don't know, nobody will tell me anything. If it wasn't for X, we would have never made it."

"Well if it wasn't for X, nobody would be shooting at you in the street either."

"No mama, it's not X fault. People are just crazy, jealous and envious. X is a good man mama. He risked his life to save mine and Rashawn. I won't ever forget that, not ever."

"I know baby, but the truth is, being with him is dangerous, don't you see? You have a son to consider. Is life with X really worth the risks?"

CHAPTER 22

3 months later...

    X nearly lost his life three times. First on the streets, and twice on the surgeons table. Consequently, while fighting for his life, Martinette was bringing a new life into the world. A healthy, 7lbs baby boy she named Devante. Ro was a happy father, passing out cigars, shaking hands for all and about 4 hours, that's when he got the test results back and the devastating truth, ranking at 99.9%, that he wasn't the daddy. It was like a Jerry Springer show up in there, Martinette screaming, him screaming and the hospital staff not knowing what to do. And no matter the truth, Martinette never admitted she cheated on him, or with whom. She's been a single mom every since.

    Moving day and Shantique's emotions wavered between excitement and sadness. She was doing like her mama wanted, moving out, finding a place of her own, and being responsible. Thanks to Marisela, she was able to return to school, and was currently working on getting that degree. In just 18 months she would be a legitimate and work fulltime for Marisela as a buyer. After so much tragedy, life was finally looking up.

    "Wahhh!" a baby cried.

"Yo Marti, I think Little Te' is up. You want me to check him?" Shantique hollered from the bedroom.

"Yeah girl, bring him down. He's probably hungry."

"Didn't you just feed him?"

"Girl that was two hours ago, that boy eats like a horse."

"That's cuz you feeding him that store bought milk, if you would have breastfed him like I told you he'd be healthier and full." Shantique's mom chimed in.

"Oh hell naw, I done had enough niggas pulling on my breast for a lifetime. I just couldn't have my baby putting his mouth where …"

Shantique's mom interrupted, "Martinette!"

"Oh I'm sorry Miss Robinson, you know how I talk…okay well you know what I mean though."

"Here he is," Shantique said, bringing Little Te' down the stairs. "He's alright now. Auntie changed his diaper, and rubbed some powder on his belly, he loves when Auntie does that."

"Girl, that boy love anybody rubbing on him. He too much like his daddy."

"And who is that?" Nikko asked.

Martinette gave her a crazy stair, "God! Now stay out my bizness!"

"Alright then, where those men at?" Nikko asked.

The door opened and in ran Rashawn, "Mommy the truck is here. It's big too!"

"Well, I don't know why they would get a big truck. I ain't taking nothing but two beds and some clothes."

Butter walked in followed by Taye. "Hey! What y'all doing? I thought somebody was moving around here. He spotted Nikko on the couch, leaned over and planted a kiss on her lips. "Hey baby!"

"Uh, y'all make me so sick!" Martinette hollered.

"Don't hate." Nikko shouted. "Ain't that right baby."

"That's right!"

"Taye!" Shantique's mom hollered from the kitchen, "When you heading to Detroit?

"Next week. Me and my mom's gonna check out some homes. They thinking about moving there." Taye said.

Shantique's mom through the towel she was carrying across her shoulder and voiced her opinion. "All hell naw," she frowned, "moving to Detroit. I know you playing pro ball and all, but your mama moving to Detroit, at her age. Shit, don't nobody want to live in Detroit. Even the rats leaving the Detroit," she said laughing.

Shantique walked into the kitchen, gave Taye a hug. "Hey thanks for helping. Mama, Detroit ain't like it was when we left; they got some real nice area's where Taye can live."

"I don't care, it's too cold and drab and the winters last forever. That's why I moved south." Her mom said.

"Mama wherever Taye lives it will be like the south, hell with all the money he's gonna make he can have someone fly in summer."

Everyone laughed.

"Shut up Shantique, you just talking stupid." Her mama said. "Anyway Taye, good luck. You sure gonna need it."

X struggled down the stairs carrying a suitcase, and a bag full of Rashawn's toys. "Y'all forgot something," he said.

"X what are you doing?" Shantique said running towards him. "You trying to bust your stitches?

"Naw baby, I just want to help out."

"Well baby, now's not the time." Shantique's mom said. "Did you eat yet?"

"No Ma'am," X answered.

"Well come on here, I saved you a plate. Shantique get

X a plate."

X struggled down the stairs, carrying a box in one hand and his other arm in a sling.

Taye stepped up and removed the box of Rashawn's toys from X's hand. X wouldn't let go at first, but then let Taye take the box.

"Thanks man." He said.

"Thank you," Taye said. "Shantique told me what you did, how you saved their lives. Man, my son is my life. And so I owe you my life and a whole lot of gratitude. I didn't think I would ever say this, not ever. But I'm glad you came into Shantique's life, and I'm glad that you were there when they needed you."

X and Taye shook hands, and hugged, which seemed to spark the rest of them into a frenzy of love that they had never witnessed before. Shantique was the most affected, even when she thought that her family, her loves, her first and her last would never unite, God had a way of making everything right. She tried fighting back the tears, and was fairly successful, Rashawn, the youngest of them all, had the forthright to say what they all wanted and finally acknowledged.

"We a family now mama, me, you, daddy and X." Rashawn screamed with glee.

"Yeah baby, you right. And you know what, ain't nothing more important than your family, not now, not ever." Shantique said gleaming at Taye, and pulling X, closer to her.

She remembered that night in the hospital, when her mom asked her if being with X was worth the risk. At the time, she didn't have an answer, all she knew was what she felt for that man. Today, she knew without a doubt that she had made the right decision to at least give it a try. Life was about trials and errors and if she shunned away from every challenge, fear, trouble because it seemed too hard, how would she learn, how would she grow. That's what she told her mom that night at the hospital. If her mom hadn't took chances, hadn't faced fear in the face, hadn't made the decisions she made, they would still be in Detroit, living in a two-room flat, with nothing but her welfare check to take care of them. But her mom made the decision to leave, and here they were.

Shantique looked over at Nikko and Butter, Martinette holding Little Te', Rashawn wrapping himself around her mom's legs and she couldn't help but feel relieved in knowing through all they had been through, she still had a family.

Braselton was not as far as she thought. And even though she was moving close to 50 miles away from where she was raised, this will always be her family, her home. 52 Broad Street was where she was raised, where she became an adult, where she learned love and the place that would forever remain in her heart.

About the Author

Diane Dorce' is the author of two books, Loving Penny and her mystery/suspense Devil in the Mist. Diane continues to write and is currently working on a follow-up novel to Devil in the Mist as well as other projects. She continues to live and work in Georgia, with family and a host of friends.